"What a night."

Beau took Dani's hand in his and led her toward the kitchen. "Do you think we're going to remember?"

The idea that she might never be able to recall not just her wedding but the conception of her first—maybe her only—child was more dismaying than Dani wanted to let on. She might not want to remember anything embarrassing, but she certainly wanted to recall the parts that weren't!

"I don't know." Dani leaned against the refrigerator door, and looked up into eyes that had never seemed so blue. "I want to—"

"I do, too." Beau's dark brows drew together as he looked down at her in mock seriousness. "So I guess there's only one thing to do."

"And what's that?" Dani prodded. Reading the sudden mischief on his face it was all she could do not to smile as well.

Beau's sexy grin widened alarmingly as he looked deep into her eyes. "We try to reenact the conception, of course."

Don't miss the next installment of

THE LOCKHARTS OF TEXAS

Pick up *The Bride Said, "Finally!"*
available next month.

Dear Reader,

Come join us for another dream-fulfilling month of Harlequin American Romance! We're proud to have this chance to bring you our four special new stories.

In her brand-new miniseries, beloved author Cathy Gillen Thacker will sweep you away to Laramie, Texas, hometown of matchmaking madness for THE LOCKHARTS OF TEXAS. Trouble brews when arch rivals Beau and Dani discover a marriage license—with their names on it! Don't miss *The Bride Said, "I Did?"*!

What better way to turn a bachelor's mind to matrimony than sending him a woman who desperately needs to have a baby? Mindy Neff continues her legendary BACHELORS OF SHOTGUN RIDGE miniseries this month with *The Horseman's Convenient Wife*—watch Eden and Stony discover that love is anything but convenient!

Imagine waking up to see your own wedding announcement in the paper—to someone you hardly know! Melinda has some explaining to do to Ben in Mollie Molay's *The Groom Came C.O.D.*, the first book in our HAPPILY WEDDED AFTER promotion. And in Kara Lennox's *Virgin Promise*, a bad boy is shocked to discover he's seduced a virgin. Will promising to court her from afar convince her he wants more than one night of passion?

Find out this month, only from Harlequin American Romance!

Best wishes,
Melissa Jeglinski
Associate Senior Editor

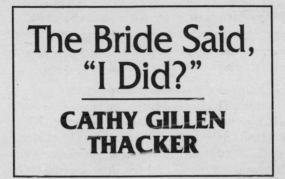

The Bride Said, "I Did?"

CATHY GILLEN THACKER

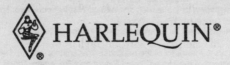

HARLEQUIN®

TORONTO · NEW YORK · LONDON
AMSTERDAM · PARIS · SYDNEY · HAMBURG
STOCKHOLM · ATHENS · TOKYO · MILAN · MADRID
PRAGUE · WARSAW · BUDAPEST · AUCKLAND

ISBN 0-373-16837-3

THE BRIDE SAID "I DID?"

Copyright © 2000 by Cathy Gillen Thacker.

All rights reserved. Except for use in any review, the reproduction or utilization of this work in whole or in part in any form by any electronic, mechanical or other means, now known or hereafter invented, including xerography, photocopying and recording, or in any information storage or retrieval system, is forbidden without the written permission of the publisher, Harlequin Enterprises Limited, 225 Duncan Mill Road, Don Mills, Ontario, Canada M3B 3K9.

All characters in this book have no existence outside the imagination of the author and have no relation whatsoever to anyone bearing the same name or names. They are not even distantly inspired by any individual known or unknown to the author, and all incidents are pure invention.

This edition published by arrangement with Harlequin Books S.A.

® and TM are trademarks of the publisher. Trademarks indicated with ® are registered in the United States Patent and Trademark Office, the Canadian Trade Marks Office and in other countries.

Visit us at www.eHarlequin.com

Printed in U.S.A.

ABOUT THE AUTHOR

Cathy Gillen Thacker is a full-time wife/mother/author who began typing stories for her own amusement during "nap time" when her children were toddlers. Twenty years and more than fifty published novels later, Cathy is almost as well-known for her witty romantic comedies and warm, family stories as she is for her ability to get grass stains and red clay out of almost anything, her triple-layer brownies and her knack for knowing what her three grown and nearly grown children are up to almost before they do! Her books have made numerous appearances on bestseller lists and are now published in seventeen languages and thirty-five countries around the world.

Books by Cathy Gillen Thacker

HARLEQUIN AMERICAN ROMANCE

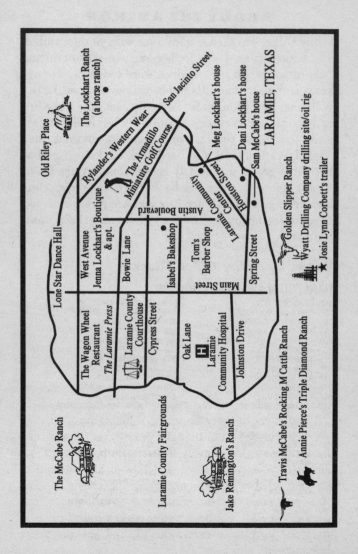

LARAMIE, TEXAS

The McCabe Ranch

Old Riley Place

The Lockhart Ranch (a horse ranch)

Rylander's Western Wear

The Armadillo Miniature Golf Course

San Jacinto Street

Meg Lockhart's house

Dani Lockhart's house

Sam McCabe's house

Houston Street

Lone Star Dance Hall

West Avenue

Jenna Lockhart's Boutique & apt.

Bowie Lane

Austin Boulevard

Laramie Community Center

Isabel's Bakeshop

Tom's Barber Shop

Spring Street

Main Street

The Wagon Wheel Restaurant

The Laramie Press

Laramie County Courthouse

Cypress Street

Oak Lane

H Laramie Community Hospital

Johnston Drive

Laramie County Fairgrounds

Golden Slipper Ranch

Wyatt Drilling Company drilling site/oil rig

★ Josie Lynn Corbett's trailer

Travis McCabe's Rocking M Cattle Ranch

Annie Pierce's Triple Diamond Ranch

Jake Remington's Ranch

Chapter One

"What you need is a man," Jenna Lockhart teased.

"According to John and Lilah McCabe, we all need a man," Dani Lockhart spouted back as she plucked the Sold sign off the front lawn and marched up the sidewalk leading to her century-old Victorian home.

Thanks to all four of the McCabe sons, who had finally found the loves of their lives and gotten married, wedding fever had swept the town of Laramie, Texas. Old family friends John and Lilah McCabe had swiftly decided that the four Lockhart girls should do the same. And, having more or less become surrogate parents to the girls since their own parents' death, had taken it upon themselves to lead the cheering campaign. Hence, Laramie residents were now looking to the four Lockhart daughters to pony up to the hitching post.

Unfortunately, Dani thought irritably as she watched the moving van drive away from the curb, it wasn't that simple. She and her three sisters had all returned to Laramie so they could once again be closer to each other, but none of them was intent on bringing a man into her life. All had been badly burned in the game of love. All were now determinedly, and she did mean determinedly, single.

"But *that* is not going to happen," Dani continued after a moment, speaking to all three of her sisters as they sat on the comfortable wicker furniture on the front porch. The furniture had been sold with the house, and it fitted the spacious veranda perfectly.

Jenna capped her pen, shut her sketchbook of dress designs and stood. "You know what I mean. Someone to help discourage Billy Carter once and for all." Jenna walked across the shady deck. "If you had a man around, showering you with attention, well, surely Billy would understand that at eighteen he's far too young for you. And then find someone closer to his own age to date."

Refusing to touch that suggestion with a ten-foot pole, Dani ran a hand through her cap of copper hair and sighed. She knew that part of this untoward situation was her fault. Billy Carter had gotten in touch with her three years ago when he'd interviewed her for his school newspaper. Since, Dani had mentored him via e-mail, answering his questions about what it was like to work in the industry and encouraging his own interest in a film career. She'd known he looked up to her, but she'd had no idea he had a crush on her until the day they finally met in person, and by then, it was too late. She'd already hired him for the summer.

Dani sighed and set the Sold sign in a corner of the front porch, so the realtor could pick it up at her convenience. "I've tried to get Billy interested in girls his own age," Dani confessed. In the few weeks she'd been back, shopping for a house and settling in, she'd tried to fix him up several times.

"And?" Jenna asked with bated breath.

Dani frowned, remembering how her young protégé had turned up his nose at each and every one of them.

"No go." Dani frowned and shook her head as she admitted reluctantly, "Billy has eyes only for me."

The four Lockhart sisters exchanged troubled glances.

"Maybe if he wasn't going to be working for you the rest of the summer," Meg suggested gently as Dani held the door and she carried in the straw basket of housewarming goodies she'd brought, "your problem would be easier to resolve."

Threading her way through the dozens of moving boxes, Dani led her sisters to the spacious country kitchen at the rear of the house. She took the basket of goodies from Meg and slid it into the refrigerator. "I can't fire him now, not after just one day, especially when he did such a super job this morning making sure the movers put all my work boxes in the library. And with over two thousand videos to unpack, sort, catalog and put away, and several thousand more coming in the next few weeks...well, you can see where I'm in a bind."

Like her, Billy had a passion for movies. The kind of passion that was just not going to go away. The kind of passion the industry needed in this day and age if it was ever going to get back to the glory days of old, where the story—not the special effects—was the focus of the film.

"Billy is an excellent student, an incredible worker. He's just young and overly romantic. I don't think I should hold that against him," Dani continued. Surely his crush on her would fade with time, she told herself.

"Then maybe you should hire someone else, too. A third party to make things less intimate," Kelsey suggested practically as the four sisters headed back out to the much-cooler veranda, glasses of lemonade in hand, to enjoy what was left of the sultry summer afternoon.

"I only wish I could. But my budget has been sorely strained as it is," Dani said. She had moved from Los Angeles, bought one of the most expensive old houses in town: a charming Victorian on Spring Street—and then set about furnishing it. She'd depleted her savings, and until she received her book advance, in approximately another month, she was counting every penny. Her sisters, all having incurred similar expenses, were also strapped for cash.

"I need someone who knows movies as well as I do. And aside from Billy—" a film buff if ever there was one, Dani thought "—I don't know a single person in Laramie who would have the patience, never mind the know-how, for the job. I mean, I can just rattle off a title and Billy instantly knows whether it was a western or a comedy. Who's in it, who directed it, how it was received by moviegoers."

"Well, then, I guess you could try dressing badly," Jenna, a clothing designer and fashion plate in her own right, teased.

"Or smelling awful," Kelsey, a cowgirl and budding rancher who knew what it was to smell to high heaven after a day in the saddle, suggested with the same mirth as Jenna.

"Or just stop bathing," Meg, who'd just landed a job as nursing supervisor at Laramie Community Hospital, said. "That'll do it."

"You all are lots of help." Dani rolled her eyes at the good-natured ribbing.

Silence fell as Meg stood, stretched and peered around the crepe-myrtle bush at the corner of the house. Dani noted the stunned look on Meg's face.

"What?" Dani demanded.

Meg blinked, blinked again. "Uh…are you expecting company this afternoon?" she asked nervously. Which was odd, Dani thought. Meg was never nervous.

"No," Dani said slowly, almost afraid to find out what suddenly had her oldest sister on edge. "Why?"

Jenna joined Meg at the veranda railing. She, too, peered around the brilliant flowers on the leafy green bush. "Oh, boy," she said. "And we thought Billy was going to be trouble."

Kelsey leaped up to see what the fuss was about. "You aren't kidding," she muttered, looking even more amused and skeptical.

Dani, who felt she'd already endured enough joking for the day, stayed where she was, remaining cool, calm and collected. And curious. "Is Billy back?" Dani demanded when her three sisters continued to gape at whatever—whoever—was coming down the walk. She'd just sent the kid home for the day half an hour ago.

"You wish," Meg said.

"Billy, you can handle," Kelsey agreed.

"But this one…" Jenna shook her head in silent commiseration.

Surely her sisters were pulling her leg with their dramatics. Dani walked over to the corner of the porch where all three were congregated, fighting for a view.

She peered around them. Seeing who was coming up the walk, all the air left her lungs in one big *whoosh*. She would have known that tall broad-shouldered silhouette and ruggedly handsome face anywhere, even if he hadn't graced the romantic daydreams of millions of women the world over.

As usual, Beau Chamberlain was wearing snug worn

jeans, custom leather boots, a bone-colored Stetson hat and a snowy white western shirt that had become his trademark both on and off the set. The only thing that alluded to his star status—aside from the knowing curl of his sensually carved lips and the exceedingly confident way he carried himself—was the movie-star sunglasses that shaded his bedroom eyes.

Already picking up her sketchbook of designs, Jenna turned back to Dani. "Should we stay or go?" Jenna asked, looking ready to bolt if so desired.

Dani frowned as Beau made a hard right and strode resolutely up the walk to her house. To her mounting dismay, he looked ready to kick some Texas butt. Namely, Dani realized on a beleaguered sigh, hers.

But that was not going to happen.

"Stay," Dani told her sisters firmly. Her heart beat slowly and heavily as she surveyed the straight black hair peeking out from beneath the brim of Beau's hat, and remembered the way it had felt beneath her fingertips. Another shimmer of awareness sifted through her, weakening her knees. "It won't take me long to get rid of him," Dani promised. All she had to do was remind Beau of the acrimonious nature of their relationship for the past two years, and he'd be gone in a flash.

Ignoring the take-no-prisoners set of his broad shoulders and the determined flare of his nostrils, Dani crossed to the top of the porch steps. She folded her arms in front of her and glared down at him, determined not to forgive him for what had happened between them in Mexico. "I thought I'd seen the last of you," she said coolly, amazed he had the audacity to show up on her doorstep after the unforgivable stunt he'd pulled on her south of the border. Never mind stand in front of her so contentiously, his legs braced apart, every inch of him taut and ready for action.

"Dream on," Beau Chamberlain replied with a grim smile. He yanked off his sunglasses to reveal thick-lashed, midnight-blue eyes that lasered into her very soul. "Wife."

DANI LAUGHED UNEASILY as she recalled all too well where and how they had last parted company. And she, at least, hadn't been wearing a wedding ring. That she knew for sure. The gauzy white dress, flowers and lacy white mantilla were another matter. But she was sure they could easily be explained. Just not by her. Not yet, anyway.

"What are you talking about?" she demanded incredulously, not sure what he was trying to pull on her now, just knowing she didn't like this practical joke any more than she had liked the first one.

Beau propped one boot on the bottom step. Leaning forward, he rested an elbow on his thigh. His sunglasses dangled from his hand.

"I am talking," he enunciated clearly, looking deep into her eyes, "about waking up in Mexico three weeks ago with you in my bed."

Dani recalled waking up *alone* in a hotel room and being naked beneath the sheets. And very little before that. Embarrassed to the hilt—as he had no doubt intended her to be, Dani thought angrily—she felt all the color leave her face. Her sisters looked similarly distressed. Darn it all, anyway. She hadn't wanted them, or anyone else for that matter, to know about this!

"Oh, dear." Meg consulted her watch with customary tact. "I think I better go pick up Jeremy. That birthday party he's attending is supposed to be over at four and it's three-thirty now."

Jenna cleared her throat and patted her chest with the flat of her hand. "That reminds me. I think I have a customer coming in for a fitting."

Kelsey dug in the pocket of her blue jeans for the keys to her pickup truck. "You know cattle and horses—they wait for no one. And I've already taken off enough time today." That quickly, all three of her sisters scattered, leaving Dani to work out what was obviously a difficult situation with as much dignity and privacy as possible.

"Way to clear out a front porch," Dani told Beau sarcastically, not sure when she had wanted to deck a cowboy more. And Beau Chamberlain was one heck of a cowboy, both on-screen and off. There hadn't been one with as much charisma and raw sex appeal since John Wayne. Worse, the man practically exuded courage, integrity and the determination to do right, no matter what the cost.

Men liked and respected him.

Women adored him and lusted after him.

Children found him irresistible.

And animals instantly trusted him.

Only Dani, it seemed, found him lacking in any way.

A fact, she knew, that had gotten to him like a spur in the side.

She regarded him in a devil-may-care way as he shrugged his broad shoulders. "You could have asked them to stay," he said. Clearly aware he was annoying her terribly, he looked her over from head to toe, taking in the delicate U of her collarbone and the shadowy hint of cleavage in the open V of her marine-blue blouse. His glance moved still lower, checking out the fit of her tailored white linen slacks before returning to her eyes. "I'm sure they'd like to know all about our marriage," he taunted softly.

"Stop saying that." Dani felt herself flush with embarrassment. She didn't know what he was up to now, but she didn't like it one bit.

"Why?" He tipped the brim of his hat back with his index finger and looked up at her with a taunting smile. "It's true."

Dani's eyebrows climbed higher. "It can't be," she countered just as emphatically, even as her knees grew weaker still.

"Really," he said, still holding her gaze. "And how do you figure that?"

"Because —" Dani marched down the steps until they stood at eye level, and poked a finger in his chest— "we've been sworn enemies for two years. I would never marry someone and not remember it! Never mind my sworn enemy," she contended hotly.

Beau moved up two steps, so they were standing on the same one and he was once again towering over her. "But you do recall waking up in that little inn in Mexico with a raging headache," he said, glaring down at her.

Dani's shoulders stiffened. Insensitive cretin. He *would* have to bring that up! She lifted her chin, drew a deep breath. "I was also alone."

"Only because I left to find out what the devil had been going on," he pointed out.

The way he'd looked at her then—as if he'd known what it was like to make love with her—sent shivers of awareness sliding willy-nilly down her spine. "What do you mean?" Dani demanded, hanging on to her composure by a thread.

Beau angled a telltale thumb at his chest. "I woke up with one helluva headache, too. I also wondered what in the heck had been going on that would have landed us both in bed and naked as jaybirds, to boot."

Dani winced at the potent fantasy his words evoked. Beau's beautifully muscled body, covered with light whorls of hair, stretched alongside her own. Everywhere she was soft, he'd be hard. Everywhere he was male, she'd be female. And surely no good could come of that! "Must you be so graphic in your descriptions?" Dani said, frowning all the more. She did not want to think about making love with him! Because that was never going to happen. It never *had* happened, no matter what things looked like. If it had, she certainly would remember it. Wouldn't she?

"As I had no memory of having gotten there with you, not to mention having shucked our clothes," he said softly, his low sexy voice doing strange things to her insides, "I decided to get up to investigate."

"Of course." Determined to irritate him as much as he was irritating her, Dani blinked her eyes at him coquettishly. "Why didn't I think of that?"

Steadfastly ignoring her goading manner, Beau continued with daunting seriousness. "Only, there was a marriage certificate on the bedside table. It had both our names on it."

If he was pulling her leg, he was doing a damn-fine job of it, Dani thought. "Let me guess. And you didn't remember getting married, either."

Beau exhaled. "Not initially, no," he told her grimly.

Despite her desire to stay cool, calm and collected, Dani's heart took on a quicker beat. She rolled her eyes, not believing a word of it. "But you do now, of course."

Beau nodded and eyed her seriously. "The more I looked at the marriage certificate that morning, the more I had a fuzzy memory—sort of a single freeze-frame image of the two of us standing in front of a priest, with candles all around us and guitar music playing softly in the background. At first I thought it was a dream, but then when I checked out the church where the marriage had supposedly taken place and spoke to the village priest, who confirmed he had indeed married us the night before, I knew it was true. Why or how I remember that and nothing else leading up to it, or following it, I don't know," he said. "But I do remember that. Just a millisecond of it, anyway."

Dani had to admit, he spun a convincing yarn. He *looked* sincere, too. But that was also his stock-in-trade as an actor, making the unbelievable believable, she schooled herself firmly. "You need a better script." She gave him an arch look and started to turn away. "So tell the writers you hired to come up with this preposterously lame joke to go back to their computers and write you a better exit scene."

With maddening nonchalance, Beau clamped a hand on her shoulder and turned her back to face him. His strong capable fingers radiating warmth through her blouse to her skin, he reached into his hip pocket and pulled out a folded piece of parchment paper. "Perhaps this will refresh your memory," he said, pushing it into her resisting fingers.

Dani stared up at him, her throat dry. She had to hand it to him. He was playing out this prank to the end. The only way she could end it was by playing out her part, too. "Fine," she said tartly. She unfolded the finely crafted sheet with stiff fingers, determined to get this farce over with once and for all. She stared down at the certificate of marriage. It was a convincing fake, she had to give him that. Even the signature of the bride— her signature—looked suspiciously real.

Her fingers began to tremble.

"Now do you remember?" Beau prodded impatiently. Sweeping off his hat, he raked his fingers through his hair.

Dani pushed the memory of a hauntingly beautiful Spanish love song from her head. "No," she retorted more stubbornly than ever, handing him the certificate right back. Her pulse picking up for no good reason, she angled her head at him. "I don't remember that," she said just as firmly. "So it can't be valid."

"That's what you'd like to think, sweetheart, but I'm here to tell you it just ain't so. I checked it out, both in Mexico and with my attorney in Los Angeles. Like it or not, legally we are as married as two people can be."

Panic surged deep inside Dani, instantly giving way to incredibly warm and sexy and totally out-of-the-question romantic fantasies. "Then we'll have it annulled," she insisted, stepping back and away, telling herself she was *not* going to get roped into any wildly exciting or potentially devastating romantic drama with him.

"With the possibility of a baby on the way?" Beau advanced on her, becoming once again the same kick-butt take-charge cowboy America had fallen in love with on-screen. He looked down at her and shook his head. "Forget it. There is not going to be—now or ever—an annulment."

"JUST TELL ME it's not true," Dani said half an hour later as she sat on the examining table in the Laramie Community Hospital family clinic, nervously awaiting the verdict from her physician friend, Lacey Buchanon McCabe, who'd been drafted to do her this enormous favor right away. Dani had only agreed to this test to quickly and efficiently and as scientifically as possible put an end to Beau's claims of possible parenthood once and for all. As far as she was concerned, Dani thought, the sooner Beau Chamberlain was out of her life the better. She knew they couldn't possibly have made love, no matter how married—or naked—they had been. The sooner Beau knew it, too, the better.

Lacey pulled up a stool and scooted closer. A newly-wed herself, she had never been happier, now that she was married to staff surgeon Jackson McCabe, and she looked it. "Can't," Lacey said gently. She regarded Dani solemnly. "You are."

Dani gulped as her heart began to gallop. Pleating the soft linen hospital gown between her fingers, she protested emotionally, "But—"

"The test I just ran is very accurate," Lacey interrupted in a firm tone. "If it says you are, you are."

Lacey paused. In full physician mode, she studied Dani's face, then eventually patted her knee. "Do you want me to call in Beau?" she asked gently.

Normally, Dani knew, that was the next step. "No. Yes." Dani ran her hands through her hair, shoving it off her face. "I don't know." This had to be a dream. It couldn't possibly be real, could it? But if it was a dream, why couldn't she wake up? And why couldn't she shake the sudden sharp image of herself holding Beau Chamberlain's baby in her arms, with Beau standing right beside her? Why couldn't she shake the image of her and Beau and their baby becoming an incredibly happy and contented family?

What was happening to her? She wasn't romantic!

She was anything but. Their public feuding had shown her that Beau was not the man for her. From the first moment they'd met at a party two years ago, he had tried to tell her that real life could be every bit as good as in the movies. While she had tried to tell him that real life was rarely as fair or kind or predictable over the long haul, as he made it out to be. Worse, he was doing the moviegoing public a disservice by making films that led people to believe that right always prevailed over wrong, because bitter experience had taught Dani that just wasn't so. *Sometimes the worst happened for no reason at all.*

"Maybe you need a minute?" Lacey asked as Dani put a hand to her tummy and let it hover there, contemplating the unexpected miracle within. She didn't feel any different. She didn't look any different. And yet, deep inside her was a tiny baby that was part Beau and part her, growing, thriving and in need of a tremendous amount of tender loving care from both of them. If that wasn't a miracle of life and love, what was?

"I definitely need a minute," Dani said firmly as she pushed the happiness and wonder from her heart. She had always wanted a baby. But not like this. And definitely not with the man who had never even been her friend!

"Jackson and I are both going to be here at the hospital all evening. We're heading up the search committee for the new family practitioner to take his dad's place as chief of Family Medicine. And we've got a hundred résumés to read through. So if you want to talk or you think of any questions, just call me or come by. In the meantime, you need to set up an appointment with an obstetrician on staff. And start taking these prenatal vitamins." Lacey sifted through the supply cupboard, pulling out samples of vitamins and several pamphlets. "Also, read these. They cover the basic dos and don'ts of pregnancy. Okay?"

"Okay." Still in shock, Dani stared at everything Lacey put in her hands.

Lacey touched her shoulder gently. "Are you going to be okay?"

Dani drew a deep breath and tried not to think about how irked Beau had been with her because she had never seen things his way and probably never would. "Sure," she fibbed. "It's just a lot to take in."

"I know, but like I said, Jackson and I are here for you, so don't hesitate to call."

Lacey slipped out. Seconds later the door opened. His expression both hopeful and wary, Beau stepped in. He looked at her. "Guess I don't need to ask the results."

Dani slid off the end of the examining table. Her legs were trembling as she put the pamphlets and prenatal vitamins aside and reached for her clothing. "I do not understand how this could have happened," Dani muttered. Under the cover of her hospital gown, she slipped on her panties, and then her white linen slacks. Her fingers were shaking so badly she could barely manage the zipper and button clasp.

Arms folded in front of him, Beau leaned against the corner of the examining table. "Make that two of us," he muttered, for a moment looking as taken aback as she felt.

Silence fell as she pulled on her bra beneath her gown.

"Well, it could be worse," he said eventually as she turned her back, removed her gown and slipped on her blouse.

"How?" Dani demanded, distressed. Turning back

to him, she found her sandals. She hated that he was now trying to make the best of this! She wanted him to be as upset—as simultaneously ecstatic and upset about her unexpected pregnancy—as she was. But now that his shock had faded, Beau Chamberlain was looking downright happy about it all! As if it was yet another example of life always working out for the best, instead of the unmitigated disaster it could very well turn out to be.

Beau grinned and shrugged. "You could be pregnant and *unmarried*."

Straightening, Dani glared at him. She did not appreciate his quip and she let him know it with a look. "That's not funny." She pushed the words through tightly clenched teeth.

He sighed, then grimaced. "Okay." He shoved a hand through his hair again. "Obviously this has caught us both off guard and we have a lot to figure out."

"You're not kidding there." Dani grabbed a brush from her purse and, stepping over to the mirror, ran it through her hair. Tucking the curving ends behind her ears, she looked steadily at Beau, who was standing just left and behind her, in the mirror. "Like when, where and how we are going to get an annulment without anyone—other than my sisters, thanks to your blurting it out the way you did—ever finding out we were married."

Instead of agreeing with her, as Dani had hoped and expected he would, Beau Chamberlain merely shook his head. He gave her a look stony with resolve. "I meant what I said, Dani. No annulment. And no divorce. I don't know exactly how or why we entered into this marriage, but I'm not about to let us look any more foolish than we already do," he warned flatly. "The two of us are staying married."

Dani whirled to face him. A pulse pounding in her throat, she tipped her head up to his. "But we don't love each other!" And as far as Dani was concerned, love was the only reason to get—or stay—married.

Beau clamped his hands on her arms, his expression no less confident. "Then maybe we'll grow to love each other," he suggested with customary optimism. His glance narrowing, he continued to hold her gently but firmly, "Meanwhile, you're having our baby. And our baby is *not* going to be born illegitimate."

Beau waited for Dani's reaction. It wasn't long in coming.

"This is ridiculous," she stormed, pulling herself free of him yet again. She stomped away, her slender hips swaying provocatively beneath her tailored linen slacks. "We don't even like each other!"

Content to go ahead and have it out with her right there in the Laramie Community Hospital family clinic, if that was what she wanted, Beau braced himself for a battle. After all, he'd known getting things worked out between them wouldn't be easy. That was why he'd taken the time to make sure he'd figured out all of the angles before he showed up on her doorstep.

Now that he was here, he found it was worth the wait. Well worth it. For she had never looked more beautiful to him, nor feistier, than she did at that moment. Soft silky hair, the color of copper gleaming in the Texas sun, framed her delicate oval face. But it was more than the soft swell of her breasts, the slender indentation of her waist, curvaceous hips and long sexy legs that put his hormones into overdrive whenever he was around her. It was the sassy tilt of her chin, the intelligence and wit that sparkled in her eyes. Without even trying, Dani challenged him in a way no other woman ever had or ever would.

Physically they were a match. Emotionally…well, emotionally was another matter. From the first moment they'd met at that party, Dani'd had her dander up. Probably because her previous romance with another actor had ended badly. But that was no reason for her to mistrust him. Especially now that a damn miracle had occurred and they were having a baby that, like it or not, would bind them together for life.

"We could like each other, given half a chance," Beau said finally. That was, if Dani would put her usual cynicism aside and let them get to know each other the way he had wanted to from the very start. But to his dismay, once again Dani wasn't about to let that happen.

"That's not very likely," Dani shot back, her amber eyes darkening defensively, "given that we have completely different views on just about everything that matters."

That was true, Beau thought resting one hip against the edge of the examining table. But once again, it wasn't something insurmountable. "Nevertheless, we need to stay married."

"Until the baby is born," Dani wearily guessed.

Beau shook his head. "Until we figure out what happened to make us go off and do such a foolish thing as get married."

Dani stared at Beau. "I already told you," she repeated impatiently. "I can't remember anything."

Beau lifted a skeptical brow, figuring if he had some fuzzy memories, she surely had some, too. "Not even why we ended up in Mexico?"

"Well, of course I remember that!" Dani retorted, incensed.

WEARY OF THE PUBLIC SNIPING that had been going on almost from the moment they'd met, the two of them had decided to try to work things out. Dani had wanted to stay in Laramie to talk. But in desperate need of some real rest and recreation after completing work on *Bravo Canyon,* Beau had insisted they take his private jet and go to his villa in Mexico. Dani had agreed for three reasons. One, she had known that getting Beau to understand *her* view of what movies should be and not his was going to be a long slow process. Two, she had seen how genuinely tired he was after the long arduous shoot in the Guadalupe Mountains of Texas. And three, because she had wanted to try to end the fighting with Beau out from under the watchful eyes of her sisters and John and Lilah McCabe, who were likely to see any personal conversations between Beau and Dani as reason for romantic speculation or matchmaking. And, Dani was reluctant to admit, they wouldn't have been far off.

The truth was, she had been secretly attracted to Beau Chamberlain from the very first. So attracted, in fact, that she'd had to use every ounce of attitude she possessed to keep him at arm's length. At first he had been amused. But as time wore on, he'd become increasingly irritated by her standoffish behavior. To the point he had begun sniping back, annoying her and getting under her skin every chance he got in much the same way the boys had used to tease her at recess. Dani—and everyone else in Hollywood, it seemed—had sensed that a mutual attraction was behind Beau's verbal sparring and increasingly public attention to her. To stop it, all she had to do was let her defenses down, talk to him with the same openness and vulnerability she showed her other friends.

But that hadn't been an option for Dani two years ago, not in the film industry. She had mixed business and pleasure once before, and been stung when she gave the movie that her boyfriend, Chris Avery, was in one star and then been dubbed the Lady with the Poison Pen. It was a moniker everyone in Hollywood, including Beau, had repeated at one time or another either in anger or in jest. Dani had no intention of letting that happen again. So she had kept her attraction to Beau to herself. And she hadn't let any of what went on between them color her reviews of Beau's movies. She had made sure she was just as tough on him as she was with everyone else.

And she had known, even if the impossible happened and they did manage to become friends when they went off to Mexico together, that would continue. Dani did not do favors for people she knew in the business; her professional reputation was much too important to her.

Which made what had eventually happened—the two of them ending up married and in bed together—even more puzzling. Not just for her, but for him.

"And what else do you remember?" Beau prodded.

Dani spread her palms helplessly on either side of her. "I remember arguing with you in sort of a flirtatious way all afternoon and into the night, and that's it." Dani paused, aware they hadn't actually gotten married until the next day if the date on the marriage certificate he had shown her was correct. That left a very big blank in her memory. A thirty-some-hour blank she found very dismaying, especially after all the bantering and teasing that had been going on prior to that. Like it or not, from the moment they stepped on that plane, her defenses had been going down. And apparently so had his.

Reminding herself not to be too trusting, Dani asked cautiously, "What about you?" Up until this afternoon, she had assumed *he* was the mastermind of this whole folly. That he had designed the whole thing as payback to embarrass her and throw her for a loop for the not-so-glowing reviews she had given his movies and the way she had deliberately held him at arm's length, refusing to let him work his movie-star charm on her. But now, given the stunned and curious way he kept looking at her, she couldn't help but wonder if he wasn't as much an innocent victim of whatever had happened to them as she was. And if that was the case, she had no reason at all to be mad at him. And that was a notion she found even more unnerving. Because it was her anger, their mutual resentment, that she had been counting on to keep them apart and prevent them from doing whatever it was they'd done down in Mexico again.

Beau frowned, stroked his jaw and continued filling her in matter-of-factly. "When it comes to that night, I draw a complete blank. I'd like to think it's because the whole evening was so traumatic," he teased, beating her to the punch with a wink.

"Har-de-har-har, cowboy," Dani responded, determined not to let him joke his way out of anything when it came to the two of them. "And if that evening was traumatic," she asserted stubbornly, "it was traumatic for both of us."

"True." Beau paused, stroked his jaw again. As the thoughtful moment drew out, his eyes sparkled wickedly. He rolled his weight onto his toes and leaned toward her conspiratorially. "And yet there must be some reason we got married that night and made a baby," he said.

"Complete utter insanity?" Dani quipped drolly. The only reason she would ever have gotten married—knowingly anyway—was for love. Her heart quickened its pace as she feared where this line of questioning was leading. Deftly she stepped back.

He stepped toward her. "That, sweetheart, goes without saying." He laced his hands around her waist and tugged her against him until they were touching breast to chest, tummy to tummy, thigh to thigh. "The truth is," Beau continued resolutely, looking down at her with soft serious eyes, "whatever happened that night had nothing to do with where we were or what we were doing at the time or even what we were arguing about. Instead—" his velvety voice dropped another compelling notch "—it had everything to do with what has been going on with us since the first day we met."

He sounded so sure. So smugly certain! "And that is what exactly?" Dani prodded, afraid from the amorous gleam in his eyes she already knew precisely what he was going to assert.

"Desire," Beau whispered softly, sifting a hand through her hair, watching it as it fell in silky copper strands across her cheek. "Pure unadulterated desire."

Dani laughed uneasily and tried, unsuccessfully, to step out of the warm confining hopelessly erotic circle of his arms. "Now I know you're insane," she claimed as she splayed both hands across his chest and felt the strong heavy thudding of his heart, so like her own. "I have never, not for one day, not for even one second, desired you!" Dani fibbed as his gaze traced the parted contours of her lips.

Beau's sexy smile widened. He slid a hand beneath

her chin and tilted her face up to his. "Sure about that now?" he asked as his head slowly lowered.

"I'm positive," Dani whispered. Trembling at his nearness, she drew in a jerky breath. This was not going to happen. He was not going to kiss her.

Beau touched his lips lightly to hers once, and then again. "Okay, let's see," he murmured seductively. The next thing Dani knew her eyes were closed and his lips were on hers, nudging them apart. It was the kind of kiss you saw in the movies. Tender, evocative, erotic. Sensitive, searching. It was the kind of kiss you never really expected—in real life—to get. But getting it she was, and she had to admit that, even as she stood on tiptoe and let herself be drawn into the seamlessly sexy kiss, it was rocking her to her very soul. Making her tingle all over. Making her want. Need. Desire. Oh, heavens, she had never felt such desire. Or experienced anything so wonderful and dangerous and right. And it was then, just as she should have suspected, that Beau let the soft kiss come to a slow effortless conclusion.

Still holding her in his arms, Beau searched her eyes. "Now do you remember?"

Chapter Two

Suddenly Dani knew what was happening and why. She couldn't believe she had been such a fool. Worse, she had almost—almost—bought the I'm-head-over-heels-in-love-with-you look in his eyes! Only her common sense had saved her from admitting something equally foolish to him. But thank heaven she was one woman who was firmly rooted in reality. She knew—better than most—that this life did not come with happily-ever-afters. Especially ever-afters that good. She might wish one of the most famous movie stars in the world was totally enthralled with her, but it wasn't happening. No matter how hard the Texas lothario was currently pushing to convince her otherwise.

"Now I get it," Dani said as she shoved away from him.

"Get what?" Beau studied her with highly exaggerated confusion.

Dani scowled and planted her hands on her hips. No way was this handsome cowboy running a scam on her. "So where is it?"

Beau quirked an eyebrow and continued to regard her with confusion. "Where's what?"

"The hidden camera."

"Camera?" Beau repeated, doing, Dani thought, a fine job of acting perplexed.

But she wasn't buying it. Not for one red-hot instant. She waved her hands excitedly. "We're on the *Celebrity Hoaxes* TV show, aren't we?" Stepping forward, she pointed an accusing finger at his chest. "This is all a practical joke. On me. And everyone in Laramie is probably in on it. My sisters, Lacey McCabe and the people right here at the hospital." Which meant, of course, she wasn't really pregnant, either, since they hadn't really made love or gotten married in Mexico. So she could stop worrying about that right now, Dani concluded with relief. Since this was all part of a giant joke on her.

"Come on, where are the cameras?" Dani began to search the examining room.

Beau followed her, looking even more nonplussed as she searched behind the cabinets, beneath the sink. "What cameras?"

Dani whirled to face him. "The ones that are taping us for the TV show, of course."

Beau placed his hands on her shoulders, then said very quietly and very calmly, "Dani, there are no cameras."

She smiled thinly, aware that she had never wanted to haul off and slug him more than she did at that minute. "Of course you *would* say that." He wanted her to make a fool of herself in the worst way!

Beau's eyes darkened. "I mean it, Dani. There are no cameras," he repeated firmly. Hands slipping back to her waist, he lifted her up and onto the examining table. Trapping her with his body, bracing a hand on either side of her, he leaned in close, "We are *not* being filmed."

Dani ignored him as another flare of mistrust swept through her. "If you say so, but for the record—" she looked straight into his midnight-blue eyes "—this is all a colossal waste of time. Since I will never in a million years give you permission to air what is taking place right here and right now." That said, she leaned back and neatly folded her hands on her lap.

"That's good." Beau looked pleased as he stepped between her knees and pulled her close. "Because I don't think I'd want what is taking place right now aired anywhere." He angled his thumb at his chest, winked facetiously. "I don't want to be made a fool of, either. I have a reputation to maintain, you know."

Speaking of reputations, they had been in here— alone—an awfully long time, Dani thought. Enough to get the local gossip mill going, big time. "Too bad you didn't think of that before you convinced me to go off to Mexico with you." Dani pushed him away with both hands, hopped off the table and exited the examining room. Dashing to the front desk, she paid her bill, then headed out the doors into the shimmering late-afternoon heat.

Beau caught up with her just past the entrance and steered her toward his vintage pickup. Made in 1960, the cherry-red truck was in mint condition inside and out, the only change to it modern safety belts and a topnotch stereo system. It was not exactly the kind of vehicle Dani would ever have expected a Hollywood star to drive. She figured he'd drive something expensive and strictly for status. But the cherished old pickup, so sturdy and reliable and masculine, suited him just the same. Maybe because it was the kind of truck a real cowboy would drive.

"Too bad we didn't think of a lot of things before

we flew off to Mexico together.'' Beau opened the door and, still holding her elbow, gallantly helped her inside.

A prickle of uneasiness moved through Dani as the next thought hit. She watched as he circled the truck and slid behind the steering wheel. "Were there cameras in Mexico, too?" she asked, aghast, noticing without wanting to the way his white cotton shirt delineated the sexy contours of his shoulders, chest and abs. Was it her imagination or could she actually remember the way it had felt to be held against that rock-solid chest, with nothing between them but heat and bare skin?

Beau turned the key in the ignition and shot her an astonished look. "I sincerely hope not!" he said, thrusting the truck into reverse. Sliding one arm along the back of the seat behind her, he pulled out of the space, then put the truck into first. His large capable hands on the wheel, he guided the truck toward the exit and onto the street.

"I don't know why I didn't see it earlier," Dani said, incensed she had been such an idiot. She shook her head as Beau stopped at the light at the corner of Johnson Drive and Main Street and turned her eyes to the people coming in and out of the businesses in the center of town. A group had gathered in front of the courthouse and were talking animatedly. A mother and two children were carrying a cake out of Isabel Buchanon's bakeshop. Men were lined up in Tom's barber shop, awaiting haircuts and shaves. The afternoon edition of the *Laramie Press* was being loaded into trucks for delivery. Comforted by the homespun familiarity of the scene, Dani turned back to Beau and continued matter-of-factly, "This is all payback for our feud."

Beau's jaw set as he drove down Main Street and then onto the street where she lived. He turned into her driveway and parked behind Dani's car. He cut the engine with a snap. Released his seat belt and faced her. "For the last time," he said quietly, "I am not playing a prank on you."

Dani wished she could believe him. Her feelings in turmoil, she glared at him emotionally. "I want to call a halt to this, Beau. Right now." She wanted not to be pregnant and not to be married.

"I just bet you do," Beau said sarcastically as he reached over and released the catch of her safety belt. "Unfortunately, my darling wife—" the words were pushed through gritted teeth, and his hot gaze glided over her from head to toe, before returning with heart-stopping accuracy to her face "—it's not that simple."

Wasn't it? Dani wondered. And darn it all, anyway, why did he keep insisting on calling her his *wife*, never mind his *darling wife?* Couldn't he see she hated that? How uncomfortable it made her? Of course he could! That, she supposed, as the word continued to echo in her head like a mantra, was precisely the point.

She knew what the evidence said, but the two of them couldn't be married. They just couldn't be! She wouldn't—couldn't—have been that foolish. No matter how secretly attracted to him she was or what movie-star moves he'd put on her! No, this was all a bad joke or a bad dream. And it would be over soon enough. All she had to do was take a page from the exasperating cowboy's book and kick a little butt. His.

"Okay," Dani retorted slowly and succinctly, letting him know with a glance this…whatever it was could not and would not go on. "If you won't call a halt to this lunacy now, then when exactly will you?"

BEAU KNEW DANI would never believe it, the way she

was feeling now, but he wished this lunacy was a practical joke every bit as fervently as she did. Heaven knew he'd initially had the same suspicions she was harboring.

Never before had he blacked out anything, let alone awakened in a bed with a beautiful woman having no idea how he'd gotten there, or when or why. But that it had happened was indisputable, Beau reminded himself sternly.

Making matters worse, kissing her at the hospital had brought back a snippet of lovemaking with her that was so incredibly spectacular it might have been a dream. And yet he knew instantly from the startling clarity of this snippet—the image of Dani naked and in bed beneath him—that it was no fantasy he was having, but a memory. Otherwise, how would he know she had a beauty mark on her left breast, right next to the nipple? How would he have such a clear image of the creaminess of her breasts, the lissome lines of her spread thighs and the sweet triangle of coppery curls the exact shade of her hair? How would he know, even as he took her in his arms tonight, that the sassy cynical-to-the-max Dani kissed with a mixture of innocence and enthusiasm that was daunting in the extreme? How would he know about the soft sexy sounds she made in the back of her throat when they made love, or how much she liked making love in the missionary position? But he did know all that. Just as he knew when he took her in his arms tonight that when they started kissing, that when they were together like that, it was all either of them could do to stop.

As for the rest, the marriage and baby part, he just couldn't imagine it. Yes, she had been a burr in his side for years now, and for one reason or another constantly on his mind, but they'd never been lovers or even close to romantically involved. Maybe they should have been, though, Beau reasoned as Dani jumped out of the truck and walked toward the house, leaving him to follow at will. Maybe if they had kissed back then, before all the trouble started, the way they had today, maybe Dani and he never would have feuded at all.

Dani paused at the top of the steps and rummaged around in her purse for her keys. Finally finding them, she unlocked the door and led the way into her house, full of moving boxes and extremely disorganized furniture. She switched on the overhead light in the foyer and whirled to face him. "You didn't answer my question, Beau," she snapped impatiently. "How long do you plan to let this scam continue?"

Beau shrugged. "As long as it takes." He didn't want to be saddled with a marriage he couldn't even remember entering into, but he was. And so was she. Like it or not, until he and Dani figured out exactly what had happened in Mexico, they were in this together.

"As long as it takes for what?"

For us to really get to know each other, he thought. *For us to be, if not loving partners, at least friends.* Because he had much preferred the idea of being Dani's friend to being her enemy. Certainly it would be much easier to bring up a baby that way.

Unable to take his eyes off Dani and the delectable picture she made in her trim linen slacks and sleeveless blouse, her bare feet peeking out beneath the strappy sandals, he edged nearer and replied, "For me to put an end to this feud between us once and for all."

"I've got news for you, Beau Chamberlain," she informed him in a soft sweet voice that set his teeth on edge. "This is not the way to do it!"

"Then what is?" Beau countered as Dani swept past him into the shadowy living room. "Reason didn't do it."

Stepping around the sofa and two club chairs, Dani began reading what was written on the tops of the moving cartons, which were stacked, one on top of the other, all over the place. Finally finding one that said "lamp," she made a soft *aha* sound and attempted to lift it down. Beau strode over to help her before she could pick it up. He set it on the floor beside her.

"There's been nothing reasonable about anything you've said to me for the past two years," Dani said. She slammed her hands on her hips, looking peeved rather than pleased by his help.

Guessing what she wanted, which was to get lamps set up around the house before darkness fell, Beau ripped open the top of the box, removed the lamp and began assembling base to shade. "There was nothing reasonable about your reviews, either!" Beau shot right back. It bugged him she hadn't liked his work. Not because he thought her reviews were inaccurate, but because they had been accurate. He'd known he wasn't doing his best work in the two-year period after his nasty divorce from Sharon. It annoyed the heck out of him that Dani had easily recognized what other reviewers had failed to see—that a part of him had lost heart. Dani's fair but kick-butt reviews of his work had been a wake-up call to him to put the past behind him. Now he was back at the top of his craft again. And soon Dani would know it, too.

"So *that's* what this is all about," Dani pronounced grimly as she found another box labeled lamp. "The fact that you, cowboy, have a movie opening next week. So what's the deal?" she asked stormily as Beau ripped

open the box. Her chin angled up. "I write something
nice about *Bravo Canyon* and no one ever sees the film
of me acting like a blooming idiot, believing we got
married and are expecting a baby?" Temper flashing in
her amber eyes, turning them a darker prettier hue, she
pulled both shade and base from the box. She shook
her head, silky copper strands flying in all directions.
Then proceeded to rip the protective wrapping from the
lamp base and shade with quick angry motions. "Blackmail will not get a good review from me, Beau."

Once again, Beau took the parts and fastened them
together. He set the reassembled lamp aside. "I don't
want a good review from you."

Dani paused, disbelief evident on her face. Her soft
sexy lips compressing stubbornly, she bent over to get
the lightbulb from the box.

"What I'd really like is no review of *Bravo Canyon*
from you at all."

Dani whirled to face him. "And you know I can't do
that," she replied stonily, looking him straight in the
eye. "*Bravo Canyon* is one of the summer blockbusters.
I have to review it. Everyone does."

That, Beau thought, taking in the flushed features of
her face, was a matter of opinion. The seconds strung
out tensely as another silence fell.

Dani clamped her arms in front of her like a shield.
"Joke's over now, Chamberlain. Go home now."

Beau shook his head solemnly, every protective instinct coming to the fore. It might be old-fashioned, but
she was his woman—at least according to the marriage
certificate. And she was carrying their baby. His personal code of honor dictated he not let anything happen
to either of them. "Afraid not," he told her, determined

to see this through. "I can't let you lift anything. Not in your condition."

Dani sighed, rolled her eyes. She swept both hands through her halo of copper hair, pushing it off her face. "You don't have anything to say about this, even if I am pregnant."

He had only to glance at her tummy and think about their future to know differently. "Afraid I do," he said.

Dani swallowed. If she didn't know better, she'd think—by the way he was looking at her—that the two of them really were meant to be together. But that wasn't true, she reassured herself. It couldn't be. And if Beau seemed to think it was...well, that was easily explained. He was a heroically responsible man. He didn't want to think they'd had a meaningless fling that had resulted in a marriage and a pregnancy. How would such reckless behavior make them look? Far better to assume something incredibly romantic and impulsive. Just because he felt that way, however, did not mean she had to.

"Fine." Recognizing he wasn't likely to leave anytime soon of his own volition, she threw up her hands in defeat and treated him to a careless smile. "You want to sign on as unpaid labor around here? Who am I to stop you? We'll get started now. Roll up your sleeves, cowboy, and get to work."

Dani expected him to bolt as soon as he saw she was serious about getting started on the unpacking. Instead, he worked diligently by her side, finding and then unpacking linens for the upstairs hall closet, bath items for the shower, sheets and blankets and pillows for her bed. He hooked up her TV, stereo and VCR, and placed them all where she wanted them—in her bedroom. When six o'clock came and their stomachs growled, he called Greta Wilson McCabe's Lone Star Dinner and Dance Hall downtown and had a nutritious dinner for two, complete with milk, delivered for them both.

During it all, Dani was as quiet and uncommunicative as could be. To her chagrin, this didn't seem to bother him, either. He continued to be as gallant and attentive as could be. And as she looked at him and saw the tenderness in his eyes, recalled the magic of Beau on screen, the one she and every woman in America had fallen in love with, she knew it would be so easy to forget everything and fall head over heels for him. It would be so easy to let herself get drawn into the fantasy of what could be. Not what was. She couldn't let that happen. Any more than she could dwell on the fleeting, but very distinct, memory of him in bed, above her.

As they slid off their stools at the kitchen counter and cleared away the empty food containers, Dani glanced at her watch and saw it was nearly 7 p.m. Bedtime was hours away, but her body felt the fatigue of moving in. Yet the last thing she wanted to do was lie in her bed alone, remembering the shattering sensuality of Beau's kiss earlier this afternoon, worrying about the foolhardy way she'd kissed him back. No, that wouldn't do. It wouldn't do at all.

Dani glanced back at the twenty-some boxes scattered around her kitchen. She hadn't touched one of them.

"Whoa now." Beau held up a staying palm before she could spring into action once again. "I think you've done enough for one day," he said sternly, reading her mind.

Actually they both had, Dani thought. "Not that I want to make a habit of agreeing with you, but I think

I have had enough for one day.'' Dani smiled. Hand against his spine, she propelled him toward the closest exit.

Beau dug in his heels and slowed their progress considerably. As they reached the back door, he wrapped an arm around her waist and looked at her curiously. ''We're not staying here tonight?'' The low sexy timbre of his voice sent a new thrill shooting down her spine.

''We're not staying anywhere together, cowboy,'' Dani corrected archly. She splayed a staying hand across his chest. ''Not now or any other night.''

Tugging her close, Beau leaned down, kissed her cheek and whispered in her ear, ''That's what you think.''

Chapter Three

Dani stared at Beau in a mixture of astonishment and disbelief. "You really can't think we're going to spend the night together."

His smile flashed, wicked and mesmerizing. "As your husband and the father of your baby, where else would I be?"

That again. Scowling, Dani folded her arms in front of her. She wasn't sure whether she wanted to deck him or kiss him. She just knew she had an overwhelming desire to do something physical where he was concerned. Deciding in the end it would be best just to keep as much distance from him as possible, she looked down her nose at him. "You're carrying this practical joke too far, Chamberlain."

She wasn't all that surprised to find *he* didn't think so. "If you really think I'm pulling your leg, or worse, that the lab work Lacey ran at the hospital was inaccurate, then put it to the test yourself," he dared with a complacent smile. "Go to the pharmacy and pick up a home pregnancy kit. Run the test yourself."

Dani regarded Beau uneasily. Why would he even suggest this, she wondered, restlessly shifting her weight from one bare foot to the other, unless it was true? Once again, Dani searched for hidden cameras, saw none. Still clinging to the hope this was all a bad dream she'd soon wake up from, Dani regarded Beau calmly. "I can't do that."

"Why not?" he volleyed back, in a low rich voice that practically oozed testosterone.

With effort Dani ignored the tremors of sexual awareness gathering deep inside her. This evening was beginning to feel too much like a date, with a kiss or two or three in the making. And it wasn't. She would do well to remember that.

Dani went over to get his hat, which he'd left on a shelf next to the back door. Marching to his side, she pressed it into his hands. "Laramie is a small town. If I went in and purchased one, the news would be all over town in an instant."

To her dismay, he merely put his hat aside, grabbed one of her hands, then leaned a shoulder against the door frame and made himself all the more at home. She tried without success to unobtrusively wrest her fingers from the strong warm tantalizing grip of his.

Beau lifted her hand to his lips and kissed the back of it, sending another tingle of awareness arrowing through her. Still holding her eyes with provoking gallantry, he murmured, "Then I'll buy it for you. Especially if it'll make you feel better to run a second test— one you've supervised yourself."

Dani swung away from him, not sure why he got under her skin this way, just knowing he did. "If you went into a store to purchase a pregnancy test, you'd definitely attract attention—even in a town like Laramie, which does a pretty good job of respecting your privacy. Then, before you know it, the story would be all over the tabloids." Miserably Dani closed her eyes.

"I can see the headlines now. Desperate for Child, Beau Chamberlain Buys Home Pregnancy Kit." She opened her eyes and regarded Beau stoically. "No thanks."

Beau rubbed his chin with his index finger and thumb and sent her a taunting grin. "You know, you seem to have a real talent for that." He winked. "Maybe you should give up reviewing movies and consider writing for the tabloids."

Dani rolled her eyes. "You're killing me, cowboy."

Beau lifted his hands in an amiable fashion. "I'm glad you have a sense of humor about this," he drawled, still regarding her appreciatively. "The way things are going, we're both going to need one."

Dani glared at him and said nothing.

Beau pushed away from the door and straightened his tall broad-shouldered frame. "You still don't believe we're married and you're pregnant, do you?" he said, closing the distance between them once again.

If she was only going on the possessive protective way he was behaving, she probably would believe it. But she knew better, she reminded herself firmly, backing up until she reached the counter. Things this crazy and romantic did not happen to her. "No reason I should," she retorted.

The doorbell rang.

Beau seemed irritated by the interruption. He looked at her impatiently. "Expecting anyone?"

"No," Dani said. "You?"

"No."

The doorbell rang again, more insistently.

She locked eyes with him deliberately. "I suppose you want me to get it?" she asked drolly.

Beau made his way through the stacked boxes to the living room, where he plopped down on the sofa and stretched his long legs out in front of him, continuing to make himself completely at home. "It is your house."

Shaking her head, Dani headed past him for the front door. She opened the door, half hoping to see a TV camera crew yelling "Surprise!" Or better yet, Dr. Lacey Buchanon McCabe, there to tell her the hospital lab had made a terrible mistake.

Instead, she found Billy Carter, the young man she'd been trying to gently discourage. His tall gangly frame was pitched forward with a determined eagerness that had Dani instantly on her guard. A liberal amount of styling gel tamed his rusty-brown hair. Round spectacles framed his intelligent brown eyes. Instead of his usual movie-slogan T-shirt and jeans, he was dressed in baggy khaki pants, a deep-purple dress shirt and vividly flowered tie, and clutched a fistful of flowers. The goatee he had grown to make him look older than eighteen was neatly trimmed, and he reeked of a seductive-smelling aftershave.

"I'm so glad you're home," Billy said breathlessly.

"You are," Dani said dryly.

Billy nodded. "Can I speak to you inside?"

"Sure." Dani let Billy into the front hallway.

"I was hoping we could go out tonight," Billy continued hurriedly, transferring the flowers from his sweaty palm to hers.

"Out?" Dani repeated, not sure where this was going.

"Just the two of us," Billy clarified seriously.

Dani decided if this pass was on the level, Beau did not need to hear it. Firmly she put the flowers back in Billy's damp hands, took his arm and directed him back to the door. Naturally, Billy dug in his heels and refused to budge. "Not here in Laramie, of course," he continued in a voice loud enough for Beau to hear every word.

Doing her best not to cringe, Dani tilted her head to the side and continued to regard her protégé warily. Behind Billy, Dani could see Beau watching with unveiled interest. Was it her imagination or did he suddenly look a little jealous, as well as disapproving? "Why not Laramie?" Dani asked Billy.

"Because." Billy shrugged and leaned forward urgently, pushing the flowers back at her. "People would see us together. No offense." He colored slightly. "I mean you seem really young to me, but—"

"I'm a decade older."

"Right. And people would, well, you know—"

"Think it inappropriate?" Deciding they'd wrestled with the flowers enough, Dani put the bouquet aside.

"But it wouldn't be," Billy rushed to assure her.

Then why was he suggesting they hide whatever they wanted to do?

Dani wondered. She sighed, shoving a hand through her hair. "Billy—"

Billy took her hand eagerly in his. "I just want us to be friends, Dani. I mean, really good friends."

As gently as possible, Dani extricated her fingers from his clammy palm. In the background she could see Beau unfolding himself from the sofa, frowning and coming toward them.

"We're going to be working together, starting tomorrow," she told Billy firmly, then spoke as if underlining every word, letting him know this couldn't—wouldn't—happen. "I'm not going to be just a mentor and a friend to you, Billy. I'm going to be your employer."

"So?" Billy shrugged again, not the least bit upset

or discouraged as, unbeknownst to him, Beau was coming up right behind him. "I know plenty of people who work together who also date," Billy told her practically.

"Not Dani," Beau said as he swaggered forward and deliberately inserted himself between them.

Billy blinked and pushed his glasses farther up the bridge of his nose. He stepped back, nearly tripping over his feet in the process. "I didn't know you were here," he stammered nervously.

What you need is a man, her sisters had said. *Someone to discourage Billy.* And clearly Billy needed to be discouraged. Big time, Dani thought. On the other hand, she didn't want to encourage Beau in the process. "Beau's here, all right, but he's not supposed to be here," Dani said sweetly, giving Beau a drop-dead look only he could see.

"But I am here," Beau corrected with a debonair assurance that made Dani grit her teeth.

"Unfortunately," Dani muttered. She did not like his possessive attitude one bit. Like everything else he'd done in the past few hours, it was a bit too convincing for her liking. Much more of his Academy Award-winning performance, she thought, willing her pounding heart to slow, and Beau'd have her believing he really was staking a permanent claim on her.

"Is he giving you any trouble?" Billy demanded, scowling and stepping between them. "Because if he is…" Billy continued, the threat in his low tone obvious.

The last thing Dani wanted was a fistfight taking place in her hallway. "No, no," she told Billy hastily as she stepped between the two males. She pushed all romantic thoughts from her mind. "It's okay."

Beau, taking advantage of the moment, placed his

hands on her shoulders. He tugged her against him, so her spine was against his chest. "Actually," he murmured, kissing the top of her head with husbandly affection, "it's very okay, isn't it, Dani?"

Ignoring the sensual feeling of his palms on her bare skin, Dani turned to face him, intending to let him know to cool it with a look. As their eyes clashed, he smiled and touched her face with the callused roughness of his palm, cupping her chin in his hand, scoring his thumb across her lips. She had the sharp suspicion he was about to kiss her as thoroughly and expertly as he had before, and the even sharper suspicion she'd be lost if he did.

Watching, Billy became even more upset. "I didn't know the two of you were friends."

"We're more than friends," Beau confirmed, suddenly becoming even more possessive. Maybe because he knew such action was guaranteed to get under her skin. He closed in on her deliberately, not stopping until there was a scant two inches between them. "In fact, I'm her—"

Dani elbowed him. "Very good friend." No way was she letting him say the word *husband*. She had enough explaining to do to her three sisters as it was. She was not adding Billy to the list. Beau merely smiled, looking more determined than ever to come out the winner in this battle of wills.

Billy, meanwhile, looked oddly relieved, now that he'd gotten over his disappointment. "So I guess you two have plans for tonight, huh?" he guessed.

Beau nodded. "Big ones. But we trust you to keep that under your hat."

"Sure. No problem." Billy looked past her at the clock that was now inching toward seven-thirty. "Look,

I don't have anything else to do this evening, so if you want me to go ahead and start unpacking the boxes of videos tonight, I could.''

"No. Tomorrow morning, nine o'clock, will be soon enough,'' Dani said. She took his elbow and escorted Billy to the front door.

Beau swaggered forward and held the door for him. "We'll see you then,'' Beau said.

"*I* will see you then,'' Dani corrected.

"You're right,'' Beau drawled. He gave her a self-assured faintly baiting look. "I'll probably be sleeping in.'' The implication being, Dani thought, that Beau planned to have a very long and tiring night. Doing what, she didn't even want to imagine. *This just gets worse with every second that passes.*

"Good night, Billy. Thank you for the flowers.'' Dani propelled him out the door. She shut it behind him, then turned and faced Beau. He looked very grim. Disapproving, almost. "What?'' Dani demanded impatiently.

Beau pointed to the moving carton with the bouquet on top. "The flowers. You shouldn't have accepted them. You should have given them back. In case you haven't noticed, he's got a giant crush on you,'' Beau continued as Billy's beat-up blue compact with the FILMBUF license plate pulled away from the curb and drove off.

Deciding Billy wasn't the only one who needed to leave, Dani opened the front door again. She took Beau by the hand and stepped out onto the front porch into the soft breezy heat of early evening. "You think that's news to me?''

"You should nip this thing with him in the bud,'' Beau continued. Taking her by the hand, he led her to the cushioned wicker love seat at the far end of the porch and tugged her down to sit beside him.

For the life of her Dani couldn't figure out why Beau was so concerned about this. Or why he seemed to think Billy could be a threat to either his or her happiness in any way. "I've tried."

His eyes glimmered with a cynicism that stung. He cocked his head and gave her a thorough once-over. "I saw."

If there was one thing Dani hated, it was being forced to defend herself when she'd done nothing wrong. And she'd done nothing to make Billy think he was ever going to be anything other than her friend. Or short-term employee.

Her nerves jangling, Dani jumped up and, irritated, began to pace the length of the porch. She shoved her hands in the pockets of her linen slacks and balled her hands into fists. "I don't want to hurt his feelings." And despite Billy's outward I'm-so-cool persona, he was just as vulnerable as she had been at that age.

Beau leaned back and clamped his arms over his rock-solid chest. "You don't think leading him on will hurt his feelings?"

Pointedly ignoring that remark, Dani stopped to perch herself on the railing to examine the fragrant magnolia bushes and brilliant crepe myrtle planted all around the front porch. "The only reason Billy is gaga over me is because I work in the film business. Trust me. What he is really feeling—he just doesn't realize it yet—is gratitude for the encouragement I've given him. I think his dreams of becoming the next Stephen Spielberg or George Lucas are possible. From what he's told me, no one else in Laramie does."

Briefly, compassion and empathy glimmered in

Beau's eyes. And Dani sensed why. An actor who had made it solely on his own, with no familial connections of any kind, Beau knew what it was like to overcome enormous odds and achieve the kind of success very few ever did. "It's quite a leap from here to Hollywood," he conceded thoughtfully after a moment, rubbing his jaw.

"Tell me about it," Dani murmured. She'd had to work like crazy to get her movie reviews published. First in a single Los Angeles newspaper and now in a syndicated column that appeared in dozens of newspapers across the nation.

"But there are other people—filmmakers—who could mentor him," Beau continued. "With your connections..."

She looked at Beau, letting him know with a glance that she was not passing Billy off like a piece of clothing she no longer wanted, even if he could be ridiculously naïve at times about relationships between men and women, what was possible, what was clearly not. She would get through to Billy eventually, and she would do it without crushing his eighteen-year-old heart. "Not that it's any of your business, Chamberlain, but I promised Billy a summer job and I intend to honor that promise. Plus, I really need his skills."

Beau pushed to his feet and waited for her to continue.

"I signed a contract to do a book," Dani explained as Beau sauntered closer. "One thousand and one reviews of 'date night' movie videos. Everything from the classics to the newest releases."

Beau stopped just short of her perch and regarded her curiously. "How did you pick which ones to review?" *And were there any of his movies in the group?*

His unspoken question hung in the air.

"That's just it." Dani bit her lip as she answered his question, and tension flooded her anew. "I haven't yet. And with every major film studio sending me several thousand films, I've got a ton to sort through. Just cataloging them is going to be a bear."

"Which is where Billy comes in," Beau guessed. He leaned forward, bracing a hand on the railing on either side of her.

Dani leaned back slightly. Her heart was pounding. She was tingling all over. She told herself it was the tension causing her body to go haywire and not his proximity. She glowered at Beau. She could feel the blood rushing to her cheeks even as she sought to get a handle on her soaring emotions. "Billy's knowledge of films, past and present, is incredible. He can help me sort through them."

Beau leaned in closer. "When is your manuscript due?"

Dani swallowed, her adrenaline pumping for a completely different reason. "A year from now." Dani tried not to feel too overwhelmed by the work still to be done or the enormous project she had taken on. "They want it in the stores by the following Christmas."

She could practically see the wheels turning as Beau did some quick calculations. "Which means you'd have to watch and review three movies a day," Beau surmised grimly after a moment. He folded his arms.

Dani studied Beau's handsome face and tall muscled form. There was nothing soft or easy about him. She sensed there never would be. He was who he was, take it or leave it. Trying not to think how much they had in common that way, Dani nodded and replied, "Approximately, yeah. In addition to writing my weekly reviews for syndication. That's why I need so much help this summer getting organized.''

Blue eyes narrowing, he continued to study her relentlessly. ''Sounds like you've taken on a lot.''

Too much, he meant, Dani noted resentfully. ''I think I know what I can and cannot handle,'' Dani retorted stiffly, releasing a slow, ragged breath, not about to admit that recently she'd had the same concerns herself. ''Not that it is any of your concern.''

Beau merely stood there.

''You were just leaving,'' Dani reminded him.

Beau nodded. ''I was.''

''But…?'' Dani hopped down from her perch and tried to sidle past him to avoid any further discussion. Not about to let her go that easily, he put up a hand to stop her, and her ribs made contact with the flexed muscles of his forearm, instead. With a sigh of frustration, she moved back so they were no longer touching and tried not to imagine a life with a man so hell-bent on having his own way all the time.

''I changed my mind,'' Beau said, a determined look on his face.

Dani's temper kicked into full gear. ''You've decided to end this lunacy of a marriage at long last?''

Beau shook his head. ''I've decided,'' he enunciated clearly, ''to protect my turf.''

Dani flushed self-consciously. Without warning, she had an idea what it would be like to really be Beau's wife, to wake up in his arms every morning, to lie in his arms every night. The thought was as tantalizing as it was disturbing. Being near him this way was like playing around a fire. Stay too far away, and you'll never get warm. Come too close, and you'll get burned. Deciding it was best just to keep a fair distance between them, she propped her hands on her hips and said, "I told you before. You can't stay here. Laramie is a small town."

"So small," Beau agreed, looking very much like he wanted nothing more than to make love to her then and there, "that all the hotel rooms are booked."

"So stay with Greta and Shane McCabe," Dani suggested, knowing it would be a dangerous proposition to have Beau too close to her for too long. Because the truth was, she did desire him and always had. She swallowed, pushing those thoughts away. Then she continued firmly, "They're close friends of yours."

One corner of Beau's mouth quirked in a smile. "They're also newlyweds," he answered, leaving no question about what he thought Shane and Greta would be doing most nights. Exactly what he probably wanted to be doing.

Dani turned away from him and walked to the other end of the porch. She reached down to touch the silky white petals of a magnolia blossom. Needing something to hang on to, she plucked it from its stem, turned back to Beau. He was still eyeing her with a depth of male speculation she found disturbing. "That didn't stop you from practically brawling with Shane in the middle of the street a few weeks ago."

Beau shifted so he was standing with his legs braced apart. He jammed his hands on his hips and narrowed his eyes. "That was a publicity stunt for *Bravo Canyon.*" He paused, still looking her up and down, from the breeze-mussed strands of her coppery hair to her bare toes and back again. "Or hadn't you heard?"

"Could this be one, too, pray tell?" Dani asked sweetly, with a lofty wave of the fragrant white blossom in her hand. Abruptly she felt a little sick, realizing there could be yet another reason for these drawn-out she-nanigans of his besides mere payback. Publicity.

"There's only one way to find out," Beau said with a smug smile. He strolled toward her. "Hang in there and see."

He stopped just short of her, looking once again as if he wanted very much to kiss her. Pulse pounding, Dani backed away from him. Try as she might, she could not get Beau off her front porch without creating a scene. The best way to play it, she decided stubbornly, was to make her responses to his macho maneuvers so dull and uninteresting that there was no way he would want to continue to spend time with her.

So she gave up trying to get Beau to leave, walked to the front door, leaving him to follow at will. She would begin to close down the house for the night, even though it was barely eight o'clock. "Fine, Beau. Have it your way," she said in a low bored tone as she tossed aside the blossom and marched into the house, him hard on her heels. Discounting him completely, she shut and locked the front door behind them. "Bed down on my sofa for the night. See if I care. Just bear in mind—" she favored him with a sweet taunting smile "—that marriage or no marriage, nothing of a romantic nature is going to happen here."

At the mention of their marriage, Beau's black brows drew together like thunderclouds over his midnight-blue eyes. "Meaning what?" he asked sarcastically as Dani headed for the stairs. Sauntering closer, he crossed his arms and girded his thighs as if for battle. "You've already decided to give up on us?"

"There is no 'us.'" Feeling hot color flush her cheeks, Dani spoke as if underlining every word. Not about to let him get the better of her, now or at any other time, she held her ground, despite the fact they were now uncomfortably close. Close enough for her to inhale his alluring cologne. Close enough for her to see the speculation gleaming in his eyes.

Beau braced his legs a little farther apart, gaze skimming her deliberately, provocatively. "Careful. You don't want to make a decision like that too soon."

Heart pounding, Dani studied him. Unwilling to think what it would be like if someone as used to getting his own way as Beau decided he wanted to be a permanent part of her life, she drew an unsteady breath. "You really aren't going to leave?" she asked rudely, knowing for Beau there were no real deterrents, only obstacles to be overcome.

"I am your husband," he reminded her with a look of utter male supremacy. "And since husbands and wives generally stay under the same roof…"

Finding his low sexy voice a bit too determined, too full of sexual promise for comfort, Dani turned away uneasily. "Fine." She put up both hands in surrender and kept walking. "Do whatever you want. But if you think you're getting a blanket or a pillow," she said over her shoulder as she headed up the stairs, "you're dreaming, cowboy."

"You're going to bed already?" he queried, not bothering to hide his disappointment over that.

Dani smiled, aware she had just won a victory in this battle of wills, albeit a small one. "You bet I am." She smiled sweetly and watched his disappointment deepen. Unable to help herself, she added, "Of course, if you get bored you can always change your mind and leave."

BEAU WATCHED Dani's slender body disappear into the master bedroom at the head of the stairs. Desire welled up inside him, but he knew for tonight anyway, it would go unsatiated. As much as he would like to wake up in bed with her again, sans clothing of any kind, he knew they had things to figure out first. Things they probably should have figured out before ending up in bed together initially.

He wasn't sure they'd be able to wait until they had all the answers they needed, given the potency of that kiss they'd shared this afternoon and the memory of how it had felt to have her warm naked body draped over his. But he wanted at least some of those answers, some explanation for what had apparently happened between them. And he knew, whether she admitted it or not, that so did she.

Deciding he might as well get comfortable, given the long boring evening ahead, he kicked off his boots and stretched out on the red sofa in the living room. He knew what she thought—that he was sticking to her like glue and staying the night merely to annoy her and prove a point. But she was wrong. He was staying because being with her was the only way to remember what had happened during that thirty-six-hour period neither of them could quite recall.

If the two of them had made love and gotten married and inadvertently or purposefully made a baby—so quickly—there had to have been a reason. And a darn good one, Beau was betting. Either they'd both taken complete leave of their senses, something he was beginning to see was a distinct possibility; been hypnotized by aliens and chosen to propagate a new species; blackmailed, drugged, tricked or somehow forced into the nuptials—by whom or what he sure as heck couldn't imagine as there was very little that could make either of them do anything they didn't want to. Or she'd been so madly in love with him and he with her that they couldn't bear to be apart one moment longer. Which seemed likely, given how physically attracted they were to each other, as their kiss this afternoon had proved. And seemed equally unlikely, given how quick they were to disagree on just about everything.

Heck, Beau thought as he folded his hands behind his head and sought to get more comfortable, maybe they'd just decided to have a baby together, despite their different views on life, and decided they needed to be married—temporarily—to do that. Whatever their motivation, they were in this predicament now up to their chins, and no crazy TV show or small-town pressures or mutual work demands were going to negate that.

Chapter Four

Beau had barely settled in when he heard the soft pad of footsteps coming down the stairs. Seconds later Dani entered the living room. She was dressed just as she'd been when she'd gone upstairs. "Lonely already?" This was working out better than he'd hoped. She'd only been up there what—fifteen, twenty minutes?

"In need of answers." Dani stopped just short of him. She looked pale, stressed out. And scared. As though the enormity of what had happened to them was finally hitting her, just as it had eventually hit him.

Beau sat up slowly. "Okay." He was ready to deal with this, as directly as possible, if she was. "Shoot." He'd tell her whatever she wanted to know.

For several tense seconds, Dani stared at Beau incredulously. Her chin tipped defiantly. Some of the color came back into her cheeks. "Enough of the playing around." Her voice was quiet, subdued, as she searched his face for any hint of duplicity or deceit. "You can't seriously expect me to believe that you have no idea what happened that night in Mexico, either."

"If I did, I wouldn't be here pressuring you for answers." With effort Beau kept his voice as neutral as possible. Simmering with a frustration every bit as potent as hers, he frowned, shoved a hand through his hair and looked deep into her amber eyes. "Initially I thought you might have set me up. When I got here and realized pretty quickly that wasn't the case—you were about as far from gloating as you can get—I hoped you'd at least know how we landed in this predicament. And then enlighten me, either through simple accusation or by just plain blurting it out. But since you don't appear to remember anything..."

"I don't," Dani said, sighing, appearing dismayed to find he really didn't know anything.

"...I'm hoping if we spend time together it'll all start coming back to us." Beau scooted over to make room for Dani on the sofa beside him. "'Cause Lord knows I've already tried about everything else I can think of to get my memory back. And thus far nothing's worked."

"I've racked my brain, too, and I can't recall much of anything, either," Dani said.

It was a peculiar feeling, finding they were both in the same boat. Beau was used to their being completely at odds with each other. To suddenly find they were facing the same dilemma, and such a personal one, to boot... He had a feeling this was about to get more complicated. A lot more complicated. Worse, he wanted to drag her into his arms and kiss her again, reason be damned. He wanted to take her upstairs to bed and make wild passionate love to her and see if that brought anything back. And then, only then, when they'd exhausted themselves, run the gamut of their feelings for each other, deal with this predicament they were in. But that was impossible when she was doing her best to keep her feelings about him and everything else under lock and key.

Dani clamped her arms in front of her like a shield. "Then I'm really not on an episode of *Celebrity Hoaxes.*"

"You really aren't." Beau exhaled slowly and continued to study her in the dusky light. "Although how you managed to even think that I'd do something like that to you, no matter how ticked off I was at you, I don't know."

Dani lifted one slender shoulder in a hapless shrug, turned her glance away and began to pace, the last of her denial fading fast. "It was more acceptable than the reality of the two of us being really married and expecting, I guess." She finally sat down next to him on the sofa, being careful to maintain a good eight or nine inches between them.

Beau turned to her, no longer sure if this was a bad dream or a lifelong fantasy come true. He only knew for certain that if a woman was carrying his child, he would want her to be Dani. He frowned. "I guess this means you don't recall us actually, uh, making the baby, either," he said.

Dani shook her head. "You swear to me this isn't a joke?" She studied him seriously.

His heart began to beat like a bass drum. Reminded how very much was at stake here, Beau said softly, "I don't joke around when it comes to that, Dani." He brushed a strand of hair from her cheek and tucked it behind her ear. "The fact that you're carrying my child is a very serious matter indeed."

"You're right." Dani's lips tightened. She let out a short little sigh. "It is." She pushed off the sofa, headed for the phone and began to dial.

"Now what are you up to?" Beau demanded. They'd

just started to get somewhere, and there she was, running away from him again.

Dani shot him a quelling look over her shoulder. Abruptly she was her old sassy self. "I'm doing what we should have done three weeks ago. I'm getting us some help!"

THIRTY MINUTES LATER, Dani and Beau were in a private conference room at Laramie Community Hospital with Jackson McCabe and his wife, Lacey, during their dinner break.

"We have to stop meeting like this," Jackson quipped, accepting the two chicken Caesar salads and fruit compote Dani and Beau had ferried over from the Lone Star Dinner and Dance Hall.

"I don't know about that." The blond and beautiful Lacey winked at her surgeon husband. "I rather like having any kind of dinner I want brought to me just for taking the time to answer a few questions."

"The way to my woman's heart is through her stomach," Jackson teased with a rueful shake of his head, prompting an affectionate glance from his beloved pediatrician wife.

"So what's on your mind?" Lacey prodded as she settled into her chair and snapped off the top of her mineral water.

"Are you concerned about Dani's pregnancy?" Jackson asked.

"Actually we're wondering how exactly she got in that condition," Beau said, looking movie-star handsome in the small but cheerfully appointed room.

Lacey and Jackson chuckled in unison. "You're telling us you two have come to us for a lesson in the birds and the bees?" Lacey said, incredulous.

"More like a lesson on amnesia," Dani replied. "Because the problem is, neither Beau nor I remember the deed."

Lacey's eyes widened. "How is that possible?"

Dani sighed. "That's what we'd like to know," she said, her curiosity outweighing her embarrassment.

"Okay," Jackson interjected, holding up a palm. "Start from the beginning. And tell us what you do remember."

Dani looked at Beau. He nodded at her, tacitly giving her permission to go first. "Beau came to me and said he thought it was time that this feud of ours came to an end. I really wanted a truce, too," Dani said on a heartfelt sigh. Cautiously she swiveled around in her seat to look directly at Beau. "That much I remember very clearly."

"I was tired of the fighting," Beau admitted. "So we flew to my private villa on the Mexican coast."

"And then what happened?" Lacey asked.

Beau looked at Dani. Dani looked at Beau and saw the hollows beneath his cheeks become more pronounced. Silence strung out between them like a tautly drawn bow. "I remember us talking a lot—" *and flirting* "—that afternoon," Dani said finally as she rubbed her palm nervously over the smooth surface of the conference-room table.

"I have a brief fuzzy memory of us walking on the private beach together late at night—right outside my villa, under the stars," Beau said in a warm hushed voice. "But that had to have happened before we got married."

"Married!" Lacey and Jackson said in unison, clearly stunned.

"Yes and I don't even remember that." Dani sighed.

"What is the next thing you do remember—either of you?" Lacey asked.

"Waking up in a hotel room in the village with Dani beside me and a marriage certificate from the chapel in the village on the bedside table."

Jackson shook his head in amazement. "And I thought my brothers and I had some wild times lassoing us our wives!"

Lacey McCabe grinned, admitting this was so. "Which is where and when you assume conception occurred?" Lacey asked, turning her attention back to Beau and Dani. "In that hotel room?"

Beau nodded. "At least it certainly appeared that way—we were in bed together, sans clothing of any kind. And there was no evidence I could see that there had been any kind of birth control used."

"And you weren't on the pill or anything?" Jackson asked Dani.

Dani shook her head. There would have been no point. She hadn't been intimately involved with anyone since she and Chris Avery broke up.

"So what happened then?" Jackson and Lacey asked eagerly in unison.

Beau exhaled shortly. "I left to check out the marriage certificate, and sure enough, it was valid. By the time I returned, Dani had left." He pressed his lips together unhappily. "I didn't see her again until this afternoon." Three weeks had passed between the trip to Mexico and now.

"Is that all you remember?" Jackson turned to Dani.

Blushing fiercely, Dani nodded. "Except I was alone when I woke up. So I assumed I had been set up or duped—that it was revenge for my four bad reviews of his movies, or maybe even a warning regarding the new movie he has coming out in a couple of weeks. Anyway I hightailed it home to Laramie as fast as I could.''

"Do you think the two of you made love?'' Lacey asked Dani.

"Actually, I'm beginning to think maybe we did,'' Dani said reluctantly, becoming even more embarrassed. It would certainly explain a lot. Why she'd felt so contented in that distinctly physical, feminine way when she'd awakened, before the shock of discovering herself naked in Beau's hotel room bed had set in. And it would explain these strange, almost dream-like flashes of memory she'd been having, of Beau kissing her and caressing her breasts and covering her body with his own. Up until now, she had almost convinced herself it was all a dream, albeit a wild and crazy one, brought on by a combination of the circumstances she'd found herself in, and the fear of possibly never being able to remember fully what had actually happened that night to land her in such a predicament. Now she wasn't so sure. Maybe it had all been real. Right down to the incredibly passionate lovemaking.

"And Beau's right.'' Dani forced herself to put her pride aside and go on. "It looks like we didn't use protection.'' A fact she had been secretly worried about for three weeks now. But like a fool, she'd kept hoping if she pretended none of it had happened, and she didn't let herself think about it, it all might just go away. And her life could return to normal. Yeah, right!

Lacey concurred. "Did you two have anything to eat or drink that might have been contaminated while you were at the villa?'' she asked, turning back to Beau and Dani.

Beau shook his head no. "We purchased all our food and water in Texas before we flew down there and prepared the food ourselves. I later had some of it tested. It was all fine. No toxins or poisons of any kind."

"Could anyone have slipped you something without your knowing it?" Jackson pressed.

Beau, who'd obviously had some of the same suspicions himself, shook his head. "I don't keep a staff at the villa. The two of us were completely alone. But just to make sure, I had some blood work done by my family doctor as soon as I got back to Los Angeles. I was going to call Dani if it looked like we'd been poisoned, but nothing turned up in the tox screen and he assured me I hadn't been. So I went back to the village—that's what I've been doing the past three weeks—and retraced our steps to try to make sense of all this. Apparently, after our wedding ceremony we went to a restaurant there, and they gave us celebratory drinks—on the house—spiked with homemade tequila that was apparently around two hundred proof. Dani drank most of one, and I drank all of one and part of another."

Dani, who'd never been much of a drinker, anyway, winced. "Do you remember any of that?" she asked Beau.

"Nope, not a thing," he replied quietly. "Not even being there. But they took our photo and put it on the wall of the cantina. I had that checked, too. It was genuine."

"Do you have a copy of the photo?" Dani asked.

Beau reached for his wallet, took out the photo and dispassionately placed it where all could see.

Dani stared down at it. She and Beau were sitting at a table, holding hands. A wedding bouquet of wildflowers was on the table beside her. A lace mantilla had been placed on her head. She was wearing the off-the-shoulder gauzy white Mexican dress she'd found in the hotel room the next morning when she woke up.

"Does this ring any bells for you?" Lacey asked.

Dani shook her head as she continued to study her glowing countenance. She sure looked happy. And sober. And very much in love. To her utter amazement, Beau appeared equally ecstatic. "It looks like we got married before we were at this restaurant, Beau. Before we had anything to drink," she said in a low puzzled voice. If they had been drunk and silly, it would have been one thing to run off and get married on a whim. But this picture hinted that they had known exactly what they were doing when they exchanged their wedding vows, and *that,* Dani did not understand at all.

Beau draped his arm over the back of her chair and leaned in so their bodies were less than an inch apart. His face was close to hers as they studied the picture together. "That's exactly what they swear we did," he said thoughtfully. "According to the locals I talked to, we got married on the spur of the moment. But we were stone-cold sober when we did it. And happy."

No wonder he kept calling her his wife, Dani thought.

In his mind, in the minds of all who had witnessed their union, they really were married. Feeling more confused and upset than ever, Dani bit her lip and looked into Beau's eyes. "I don't understand why we don't remember getting married—especially if we were sober at the time." She turned back to Lacey and Jackson. "I know this isn't your specialty, either, but you're both doctors. Have either of you ever heard of something like this happening?"

"No." Jackson frowned. "But I know someone who might be more versed to help us figure this out."

"So do I," Lacey added.

Jackson and Lacey took Beau and Dani upstairs to his office to look up the phone numbers of their psychiatrist colleagues. Without disclosing who their patients were, Jackson and Lacey took turns describing the situation over the phone. Beau and Dani sat tensely in the reception area while Jackson and Lacey bandied about medical terminology, very little of which made any sense to them at all. Finally, after about four phone calls and twenty minutes, and a brief discussion—equally baffling and full of medical jargon—between Lacey and Jackson, they had a consensus.

"Okay, here's what we think may have happened," Jackson said as the four of them sat down to hash it out again. "It's probably a combination of some sort of hysterical amnesia and an alcohol-induced blackout. The homemade tequila you drank was really potent. Which in turn caused your blood alcohol level to rise very quickly. Whatever chemical process it is in your brain that allows you to make memories was then all messed up. Since you both drank the same thing at the same time, you probably got inebriated at approximately the same rate. Hence the dual blackout or loss of memory."

Dani and Beau breathed a sigh of relief at the same time. It was good, finally, to have a medical explanation for their memory loss. "Are we ever going to remember what happened?" Dani asked anxiously.

Jackson frowned. "It depends on what kind of blackout it is. There are two kinds. One, where you will remember in hazy fragments or with prompting what went on. And the other kind where the memory is gone forever."

"We think you will remember this, though, because of the other component," Lacey added matter-of-factly.

"The one that caused you both to forget everything up to and including the actual marriage and jaunt to the restaurant."

"Which is where the hysterical amnesia comes in," Jackson explained.

Lacey nodded. "It may be, and again we're all just guessing here, that the fact that the two of you got married—given your feuding history with each other—when combined with the alcohol's and resulting blackout's upset to your system caused a sort of dual hysterical amnesia about everything that went on, not just at the time you were accidentally inebriated but in the twenty-four hours or so preceding that, too."

"Sort of like what happens after a head injury or an accident or anything that is really traumatic," Jackson explained.

"In which case...?" Dani prodded nervously, wondering what the prognosis was.

"You'll remember when and as you're able to deal with it emotionally and not before. And, as with a blackout, it probably won't be all at once, but in little fragments," Lacey counseled gently. "Dani, you'll remember something. And then if you tell Beau, he may remember something else. Until all the pieces finally fit together. At least that's what we hope will happen for you two."

"And you're saying the more we stay together, the better the chances of remembering?" Beau asked. His arm moved from the back of Dani's chair to her shoulders, cloaking her with a steadying warmth.

Lacey and Jackson nodded. Speaking for them both, Lacey continued, "Frankly, so much time has already gone by—a good three weeks—for the best chance of success, we advise you to stay together until you do remember.''

Dani let out a wavering breath. "I'm not so certain I want to remember everything," she muttered. What if it turned out she'd done something really embarrassing? Like a striptease? Her clothes had been draped all over the hotel room. Her slip here, panties, bra, garter belt and stockings there...

"Don't worry," Jackson soothed. "A person isn't likely to do anything during a blackout they wouldn't do when just plain drunk."

"Are you sure about that?" Beau asked.

Jackson and Lacey nodded. "Psychological studies have been done on that."

Dani rolled her eyes. This was not helping. Although now that she noticed, Beau was beginning to look all the more intrigued. As if he wanted to remember every little thing, down to exactly how and when and why her clothes had been draped on chairs, windowsills, bureaus and lampshades, even the drapery rods! Had it been just *her* clothes scattered willy-nilly around the room? Or his, too? Dani wondered as a self-conscious flush heated her cheeks. Again, she was not sure she wanted to find that much out.

"It's just the inability to remember that makes the gap in memory seem filled with awful possibilities," Jackson continued.

You can say that again, Dani thought. The last thing she wanted to find herself doing around Beauregard Chamberlain was shedding all her inhibitions. But that was apparently what she had done. What they both had done.

"Jackson's right," Lacey said. "The things you imagine you did together or are afraid you did may be much worse than the actual events. It's just the uncertainty of it that's going to drive you crazy until you do remember.''

Dani fervently hoped that was the case, because right now she was imagining all sorts of things, none of them good. And not just for her.

''What about the baby?'' Dani asked Lacey, her teeth worrying her lower lip as she expressed the most riveting fear of all. ''If I did become pregnant while I was that inebriated, is the baby going to be okay?'' This much was Lacey's field of expertise, as she was a crackerjack pediatrician with an excellent reputation.

''Not to worry.'' Lacey smiled reassuringly. ''It takes three to five days for the fertilized egg to move down the fallopian tube, another three to five days for the zygote to be implanted on the uterine wall. And nothing will pass from your body to the baby's body until that occurs. So Mother Nature had your baby well protected.'' Lacey paused, then asked, ''You haven't been drinking since?''

''Haven't had a drop,'' Dani said. In fact, the way she was feeling now she didn't care if she ever had another drink of alcohol of any kind.

''Neither have I,'' Beau said. He didn't look as if he wanted to drink anything again anytime soon, either. *Another thing they had in common,* Dani realized reluctantly.

''Well, good, keep it up, parents-to-be,'' Lacey said, patting Dani on the shoulder.

''Meanwhile, let us know if there is anything else we can do to help,'' Jackson said as he and Lacey walked them out. Dani and Beau promised they would, then left the hospital together in thoughtful silence.

''What a night,'' Beau said twenty minutes later as

he ushered Dani from his pickup truck to the front porch of her newly-purchased house.

"Tell me about it." Dani sighed wearily as she let them inside and tossed her purse on top of a box.

Beau took her hand in his and led her toward the kitchen. "Do you think we're going to be able to remember?"

The idea that she might never be able to recall not just her wedding but the conception of her first—maybe her only—child was more dismaying than Dani wanted to let on. She might not want to remember anything embarrassing, but she certainly wanted to remember the parts that weren't. She shrugged as she peeked into the refrigerator, then, finding nothing she wanted, despite the bounty of groceries her sisters had brought her as housewarming presents, shut the door again. "I don't know." Dani leaned against the refrigerator and looked up into eyes that had never seemed so blue. "I want to—"

"So do I." Beau's dark brows drew together as he looked down at her in mock seriousness. "So I guess there's only one thing to do," he said, slipping back into his native Texas drawl.

"And what's that?" Dani prodded. Reading the sudden mischief on his face, she found it was all she could do not to smile, too.

Beau's sexy grin widened alarmingly as he looked deep into her eyes. "We try to reenact the conception, of course."

Chapter Five

Dani tossed her head and stepped past him. "Dream on, cowboy." She threw the words over her shoulder like discarded bits of sand.

For three weeks now Beau had been telling himself that circumstances had exaggerated the potent chemistry between them, the impact of her stunning good looks and feisty personality combined. But it just wasn't so. He had only to be near her to realize what a truly beautiful woman she was. Sassy, spirited, determined, and no one challenged him—no one wanted to know him—the way Dani did. As for her stunning good looks, he had only to be near her to appreciate the flawlessness of her complexion and the delicate features of her oval face. He dreamed about her pert nose, full lips and perfect chin. Longed to see the intelligence and quick wit in her amber eyes and hear the throaty softness of her voice.

Aware he had never wanted to possess a woman more, heart and soul, Beau closed the distance between them. Maybe it was time she learned she couldn't shut him out that way, not out of his own child's life and not out of hers, not if he wanted in, and right now, as it happened, he did want in. The best way to do that, of course, was to drag her into his arms and kiss her again, the complications of their situation be damned. He wanted to let their feelings—not logic and reason—take over. He wanted to take her to bed and make wild passionate love to her again, so thoroughly and completely neither of them would ever forget a single instant of it. And then, only then, when they'd exhausted themselves, run the gamut of their feelings for each other, deal with all the unresolved specifics of their situation. Which, he admitted, were considerable. But they couldn't take it all on now. They had to take on each issue one at a time. Starting with the return of their memories.

"Can you think of a better way to bring it all back to both of us?" Beau asked silkily as they continued their silent two-step around the kitchen until her back was to the wall and he was directly in front of her. *He* sure couldn't!

Dani blushed and drew in a quavery breath as he braced a hand on the wall on either side of her. Their bodies weren't quite touching, but he could already see her trembling with desire. Her palms flattened against his chest, holding him at bay. Even as the full brunt of her temper shone in her eyes, her body shuddered and softened toward his. "I'm sure this isn't it!" she shot back breathlessly, tilting up her chin.

Beau smiled as he read the desire in her eyes. He tunneled his hands through the coppery softness of her hair. "We'll never know for sure," he murmured softly, smiling down at her, "unless we give it the ol' Texas try."

"I don't want to give it the ol' Texas try," she said stubbornly.

"Sure about that now, Dani?" he taunted, noting her

eyelashes already beginning to close. '''Cause you look to me like you're just dying to be kissed.'' And then, waiting be damned, his lips were on hers. He knew she didn't mean to kiss him back, any more than he could help kissing her, and somehow that made the culmination of their desire all the sweeter. Groaning, he deepened the kiss, exploring her mouth with his tongue, leaving not a millimeter untouched. He knew, married or not, they were different as night and day. It didn't matter. She made him aware of needs that until now he had been unaware of. She made him feel like half of a whole. She made him feel married. Not just for now, but forever. And heaven knew he had never felt anything like this in his life. Never wanted a woman so much. Never wanted to possess her so thoroughly and so quickly. Never wanted to give her his heart and his soul. But with Dani, he did.

Dani struggled to keep her feelings in check, but it was an impossible task when his body was flush against hers and his arms were wrapped around her. Over and over, his tongue plunged into her mouth, stroking and exciting. No one had ever asked her to give so much, and a few more kisses robbed her of the ability to protest at all. When his hand slipped beneath her blouse and cupped her breast through the lace of her bra, she arched her back and trembled with helpless pleasure. So this was what had happened, she thought. This was why and how they had made love. She was drowning in the pleasurable sensations sweeping through her. He'd made her want him to the point of madness. And he, too, had wanted her in exactly the same way.

Warm ribbons of pleasure flooded her as he caressed the taut aching tip of her breast and covered her mouth in a searing kiss. And it was then that Dani began to remember. Then that she had a brief potent mental image of the two of them in bed together, intimately entwined. Beau's hands on her breasts, kneading and caressing…then his lips…his thighs spreading hers even as she ached and writhed…her whole body surrendering, straining, wanting, needing…his hands beneath her hips, lifting her…as if to possess…

Startled by the vividness of the imagery, the knowledge of her own unprecedented wanton behavior she pushed him away, her breath coming raggedly. She couldn't believe he'd made her feel so vulnerable so fast. Any more than she could believe she'd responded as passionately as she had. "I can't believe you just did that," she fumed, as angry at herself for the thoughts running through her mind as she was at him for his actions. She knew the difference between sex and love. And she wanted love. Until she knew he loved her as a husband should, there would be no more making love. Making love too soon was one of the things that had gotten them into this mess.

"I can't believe we stopped." Clearly he wanted to take their lovemaking to the limit and beyond.

"It shouldn't have happened," Dani insisted stubbornly.

His glance dropped to the nipples visibly protruding against the material of her blouse. "We *are* married."

Dani glowered at him. "Legally—temporarily—maybe," she allowed.

Beau's eyes clashed with hers as he corrected softly, reasonably, "At least for the next nine months."

"You can't—we—"

He stepped closer and, before she could run, cupped her shoulders warmly. "We may not know exactly *how* we went from fighting to loving in such a short period of time, or even *why* we acted like lovestruck lunatics, rushing off to get married, but that no longer matters.''

Dani was still as a statue as she studied his face. "It doesn't?''

"No," Beau replied. "And you know why not?" He looked deep into her eyes. "'Cause we are having a baby together, and that baby is coming into the world the best way possible, with two parents who love him or her enough to put their own needs aside and concentrate on their child. Our baby is going to be born legitimate, Dani.''

As much as Dani wanted to, she couldn't argue the wisdom of that. They did owe it to their baby to give it the best possible start in life, and that meant having two parents who were married at the time of his or her birth. The real problem was what followed. She didn't want to let herself fall in love with Beau or grow to depend on him, only to have him walk out on her. She'd endured the loss of her parents. She couldn't endure another loss of that magnitude. And if he kept kissing her that way, kept looking at her that way, kept hanging around that way, acting like a husband and calling her his wife, Dani knew odds were good she would fall head over heels in love with him.

Marshaling her defenses, she stepped away from him. "And after the baby's born, then what?" Dani pressed, looking Beau straight in the eye.

He shrugged and flashed her an unapologetic grin. "It'll all depend on how we get along in the meantime, I guess." He seemed to think they were going to get along just fine.

Dani studied him in silence. His optimism was contagious, though some of her reservations remained. It had not been her experience that happiness landed on her doorstep very often. And yet, the more she looked at him, the more she wanted to believe this could all work out for the best, despite the odds against it. "You're really serious about this," she said slowly.

Beau raked his hands through the inky-black layers of his hair. "The more I think about it, the more I know we had to have done whatever we did for a reason, Dani." He paused. "Because you and I both never do anything without a damn good reason."

That was certainly true, Dani thought. His career and rise to fame had been one of the most well-orchestrated campaigns she had ever seen. Just as her own achievements had taken a lot of planning and determination. Both of them had guts and singularity of purpose in abundance.

Beau ran his palm across his jaw. Seemingly aware of just how ruggedly handsome he was to her with the hint of evening beard on his face, he flashed her a sexy grin. "Unfortunately I don't happen to recall what that reason was." He planted his hands on her shoulders encouragingly. "But ten to one, it's there. In both our memories. And when we do remember everything, we'll understand why we did what we did down in Mexico."

Dani sighed. She hoped that was the case. She didn't know how much more of this she could take.

TEN MINUTES LATER, Beau and Dani were squaring off again. This time over sleeping arrangements. "You honestly expect me to sleep on the sofa?"

Dani thrust the pillow and blanket she had culled from one of the moving boxes at him. "Be glad it's not the floor."

Beau cradled the blanket and pillow against his chest. He did not look inclined to use either. At least not alone.

"I saw your bed," he said, a mixture of mischief and desire glimmering in his eyes. He tossed the bedding onto the sofa and followed her to the L-shaped staircase leading up to the second floor. "It's a double."

"Actually," Dani drawled as she halted on the bottom step with one hand resting on the banister, "it's a queen."

"See?" Beau shrugged, patiently waiting for her to stop blocking his path. "Plenty of room for two."

He was doing it again, looking at her as if he was already making love to her. She could feel the desire pouring from them both. Only this time she knew he wouldn't be satisfied with a fleeting touch and a few kisses. If he joined her in her bed, he would want more. And she wasn't ready for the next step.

"Think again, cowboy." Dani stood firm, not sure what was more annoying—his persistence in pursuing her or his thoroughly male confidence that one day he would win this battle of wills. "There will never be enough room in my bed for you, Beau Chamberlain, no matter how married we are or what size mattress I sleep on," she told him hotly, not about to forgive him for the kisses in the kitchen just now or the passion they had engendered. A passion that was bound to keep her up all night! She was still tingling from head to toe!

Want to bet? Beau's look said. "Now, honey, don't make promises you can't keep," he taunted playfully, sidestepping the moving boxes that were stacked at various places in the hall and stopping just outside her bedroom door. "If we made love once, we can—heck, we probably will," he finished with a knowing wink, "do it again."

Which was exactly what Dani was afraid of. She didn't want to add any more memories to those that were already starting to come back, unbeknownst to Beau. But not about to let him see how vulnerable she felt when she was around him, or how much she was beginning to want him, too, she volleyed back, "You just keep telling yourself that, cowboy. Meanwhile," she told him in her soft Texas drawl, "I'm going to bed."

Beau grinned as happily as if she'd invited him into her bedroom. He stuck his thumbs through the belt loops on either side of his fly and retained his arrogant stance. He held her eyes with his mesmerizing gaze, making her feel all hot and bothered inside. "Try not to dream about me too much."

Dani rolled her eyes and ignored the tidal wave of heat starting deep inside her. "Don't you wish that was going to be the case?"

"I'M GLAD YOU CALLED," Dani's sister Meg said fifteen minutes later as Dani curled up in bed, newly installed telephone in hand. "I was going to check in with you in a few minutes."

"Jeremy asleep?" Dani asked, referring to Meg's son, who was almost six.

"Out like a light," Meg replied happily. "That birthday party he went to this afternoon really tuckered him out. But we digress," Meg said. "What we really need to be talking about here is Beau Chamberlain. What in the world was he talking about today when he called you his wife?"

"The truth, apparently," Dani said dryly, then went on to explain about their apparent marriage and resulting pregnancy, as well as their mutual memory lapse.

Meg listened quietly to Dani's entire recitation. Like Dani, Meg was happy about the baby. She knew Dani had always wanted to have a baby of her own someday. Meg was less certain about the baby's daddy.

Meg was silent for a long moment on the other end of the phone connection. Finally she said, "You really think you can trust Beau to be there for you the way you and the baby are going to need him to be? I mean, the two of you have carried on quite a feud the past few years."

"I know." Dani sighed.

"But…?"

Dani paused, recalling the look in Beau's eyes when he had finally confessed he had amnesia about almost everything that had happened in Mexico. She had only to think about his gotta-do-right-by-our-kid attitude when it came to the baby to know he was telling her the truth. They were really in a jam here. And like it or not, they were in it together. Dani swallowed. "All I know is that Beau is serious and responsible enough to want—no, demand—that we stay married until the baby is born and we can figure out what to do."

Meg sucked in a breath. "Whoa now, little sis. Is that really what you want?"

Dani knew it wasn't a choice Meg had made. She had decided to rear Jeremy alone, to this day never even revealing who her son's father was.

And that had been a surprise, too. The oldest of the four Lockhart sisters, Meg had always been the responsible one. Looking after all her sisters, making sure everyone was okay. And that trait had intensified after they'd lost their parents. Maybe, Dani mused, because Meg had been away at college in Chicago when the tornado that had killed their parents had hit and unable to get back home to her sisters for a good twenty-four hours after the catastrophe.

Dani knew even if she never said so that Meg still felt guilty about that. But she also knew it wasn't Meg's fault. It wasn't anyone's. Thanks to the high winds and fierce storms that had accompanied the tornado, phone lines had been down all over Laramie County. They'd had trouble finding Meg—who hadn't been listening to the news and had no idea anything was wrong.

Once they'd finally located her at the college medical library around midnight, they'd had to wait until early the next morning to get her on the first available flight home. Then they had to arrange for someone to go to the Dallas–Fort Worth airport to pick her up and bring her back to Laramie to console her sisters, make funeral arrangements and decide what to do next.

None of which had been easy tasks.

Afterward Meg had dropped out of college, where she'd been working toward a master's degree in nursing, and returned home to Laramie to sell the Lockhart Ranch and care for her three younger sisters.

Her sacrifice had kept Dani, Jenna and Kelsey from being split up and put in foster care. And since then, Meg had done everything possible to protect, nurture and care for her three younger sisters. To the detriment of her own life and happiness, Dani sometimes thought. Because Dani couldn't help but think, had it not been for them, Meg—who had also found herself unexpectedly pregnant shortly after returning to Laramie—might have married or built more of a life of her own.

"Do you want to stay married to Beau?" Meg continued, sounding quite frankly aghast.

Dani took a deep breath and clutched the phone even tighter. "I don't know," she said finally. The heck of it was, marriage to Beau wasn't as unpalatable an option as it should have been. Not nearly.

But that wasn't even the worst of it, Dani thought several minutes later as she snuggled under the covers and attempted to get comfy enough to sleep. The worst of it was, she had fibbed when she'd said she didn't remember anything else about their time together in Mexico. She did. She just hadn't been sure it was real until Beau had kissed her downstairs in the kitchen. But once he had taken her all the way in his arms and covered her lips with his, she had known those recollections that had seemed more dreamlike than real had been rooted, not in fantasy or imagination as she had first supposed, but in something that had actually happened.

And if she could remember how gently and intimately he kissed, how thoroughly and passionately he loved, what else, Dani wondered nervously, might she eventually remember?

BEAU STRETCHED OUT on the sofa that was a good foot short for his six-foot-plus frame. It had been a long time since he had been banished to the sofa for the night. Even longer since he'd had his life turned upside down by a woman. And never to this degree. He had never expected to get married again.

Never *wanted* to get married again.

And yet, at least part of being married to Dani, the physical part, didn't seem all that bad. The kiss they had shared, not to mention the fuzzy recollection he had of their wedding night in Mexico, had let him know that their lovemaking was the kind of lovemaking that came along once in a lifetime, if you were lucky.

The problem was, the two of them were as different as night and day. Dani didn't believe in happy endings or happily-ever-after anything. Beau not only believed such happy outcomes existed, he believed they were within everyone's reach.

Which wasn't to say he hadn't gone through his jaded period, too. After his divorce from Sharon, there'd been a two-year period when he'd been so wary of being made a fool of again or getting involved with the wrong woman that he'd had trouble believing in anything or anyone. Two things had kept him going. His need to make movies. And his flirtatious feud with Dani Lockhart. She'd not only gotten to him as no woman ever had, she'd also inspired him to do some of the best work of his life in *Bravo Canyon*.

Now it was Dani's turn to face reality. He had to make her see that he was interested in her, not just the baby. He had to transform her inherent cynicism—the prevailing feeling that nothing wonderful or magical would ever happen to her—to the feeling that something wonderful surely would.

On the surface it was an impossible task.

Or would have been if his niche in life hadn't been what it was. He knew what people thought—his job wasn't just about pretending to be someone or playing a role. With every performance, every role he took, he was selling hope. He was selling dreams. The idea that it was worth whatever pain or grief a person endured to stand up and fight for what he or she believed in. The idea that if a person put his or her heart and soul into an endeavor, he or she would succeed. That, ultimately, right always prevailed over wrong, good over evil. That was why he'd always done westerns in the past and always would. Because he wanted to make movies that showed the measure of a man was more about his honor and integrity than his personal wealth. He'd given up his house in L.A. and returned to Texas because he needed to be partnered with a woman who shared his time-honored values and loved the Texas way of life, where home and family were everything, as much as he did. That woman was Dani. He knew it. And soon, with his help, she would know it, too.

DANI WAS STILL SLEEPING upstairs and Beau had just gotten the coffee started the next morning when the doorbell rang. He wasn't as surprised as he would have liked to see his attorney/agent and publicist standing on Dani's front porch. Edie and Ellsworth Getz were one of the power couples in Hollywood these days, presiding over a stable of the most gifted actors, directors and writers in the business. Having nurtured Beau's talent and career from his first days in Hollywood, they were also like a father and mother to him. With a father and mother's penchant for meddling.

"I don't even want to know how you found me," he grumbled. He had visited Laramie, Texas, often when he was a kid. He'd had an aunt who lived there. But he hadn't been around much since his aunt had moved away ten years earlier. And he hadn't yet told either Edie or Ellsworth of his plans to open an office of his production company there.

"It wasn't easy," Edie admitted as she breezed in, looking as smart as ever in a summery blue designer pantsuit. She patted her sleek blond chignon. "No one in the industry seemed to know where you were."

They hadn't, Beau thought. Until now. "I'm supposed to be on vacation," he reminded her. He had worked nonstop for the past three years, with no more than a few days off here and there. The five weeks he had allotted himself were vital to his mental health. And his personal life.

"Your vacation was over four days ago," Ellsworth said, looking just as chic as his wife in his Saville Row suit and carefully trimmed pewter-gray beard. He gazed at Beau shrewdly. "You were supposed to be back in Los Angeles last Friday."

Beau shrugged and offered no apology. "I had a change of plans."

"There's no time for that. You have a movie coming out in two weeks. The premiere in Dallas is five days from now. Back-to-back interviews and publicity blitz start in seven days," Edie said as she put on her publicist hat. All of which, it went without saying, took quite a bit of preparation. There were wardrobe fittings. Photo sessions. Question-and-answer sessions to sit through.

"I know all that," Beau said, beginning to get a little irritated.

"Then why haven't you been checking with your service or returning any of your calls?" Ellsworth demanded.

"I have more important things going on here in Laramie."

"Like romancing Dani Lockhart to try and get a good review out of her?" Ellsworth accused.

Gently Edie took up where her husband left off. "There's no doubt she's fast emerging as the leading movie critic in the country. But to think you could seduce her into writing you a favorable review...well, you'd be wasting your time."

"I quite agree," Dani said icily, joining them in the kitchen. She had on blue-and-white-striped pyjamas. A matching calf-length robe was tugged on carelessly over that, the front falling open, the belt drooping on either side of her. Her coppery hair was all tousled, her cheeks pink from sleep, her eyes glittering with fiery amber lights. She looked beautiful and kissable—and ticked off as all get-out. Knowing what she must have heard, Beau couldn't say he blamed her.

Beau bit back an oath. He hadn't meant for Dani to be privy to any of this. Determined to end this unscheduled business conference as soon as possible, he turned back to his agent and publicist. "I'll be in New York when I need to be in New York. And I will also be at the premiere in Dallas in ten days," he promised flatly. "Until then I have personal matters to attend to." And about that, he wasn't budging.

Ellsworth jerked at the knot of his tie. "More than you know," Ellsworth muttered, looking stressed out.

Edie looked at Beau steadily. "We need to talk, Beau. Something serious has come up, and I'm not sure Miss Lockhart should hear it."

Dani glared at Beau, obviously believing the worst, and turned to go.

Acting on impulse, another thing he almost never did, Beau reached out, grabbed Dani's hand and tugged her back to his side. "Stay," he said. He drew a padded swivel chair up to the glass-topped breakfast table. "There's nothing you can say Dani can't hear," he told Edie and Ellsworth.

Dani's jaw dropped.

As did Ellsworth's and Edie's.

The pair thought about arguing with him, until they took a good look at his face and realized he was not going to budge about this.

"Fine," Edie huffed after a moment. "As long as it is agreed nothing said here leaves this room." Edie gave Dani a pointed look.

Dani sighed, looking more irritated to have her integrity questioned than her home commandeered for an impromptu meeting between Beau and his representatives. "You have my word." She pushed the words through her teeth.

"It's Sharon," Edie said as Beau got steaming paper cups of coffee for everyone. "She's secretly peddling a tell-all about her marriage to you to one of the television networks."

At the thought of having the most intimate details of his private life splashed across the TV screen and being made a fool of, not just in private but in public this time, Beau clenched his jaw.

"It gets better," Ellsworth warned wearily as he stirred sugar into his coffee. "She's planning to close the deal and go public on the same night your new movie opens in Dallas."

Edie looked really worried. "She's planning to say that in your case art is imitating life, that your playing the pursuer of a married woman in the movie is more true to life than everyone knows. And that it was your secret sexual involvement with a string of prominent married women that prompted her to end the marriage to you."

Beau shook his head in disgust and shot a look at Dani. He wished he knew what she was thinking, but her expression revealed nothing except a sort of subdued wariness where he was concerned. He turned back to his agent and publicist. "That's complete bull and you know it." For the first time Beau was regretting his decision to keep the real reason behind his divorce from Sharon private.

"Yes, *we* know it," Edie said, her eyes full of sympathy for her client. She stirred artificial sweetener into her coffee. "But we're not the movie-going public, and they may not think so. A scandal like this, timed to coincide with your movie's debut, could dramatically hurt ticket sales. If ticket sales on *Bravo Canyon* are low the first week, well..." Edie looked steadily at Beau. "I don't have to tell you how quickly films are leaving the theaters and going to video these days."

Beau made no effort to hide his displeasure. "Can't we stop her?" he demanded impatiently, drawing on his agent's experience as an attorney.

Ellsworth shrugged. "You could ask for an injunction. But that would probably only bring more negative publicity and more speculation about whether or not Sharon's allegations are true. Meanwhile, the new movie debuts..." Ellsworth's voice trailed off. It wasn't necessary to say more.

Beau took a long sip of coffee, then put his cup aside. "So what are you asking me to do?" He sat back in his chair and folded his arms.

"Talk to her," Edie said.

Beau would sooner burn in hell. He noted Dani didn't seem to like that option much, either. His jaw shot out pugnaciously. "No."

Ellsworth looked at Beau sternly. "Her representatives, then. She must want something. If you don't want to do it yourself, then authorize us to do it for you."

Beau shook his head. "I'm not paying her off again." He'd done that once, just to end the marriage, get it over with. And he'd regretted it ever since. "Besides, Sharon and I had an agreement. Neither of us was going to talk publicly about the reason the marriage ended. That agreement was a prerequisite of her getting any money from me. If she breaks it, she loses the settlement she won in the divorce."

Edie sighed. "You'd have to sue her to get it back,

and word around Hollywood is she's already spent it all and then some."

"All going after her that way would do is tie you up in more litigation for years and further the scandal." Ellsworth backed up his wife.

"On the other hand," Edie continued persuasively, "if you could figure out a way to get her to stop this before it goes any further and does damage to either of your careers…"

"Maybe use your influence to get her a plum role in an upcoming film?" Ellsworth suggested.

"No," Beau said firmly. He stood, signaling this impromptu meeting was over. "I paid her off once." He looked at his agent and publicist grimly. "It was a mistake. I am not—I repeat *not*—doing it again."

BEAU WALKED EDIE and Ellsworth to the front door and stood watching as they drove off. His expression was so dark and brooding that eventually Dani joined him on the wide front porch. She knew, even if he was far too much the strong silent type to admit it, that he really needed to talk about what was going on in his life. As his wife, albeit only temporarily, she needed to know so she could be braced for whatever else might be coming next from Sharon Davis and her bogus claims and the resulting public furor.

The only problem was finding a way to get Beau to talk to her about what he clearly did not want to talk about. To anyone. "What are you thinking?" she asked gently after a moment, hoping a little kindness and understanding would break the ice.

He turned to look at her, his eyes scanning her face. Searching for what exactly, she couldn't say. "Breakfast,'' he told her in a low hushed voice, his warm breath brushing her hair.

She became aware her pulse had picked up marginally. He looked so right, so natural, standing next to her on the porch. For a second Dani let herself fantasize how it might be to live there with him as husband and wife, to go to sleep with him every night and wake up with him every morning. Even if she didn't believe for an instant what he was currently telling her—that he'd put the problem with his ex-wife completely out of his mind.

''I'm hungry,'' Beau continued with the sort of lazy male insistence that had made him an international movie star. His sexy smile deepened as his gaze moved from her eyes to her lips and back again. Turning so he faced her, he wrapped both arms about her waist. ''How about you?''

Dani was hungry. She wasn't willing to be diverted from her quest. ''Then we should get dressed and head to one of the restaurants on Main Street,'' she suggested, figuring they could talk on the way. She took his hand, intending to lead him back into the house.

Instead, Beau let go of her and lounged against one of the posts supporting the porch roof. He was wearing the same clothes he'd had on the day before. Only this morning the white shirt was unbuttoned and untucked, revealing a two-inch strip of golden skin, covered with tufts of velvety black hair. His eyes were a very sexy dark blue. His black hair was rumpled, his lips soft and sensual. A day's growth of beard lined his handsome face, giving him sort of a desperado aura and reminding her just how good he looked, in and out of bed, on and off a movie screen.

"No need for that," Beau drawled. "Last time I checked, we had plenty of food in the refrigerator."

Dani fastened on the *we*. He had certainly taken to the idea of couplehood awfully fast. She wasn't sure she liked him making himself so much at home in what was still her place.

"Only one problem with that, cowboy," Dani retorted. Knowing how easy it would be to find herself in bed with him again, but determined not to be sensually distracted, Dani stepped back and crossed her arms. "I don't have any dishes unpacked yet. Nor am I even sure where any are." There were so many boxes. None of them all that well marked. Trying to find even a couple of cereal bowls and spoons to use—never mind the dish detergent to wash them with—would be a nightmare. Besides, the less they were alone right now, she thought, the better. She didn't want Beau getting any ideas about reenacting their baby-making session as a method of jogging their memories.

Beau's smile only deepened. He pushed away from the support post, reassuring her with a wink, "Not to worry, sweetheart. I've got Old Faithful with me."

Old Faithful! That sounded like a horse. Or a dog. Dani scanned the pickup truck he had left sitting at the curb and saw neither. "And what might Old Faithful be?" she inquired, wishing all over again he weren't so darned appealing to the eye, even this early in the morning. She knew he wasn't talking about some geyser.

"Hang on a minute and you'll see." Beau trotted down the steps, across the yard and over to his pickup. While Dani watched, he reached in behind the front seat and pulled out a saddle-brown leather satchel. Seconds later he had her back in the kitchen and was opening the custom-made case. Dani blinked at the contents. She wasn't sure what she expected, but certainly not this. With effort, she closed her jaw, which had fallen open. "You travel with a black cast-iron skillet?" she asked in surprise.

"A perfectly seasoned black cast-iron skillet," Beau boasted. "There is nothing worth eating this fine utensil can't cook."

Dani shook her head at the mischief shimmering in his eyes. "You're speaking from experience, of course," she guessed.

"Of course." Beau took out two tin plates—suitable for using at a campsite—matching mugs, silverware and a velvet-wrapped set of professional-quality cooking utensils that included a grater-shredder, spatula, slotted spoon, vegetable peeler, paring knife and carving knife. He opened her refrigerator, peered inside at the wealth of groceries her sisters had brought over. Grinning, he shot her a look over his shoulder. "You up for some campfire eggs?"

Dani shrugged. "As long as you do the cooking." Truth be told, she had never been all that great in the kitchen.

"No problem." Beau broke open a package of bacon and layered six slices into the bottom of the pan. While it began to sizzle, he peeled, sliced and shredded two potatoes from the mesh bag on the counter. Entranced by his culinary know-how, which put hers to shame, Dani helped herself to some more coffee and watched for several minutes. He still hadn't buttoned his shirt, and as he moved around the kitchen, she could see the muscles in his stomach and chest contract and expand as he moved. Not to mention the iron hardness of his thighs and calves, and the sexy shape of his buttocks beneath the soft blue denim of his jeans.

With effort, she forced her thoughts back to what had happened earlier. What she still wanted to know. And he was keeping purposefully mum about. "You're not going to tell me, are you?" Dani surmised as she poured herself the last of the decaf in the pot, then set about making some more.

Beau removed the bacon and put it on a paper-towel-covered plate to drain. Then he gave her a sidelong glance that took in the sleep-mussed tangles of her hair and her cotton bedtime ensemble. "Tell you what?"

"Why your marriage to Sharon Davis really ended."

His expression guarded, Beau studied her. "You really want to know, don't you." Beau slid the potatoes into the skillet.

"I'm curious."

He shrugged his broad shoulders as he added a little bit of salt and a lot of pepper and cut off the rest of her questions with a don't-mess-with-me look. "So is the rest of America."

Knowing she would never understand him any better than she ever had unless he started telling her what was in his heart and on his mind, Dani ignored his demand she back off. "Only because you and Sharon kept it such a secret," she said.

Beau reached for an onion and after peeling it, began to chop that up, too. "You don't believe in privacy when it comes to a someone's personal life?"

Dani shrugged, not sure how to answer that. The truth was, she wouldn't be asking personal questions if she didn't care about Beau. But she did care about him and had from the very first, even—to her amazement—when they weren't getting along. Figuring that was a revelation that could be withheld for a more appropriate time, she tried another tack. "But you give up your privacy when you become a celebrity or a public figure, don't you?''

''To a point,'' Beau allowed reluctantly as he added the onion to the pan and stirred it in with the potatoes. Putting his spatula aside, he wiped his hands on a towel and turned to her. ''Which is why it's so great hanging out in a small town like Laramie.'' His eyes roamed her face with disturbing intensity, taking in the contours of her softly parted lips before returning to her eyes. ''Once the newness of seeing somebody like me wears off—'' he reached up to tuck a wayward strand of hair behind her ear ''—I'm just a regular guy.''

Well, maybe not exactly regular, Dani thought, but she knew what he meant. Since he'd landed in town several weeks ago, people had taken great pains to respect his privacy and not fawn over him. They had, in fact, with the exception of that one giant publicity stunt he'd concocted with Shane McCabe, let him be just a regular guy. Beginning to tremble all over, from the heat radiating from his tall muscular body in mesmerizing waves, Dani stepped back. ''So are you going to tell me or aren't you?'' She was aware her heart was pounding.

Beau leaned close enough to kiss her—and didn't. ''You really want to know?'' he asked softly.

Dani nodded. ''I really want to know.'' Maybe it would give her the clue she would need to understand him the way he needed to be understood.

Beau exhaled and turned back to the stove. His back to her, he pushed the sizzling potatoes and onions around to the edges of the pan. ''The pool guy,'' he said gruffly.

Dani blinked, not sure what he was talking about. ''What?''

"And the pizza delivery boy." With a great deal more concentration than necessary, Beau broke four eggs, one right after another, into the center of the pan. "And the guy that delivered our groceries in Malibu." He grimaced. "She slept with them all. Of course, I didn't know it at the time." His voice filled with bitterness as the corners of his mouth curved grimly. "Like a fool, I thought they all just had big crushes on her." He paused long enough to shoot Dani a remorse-filled look. "They were a lot younger than her and in most cases were just completely gaga over the fact that she was a movie star. I didn't think much of it at the time. Sharon's incredibly beautiful and a well-known if not abundantly talented actress. It was normal for them to act funny around her. And me, too, for that matter, because of my celebrity status."

"How did you find out?" Dani asked as Beau placed a lid onto the skillet.

His eyes darkened unhappily. "I came home and found her with the twenty-year-old pool boy in our bed."

Dani had only to look at the expression on his face to know how much that must have hurt. "What did you do?" she asked quietly.

Beau rubbed the tense muscles at the back of his neck. "I turned around and walked out. When I came back a couple of days later to get my things, she swore to me it had been a one-time thing. A mistake. She begged me to take her back."

Beginning to feel pretty tense herself, Dani edged closer. "Did you?" The heartache she felt for him echoed in her voice.

"No." Beau's expression was grim and unrelenting as he crumbled the bacon in his fists. He lifted the skillet lid and sprinkled the bits over the sizzling potatoes and eggs. "In my view, the fact that the sex was meaningless made the betrayal even worse," he said.

Dani could understand that. She brought out the jug of orange juice and filled two paper cups. She carried them to the glass-topped table in the breakfast nook. "How did you find out about the others?" Dani asked.

Beau slid two eggs and half of the potato, onion and bacon mixture onto each plate. "I had a feeling from the way she acted that the pool-boy thing was just the tip of the iceberg. Whatever the truth was, I had to know it."

That sounded like him, Dani thought. He'd behaved the same way about their predicament.

He scowled as he carried their plates to the table. "So I thought about it and then went to have a man-to-man talk with each and every one of the guys that had seemed a little too attentive to my wife. Most of them were pretty young and woefully inexperienced—at least until Sharon came along and indoctrinated them into things—and it didn't take long for the facts to come out." Beau sighed, suddenly looking weary to his soul. A distant look came into his eyes. "In some cases it took a little money, but eventually all of them understood the wisdom of not discussing my wife's hankering for men other than her husband."

"And then?" Dani asked as she ate a forkful of the hot delicious eggs.

"I advised her to get therapy." Beau dug into his potatoes.

"But she refused," Dani guessed.

Beau rolled his eyes. "You bet she did. She said as long as she was of legal age and they were of legal age and everyone consented, it was okay. Forget that she was making a damn fool out of me, and our marriage. She thought of herself as sort of a sexual fairy god-mother, for initiating them into sex.''

"Oh, dear," Dani said.

Beau's jaw clenched as he thought about what had happened between him and his ex-wife. "I could have gone public with the truth and probably kept her from getting anything other than what she had brought to the marriage in a financial sense, which wasn't much. But I didn't want to involve the guys she'd slept with—they were little more than kids themselves and I figured they'd already been misused enough. That no good could come of making the sordid mess public. Any-way—" Beau shrugged "—you know the rest. The set-tlement, the agreement to keep the reasons behind the divorce private."

For several minutes they ate in silence as Dani re-flected on what Beau had been through with his ex-wife. No wonder he had become bitter, cynical and wary at the time of the divorce. Yet he seemed to have finally risen above it. At least he had until Sharon had come back to make more trouble for him. Dani's fingers tight-ened on her fork as she regarded Beau anxiously.

"What are you going to do now?"

"For the moment?" Beau suddenly seemed weary of the whole mess. "Let it ride."

He was certainly more generous than she would have been in the same situation, Dani thought, admiring him all the more. She would have wanted revenge, retalia-tion, something. She reached across the table and took his hand. "Why?"

Beau tightened his grip on her fingers and looked deep into her eyes. "Because you and I have more im-portant things to do."

Chapter Six

"Oh, really," Dani echoed dryly, wondering what in heaven's name he was going to try to commandeer her into now. "Like what?" She moved carefully away from him, determined not to put herself in a physically or emotionally vulnerable situation with him again.

"Like get this place organized." Beau flashed her his movie-star I-can-conquer-anything grin. "We won't be able to concentrate on us until there's a peaceful environment to concentrate in. Therefore—" he shook his head disparagingly at the moving boxes stacked in every nook and cranny of the first floor "—we need to unpack."

"Only one problem with that," Dani said, resenting that his immediate ambitions so clearly mirrored her own. She didn't want them to think alike on anything. Except maybe about the baby. She wanted them both to care about the baby.

Beau's glance ran over her face, lingering on her lips for a long heart-stopping moment before returning to her eyes. Adding to her dismay was the fact that he seemed to like her low-flash-point temper. "And that problem is?"

Dani blew out an exasperated breath, not sure when

a man had gotten under her skin so swiftly. All she knew was that he was fast taking over her life. And she did not want that to happen. Letting Beau into her life meant taking chances she was not prepared to take. She was happy just the way she was, even if she was a little lonely from time to time. But knowing she would soon have a child she wanted with all her heart and soul and living near her sisters again would take care of that, she assured herself. She didn't need Beau to see her through the pregnancy or help her take care of the baby. Her sisters could do that, too.

Steeling herself against any passes he might make, she propped both hands on her hips and took an equally insouciant stance. "Billy Carter will be here in a few minutes and I'm still in my pajamas." She might be working at home now, but she didn't intend to greet her employee in her nightclothes.

"I can remedy that." Beau's dark-blue eyes glimmered mischievously. "Where are your clothes? I'll get you dressed in no time flat."

"Undressed is more like it."

"I admit it. I'm pretty good at that, too."

"Well, that's a skill you are not going to be called on to use here," Dani said as hot embarrassed color bled into her face. Honestly, what was wrong with her? He hadn't even touched her and she was tingling all over!

Beau leaned against the counter and crossed his arms. The look he gave her was direct, uncompromising and confident. "You never know," he offered cheerfully.

Dani shook her head imperiously. "I know."

He merely smiled in a way that made her feel all hot and bothered inside and continued looking at her.

"However, I think I will get dressed," Dani said,

knowing the less time they spent together in an intimate fashion the better. Their situation was complicated enough without bringing sex back into the equation or allowing herself to think their marriage was anything but a temporary solution for the benefit of the child they were unexpectedly expecting.

Looking as if he had no such reservations himself about either their present or their future, Beau took her in from head to toe. His glance lingered appreciatively on her breasts before returning to her face. "Need any help with that?" he teased.

Dani rolled her eyes and drew in a short stabilizing breath. "Don't you wish."

"No," DANI TOLD BEAU and Billy for the twentieth time that morning. "I don't like that arrangement, either."

Beau and Billy put the sofa down in front of the bay window overlooking the front lawn. Wordlessly they traded impatient man-to-man glances and shook their heads.

"Why don't we just put them somewhere and worry about it later?" Beau told Dani, not sure when he had been so thoroughly exasperated by a woman. As far as he was concerned, every single way they'd had the living-room furniture arranged so far was just fine. Who cared, anyway, as long as you had a place to sit down? Or in his case, as the husband-relegated-to-the-sofa, to sleep?

"No," Dani shot back. "I won't be able to work unless it's right."

"Well, I won't be able to keep a lid on my temper unless we stop now," Beau said just as firmly, ignoring Billy's wide-eyed look of dismay.

Dani gave Beau a deliberately provoking look. Smiled with all the steely resolve of a born and bred Texas belle. "Maybe that's a sign, then, you weren't cut out for…this and should run on home now," she suggested sweetly.

Beau knew what she meant, even if Billy didn't. And he didn't care what Dani did or how many hoops she tried to make him jump through. He wasn't about to give up on this marriage of theirs. If he had married her, against his decision never to marry again, he'd had a reason. And he was damn well sticking to her like glue until he found out or remembered what that reason was.

Beau glanced at his watch. "Maybe we should break for lunch." And maybe it was time he made a few calls, without Dani's knowledge, and took care of this problem once and for all. Their lives would be much simpler, much sooner, if he did now what he'd been tempted to do all along.

"Suit yourself, but I'm staying where I am," Dani said sweetly, looking at Beau in a way that made him want to haul her into his arms and kiss her until she went weak in the knees and melted against him.

Billy looked from one to the other. Clearly he felt as caught between the two of them as he was tired of moving furniture. "Maybe I should, um, go into your office and start setting up your computer," Billy suggested to Dani nervously.

"Good idea," Dani said, her stubborn glance still trained on Beau.

"Meanwhile, I'll go out, make a few phone calls and bring us all back some lunch," Beau promised, heading for the door.

AS SOON AS BEAU LEFT, Dani went into the library/ study, with the floor-to-ceiling bookshelves and beautiful marble fireplace, to help Billy. Although still cluttered with dozens of boxes stacked one on top of the other, she knew this large room with its abundant storage and floor space was going to be the perfect working environment for her. Not to mention that there was also plenty of room for a playpen or crib and a child-size play area, so her baby could come to work with her, in comfort and style. Dani hadn't planned to mix motherhood and work just yet, but now that she was living in Laramie again, surrounded by family and friends and pregnant with Beau's child, she had to admit, she couldn't have been happier. Despite the fact the baby would link her and Beau forever.

"I never knew you and Beau Chamberlain were such good friends," Billy said as he tore open the box that contained her computer monitor.

Dani cleared off her computer table, which had already been placed next to an electrical outlet, and began looking for the surge protector. "I wouldn't call us that, exactly."

Billy carried the monitor over to the table, then went back to the box that contained the hard drive and carried it over. "He's here helping you move in."

Dani sorted out the half-dozen cables that would connect the components of the computer. "I know."

Billy went back for the keyboard and brought that over, too. His expression puzzled, he asked, "Why would a big movie star like Beau be going all out to help you when he obviously doesn't really like this moving stuff unless—" Billy stopped abruptly, a stricken expression on his face.

"Unless what?" Dani asked, wondering what had

Billy so upset. He didn't know about her pregnancy or marriage.

"Unless Beau's trying to butter you up to write a good review of his next movie!"

"When it comes to my reviews, I tell the plain unvarnished truth. Everyone knows I can't be bought. And I don't give favorable reviews for friends to help sales, either."

Billy stopped in the act of connecting the keyboard to the hard drive. "Sorry. I didn't mean to imply otherwise, but you gotta admit, Dani, you were awfully hard on him in your reviews of his last four movies."

So others had said. "Every word I wrote was dead on," Dani said irritably. Beau's movies had been good. She'd just thought they could be better. "Furthermore, other critics feel Beau could pick material that's a little more realistic and a little less idealistic, too."

Billy shrugged that off. "That's true. But your column is in a lot more than just one newspaper, Dani, now that your reviews are syndicated. Heck, you're almost as famous as Ebert or Pauline Kael."

Dani knew that was true. In some ways the importance of her opinion had begun to weigh on her. She had never wanted to be responsible for a movie's success or failure. She'd just wanted to review them. Let others know what she saw in them or didn't see.

"Beau is not here for that," she said firmly, cutting open the box that held her printer, then signaling to Billy to come over and lift it out for her. Like her, Beau was far too ethical for that. He wanted to stand or fall on his own merits. He would never ask her to write something about him that was not true. He would never ask her to write good things about his movies she didn't believe or be selective about telling the truth, the way Dani's ex-boyfriend, Chris Avery, had.

Billy carried the printer over to the stand and set it down. Scowling, he persisted, "Then how come he's here so much?" Billy jerked in a breath as his next thought hit. He leaned urgently closer. "You two aren't dating, are you?"

Dani flushed self-consciously as she struggled to untangle the cord and plug the monitor into the hard drive. "No, we're not dating." *We're married.*

"Good." Billy blew out a sigh of relief. "Because—" Again, he stopped abruptly. And grinned at her as if she'd just given him an unexpected Christmas gift.

"Because what, Billy?" Dani asked softly. Maybe it was time to get this all out on the table. Discuss Billy's obvious crush on her, openly and honestly, and then move past it. She looked at him gently, waiting for him to tell her what was on his mind and in his heart. And that was when he made his move. Closed the distance between them swiftly. Put his arms around her in a fierce hug and planted a big wet one on her lips. Dani gasped, struggled and clamped her lips together. Billy held her all the tighter and continued the hopelessly clumsy kiss.

And that was when Beau walked in.

He took one look, set down the bags containing their lunch, strode over. One swift yank and Billy was off Dani and held aloft in Beau's fist. "You have," Beau said through clenched teeth as Dani wiped her mouth with the back of her hand "exactly two seconds to explain."

Quaking from head to toe, Billy shouted, "*Summer of '42!*"

Dani blinked at the movie analogy, as did Beau. Then she put her hand on the flexed muscles of Beau's arm and stepped in to intervene. "Put him down, Beau," she said, still struggling to catch her breath.

Beau let Billy's feet touch the floor again, but did not release the powerful grip he had on Billy's T-shirt. "Keep talking," Beau growled at Billy, looking as if he was ready to punch out Billy at any second.

"Didn't you see the movie?" Billy sputtered anxiously, putting up both hands to ward off the blow he was sure was coming and obviously knew he no doubt deserved. "Where the sexy older woman falls for the young kid and takes him into her…well, you know." Billy turned bright red.

Yes, Dani did. And so, unfortunately, did Beau. And she had no intention of taking Billy into her bed. "This is not the movies, Billy," Dani said sternly.

"With one exception," Beau growled. Keeping his grip on Billy's shirt, he lifted him off his feet again so they were face-to-face. "You ever ever lay a hand on her again and you're going to have your lights punched out—by me. Only these won't be the fake punches you see on-screen. These will be the real thing. You got that?"

Billy was shaking from head to toe. "Yes. Yessir!"

"That's good." Beau lowered him to the floor. Releasing his grip on his shirt, he gave him a shove. "Now go home. Now!" he thundered, all the louder and more forcibly when Billy hesitated.

"Yessir!" Billy shouted, and darted for the door.

"And don't come back!" Beau thundered, shutting the door behind him.

Stunned, furious, Dani stared at him. That had been a terrible scene. No doubt about it. But she hadn't wanted to end it that way. She hadn't wanted *Beau* to end it at all. "You have no right," she sputtered furiously. She was the one who should have put Billy in his place.

Beau folded his arms and leaned against the front door. His eyes met hers. Once again he seemed to be watching and weighing everything she said and did. "I have every right," he reminded her mildly. "Unless you have forgotten, you are my wife."

Her feelings wounded by Beau's obvious lack of faith in her, Dani marched forward and stabbed a finger at his chest. "And Billy is my employee," she countered, feeling a crazy mixture of emotion running riot inside her.

Beau brushed past her, a censuring light in his eyes, a downward slant to his lips. "Not for long."

If she didn't know better, she would think it was Beau's heart that was hurting, instead of just his pride. Dani's heart soared at the possibility even as she worried about the problems Beau's feelings would cause. The truth was, she wasn't any happier about Billy's pass than Beau was, but she saw no reason to let Beau know that. He would just use it to further his own argument.

Her temper soaring, Dani followed Beau across the foyer. "You can't fire him, Beau. Only I can do that."

She gave Beau a quelling look that, to her chagrin, didn't seem to weigh on him in the least as he turned and smiled back at her, at that moment looking every bit the kick-butt cowboy he played on screen.

"Want to bet?" Beau drawled, and started for the door as if to go after Billy.

Dani intervened, putting herself between Beau and the front door. When he would have stepped right by her, she took him by the arm. There was no doubt Beau was bigger, taller and stronger than she was. But she had one weapon to use against him in this battle of wills—her words. "Listen to me, Beau Chamberlain," she told him, her fingers curling around the powerful muscles in his arms. "I will *not* allow you to come in here and take over my life."

"Meaning what?" Beau regarded her with growing impatience, irked by her refusal to let him go all out to defend her. He looked as if he wanted to either shake her or kiss her senseless, she couldn't tell which. "You're actually encouraging the kid?" he asked, incredulous.

He didn't have to say it. Dani knew what he was thinking. He was comparing her to his traitorous ex-wife, Sharon Davis. "Of course not," Dani replied, echoing his harsh pragmatic tone. He was furious with her for not seeing that kiss of Billy's coming, but that didn't mean he had a right to pass judgment on her. Especially since she would have handled that situation just fine on her own if Beau hadn't come along and gone all caveman on her.

She stormed back into the library, figuring if nothing else she could get back to work. Beau, however, had other plans, as he backed her up against the edge of her desk. "I didn't see you hauling off and slapping his face."

Dani didn't know exactly what it was, but there was something dangerous about him now, something overly watchful and faintly predatory in his manner.

Giving him an innocent smile that belied the sudden wobbliness of her knees and the racing of her pulse, she looked at him equably and remarked calmly, "That's because you didn't give me a chance." Dani tried to back up farther and ended up sitting on the desk.

"You're saying you would have?" Beau planted his hands on either side of her and leaned over her, so she was pinned between his body and the smooth uncluttered surface of the desk.

Dani paused, torn between her desire to make him suffer for thinking her capable of who only knew what with Billy and her even stronger desire to see that he was never hurt again the way his ex-wife had hurt him. She only knew that, used to total freedom her whole adult life, she resented having her actions and her integrity questioned now—a lot. Especially by him. "I...no," Dani said honestly. "I wouldn't have. I would have *told* him it was inappropriate." So there were similarities in what was happening here and what had happened with Sharon Davis. So Billy was gaga over Dani and her celebrity and her career in the same way those young guys had been gaga over Sharon—but it didn't mean she would go to bed with him the way Sharon had gone to bed with her youthful admirers! And darn it all, Dani thought, her resentment building, Beau should know that!

Beau glared at her, desire and a wealth of feeling glimmering in his eyes. His glance slid over the inviting curves of her breasts, her flat abdomen and slim sexy legs before returning to her tousled hair, soft lips and wide amber eyes. "I'm sure he would've gotten that," he said sarcastically. Disgusted by what he apparently saw as her naiveté regarding Billy, Beau refrained from touching her and turned away.

Knowing this was one conflict they needed to resolve, pronto, before his suspicions and her pride tore them apart, Dani pushed herself off the desk and followed him, not stopping until she was face-to-face with Beau again. Ignoring the combination of hurt and anger flashing in his eyes, she angled her chin up at him and demanded, "What exactly are you implying?"

Beau braced his hands on his waist and towered over her. His eyes lasered into hers. "I'm not implying anything, Dani," he said very very softly. "I'm telling you. As long as we're married, *the only man you are making love with is me.*"

Before Dani could do more than gasp, Beau caught her beneath the knees, swung her up into his arms and headed for the stairs. He looked as if he wanted her in his bed again, Dani realized with equal parts anticipation and anxiety. And that was a dangerous proposition. Beau was not just her temporary husband. He was the kind of man she could fall in love with. Part of her felt she had already fallen in love with him. Maybe would always be in love with him, at least a little bit.

Doing her best to remain imperious as Beau carried her up the sweeping staircase to the second floor, Dani linked one arm about his neck and used her other hand to push at his chest. "Just what do you think you're doing, Beauregard Chamberlain?" she demanded.

Beau's blue eyes twinkled at the use of his full name. "What do you think I'm doing?" he murmured sexily, his gaze ardently roving her flushed upturned face.

Getting ready to make me yours all over again, Dani thought as shimmers of desire swept through her. The only problem was, she wasn't sure she was ready for that. "You cannot just carry me up to the bedroom like...like some conquering hero in a movie!" Dani sputtered, feeling both excited and incensed.

"Really?" Beau paused on the landing. He looked down at her. His grip tightened possessively as he shifted her closer to his chest. "How come?"

Trying hard not to notice how warm and strong and

solid he felt, Dani shot right back, "Because you and I are not John Wayne and Maureen O'Hara, or Clark Gable and Vivian Leigh!" Even if it temporarily felt as though they were right up there with the hottest most combustible couples ever to grace a movie screen.

"We're ordinary people." Ordinary people did not do exciting things like this. At least not in Dani's experience.

"You're right about that, all right," Beau acknowledged with a mock gallantry that kindled her senses. He grinned confidently, then continued on up the stairs, looking all the more pleased. He strode into Dani's bedroom and set her down with unexpected gentleness onto the rumpled covers of her bed. Pausing only long enough to kick off his boots, he stretched out beside her and draped her body with his own. "We're not actors playing a part."

Dani flushed hotly as his lips tugged on the lobe of her ear, sending another frisson of sensation soaring through her veins. Suddenly his hands were framing her face and he was lifting her head to his. "We're a man and a woman. A husband and wife. A couple who is expecting a baby in a little over eight months." Giving her no chance to argue, he lowered his mouth to hers.

Dani tasted the masculine force that was Beau, felt his wildness in the plundering sweeping motions of his tongue. She didn't want to give in to him, but his will was stronger than hers. With a low moan of surrender, Dani tilted her head to give him deeper access. His tongue twined with hers, and he delivered a kiss that scored her soul and left her limp with longing and faint with acquiescence and wondering at the magical power he seemed to hold over her heart. They weren't supposed to be together—ever—given how acrimoniously they'd behaved toward each other. And yet Dani couldn't remember ever feeling anything as right as being held in his arms and kissed like there was no tomorrow, no yesterday. Only today.

"Besides…" Beau eventually lifted his head. He rolled onto his back, keeping his arms wrapped around her and taking her with him, so that she ended up draped over the length of him. "In the movies you talked about," he continued, threading his hands through the copper-colored silk of her hair, "the screen always faded to black when they got to the good part. I assure you," he said, dropping kisses along the curve of her cheek, down the nape of her neck, into the open V of her blouse, "I am not going to let that happen here."

"Beau…" Dani moaned, already feeling herself begin to surrender to him, and all he'd done was carry her to bed and kiss her.

"Not that the fault here is all yours," Beau said between sweet seductive kisses. He looked at her lovingly as he traced the bow shape of her lip with his fingertip. "It's mine, too," he whispered gently. "For not making it clear sooner to you and everyone else that you are *my* woman now. And no one else's."

Another shiver of excitement went through her. And then he was on top of her again, his body covering hers. His weight was as welcoming as a warm blanket on a cold winter night. Then his mouth was on hers in a kiss that was shattering in its possessive sensuality. He kissed her as if he was in love with her and would be for all time. He kissed her like he meant to have her. Longing surged through her, overwhelming her heart and her mind. Coupled with his wanting, it was enough to drive her toward abandon. Dani made a low helpless sound in the back of her throat. "Beau—"

"That's it, sweetheart." Beau unbuttoned her blouse, dropping kisses across her skin, while Dani's heart pounded every bit as erratically as his. "Say my name," Beau whispered, and then he kissed her again, hotly and thoroughly. "Say it over and over again." He dispensed with her blouse and her bra. And then his mouth was on her once again, moving from her throat to her breast, tempting, caressing, sending her into a frenzy of wanting. Dani arched against him, burying her hands in his hair, bringing his lips back to hers. She could feel the rigidness of his arousal as he settled himself more fully on top of her. Then need took over once again, making them both reckless and relentless. She wanted him. Needed him. Needed this. Her lips parted and she drew his tongue more intimately into her mouth, continuing to kiss and caress, touch and love, even as they struggled to free themselves of their clothes. Her skirt, panties and sandals were kicked off. His jeans, briefs, shorts and socks quickly followed. Her muscles trembled, tensed, as once again he settled between her thighs, his hips nudging them apart.

Over and over, Beau kissed her, until desire streamed through her, until she was warm and safe, until she knew, as well as he, that this—loving each other again—was inevitable.

Beau hadn't meant for any of this to happen. He'd wanted to make love to Dani, but not until they had their memories back. Not before he was certain with every fiber of his being that she was his and his alone. But when she had started challenging him, refusing to acknowledge she needed him to watch over and protect her, everything had taken a different turn. The truth was he wanted Dani as he had never wanted any woman. More telling still was the fact that he *needed* her just as desperately.

Knowing he hadn't yet looked his fill, he studied the rounded fullness of her breasts, the pouting apricot nipples. Lower still, the flatness of her abdomen, the slenderness of her waist, the enticing curve of her hips, her long sleek thighs. She was as beautiful as his earlier brief flashes of memory had allowed. His whole body tightened as he caressed the curves of her breasts, her pearling nipples and the shadowy valley between.

Surging against him as if she wished his loving would never stop, he slid ever downward, inhaling the sweet lilac scent of her and tasting the silky stretch of skin across her ribs. Dipping his tongue into her navel. Her whole body straining against him, she gave a little cry as he slid lower yet, ran his palms across her legs and gently parted her thighs. The swiftness of her pinnacle caught him by surprise, as did her wantonness and lack of restraint.

She wanted him. She let him know it. With hands and lips, teeth and tongue. Until there was no more holding back for either of them. Until once again she was beneath him. Hands under her hips, he lifted her to him. Took her slowly, sweetly. Until her heart was beating in urgent rhythm to his. The softness of her body giving new heat to his, he took her to heights and depths. He showed her they didn't need to do anything but feel. And he groaned as his body took up an urgent primitive rhythm all its own.

Until then, he hadn't known his own control could be so easily lost, but it was. Beau was aware of every soft warm inch of her, inside and out. Every sigh of surrender, every whimper of desire and pulsation of need. Lost in the sweet swirling pleasure, he went deeper yet. The bedroom grew hot and close. And yet mostly he was aware of Dani, and the wild yearning he felt rising from deep inside her. As she clung to him, his blood ran hot and quick. And then all was lost in the long slow climb and the shattering pleasure.

IT WAS A WHILE before either of them came back to earth. They lay there quietly, trembling still, breathing hard, wrapped in each other's arms. Beau had never known a moment of greater contentment. Although as the moments drew out, he could feel Dani begin to tense. Sensing she was feeling some remorse—for how quickly and unexpectedly they had ended up in bed again—he stroked a hand down her back. He knew Dani didn't do things like this any more than he did. What she didn't know was that it was okay. And not just because they were married, Beau thought, but because feelings that strong—feelings that came along maybe once in a lifetime, if you were lucky—deserved to be acted on.

Yet, as the seconds ticked out and Dani went from warm and pliant and completely his to tense and edgy, he knew it was not going to be that simple for his new bride.

He had known the inevitable shift in their relationship would be difficult for her. They had gone from sworn enemies to unwitting newlyweds and parents-to-be in a very short period. The fact that they had been at one time, several years ago, before their careers got in the way, fast friends was of little consequence, at least to her. What did seem to matter was that the idea of tumbling into bed—with anyone—was something Dani Lockhart just did not do. Considering that, maybe he should have expected this kind of conflicted reaction from her, Beau thought as Dani extricated herself from his embrace.

He watched as she rolled away from him and, clutching the sheet to her breasts, sat up on the edge of the bed. Coppery hair all tousled, cheeks flushed, amber eyes glowing with feisty lights, she looked so beautiful he wanted nothing more than to make love to her all over again. "Well, now we know how we ended up in bed in Mexico," Beau said softly, taking her hand in his, letting her know with a look and a touch they had nothing to be ashamed about. He tightened his fingers reassuringly over hers. "As soon as we start to let our guard down, one touch and it's spontaneous combustion."

Dani stiffened all the more as she removed her hand from his. She regarded him with a haughty confidence that surprised him. "Precisely why something like this shouldn't happen again," Dani said. She rose, wrapping the top sheet around her toga-style, leaving Beau with just the comforter. "With everything we have at stake, we need to keep clear heads, not just recklessly give in to our desire whenever the mood strikes," Dani said as she stalked around the room, picking up pieces of discarded clothing one by one. Carrying his shirt, jeans, briefs and socks over to the bed, she dropped them on his chest. "I don't make love casually, Beau. I want it to mean something."

Beau frowned. As far as he was concerned, it *had* meant something. Furthermore, even if Dani was too proud to admit it, he knew what was really getting to her. The fact they'd made love when so much of their life—past, present, and future—was still unresolved. "What's wrong with giving in to our desire?" he demanded, knowing if he'd had his way they'd be starting to make love again right now and work out the details of their life together later, when their emotions had settled. "We are married, you know."

Dani frowned as she gathered her own clothes. "For starters, recklessly giving in to our desire, with no thought to the future, is how we landed in this dilemma."

"Our having a baby together, you mean," Beau supplied less than graciously as he, too, got to his feet.

Dani nodded. "When we don't even like each other," she said, making what seemed to be a concerted effort not to let her eyes drop any lower than his shoulders.

Realizing more lovemaking was not going to happen—not that afternoon, anyway—Beau stepped into his briefs. "You don't make it easy on anyone, do you?" Beau said sarcastically, aware he was hard as a rock again and they hadn't even kissed. All he had done was *look* at Dani in that ludicrously wrapped sheet masquerading as a toga.

"Life is not a movie," Dani said wearily. Her fingers shook as she pushed them through her hair, trying—without much success, Beau noted—to restore order to the silky copper strands.

"So?"

With effort Beau tried to tamp down his resentment. Dani's eyes were dark and unrepentant. "So everything does not always wrap up neatly, Beau."

Beau lifted a dissenting brow and, still aching mightily, pulled on his jeans. "In our case, it could," he said curtly, although inwardly he was already acknowledging that this new tension was as much his fault as hers. He shouldn't have rushed her. But it was too late now.

They couldn't take it back, any more than they could take back her pregnancy or their marriage. All they could do was move on. With a bit more caution and foresight this time.

But Dani, it appeared, didn't seem likely to even give them that.

"We'll work this out," Beau said. "No matter how hard it is or how long it takes." He personally was hoping not long.

Dani looked at him in a way that let him know there was no possibility of further physical intimacy between them, at least as far as she was concerned. "You delude yourself if you want, Beau Chamberlain," she said very softly. "As for me—" hurt flickered briefly in her eyes "—I don't believe in fairy-tale endings or happily-ever-afters. And that is not going to change."

Knowing nothing could be gained by continuing to talk about what Dani clearly did not want to talk about, Beau watched her take her clothes and go across the hall. She stepped into the bathroom, shutting the door firmly behind her.

So they hadn't made love right away, as he wished. It would happen, he reassured himself firmly, as he continued to dress. He would make it happen. And when it did, Dani would realize there was no pretending the physical passion between them did not exist. It was there. It was real. It was a force too powerful to be denied.

Alone, it might not be sufficient foundation for a marriage. But it was a start. And a damn good one.

Chapter Seven

"So, you're not the only one moving in this week," Jenna Lockhart said at seven-thirty the next morning when she stopped in to see Dani on her way to work.

Dani looked past her sister at the monster moving van parked several houses down on the opposite side of the street. Five boys, ages six to seventeen, were scattered across the lawn. A handsome man was supervising the unloading. "Is that…?"

Jenna grinned. "Sam McCabe in the flesh."

"Doesn't he have some sort of super-successful computer firm in Dallas?"

"Yep. According to his aunt Lilah, he'll be commuting. Meanwhile, he and his sons are moving into the house he inherited from his folks. Apparently he's been having a hard time keeping track of his boys since their mom died. He figured it'd be easier to ride herd on them in Laramie."

Dani studied the six McCabes. "John and Lilah McCabe must be happy about that. They've always been fond of all their nieces and nephews. Sam in particular."

Jenna nodded. "I think they'd like to see Sam married again. Although from what I hear there's not much chance of that. No woman will ever replace Ellie in either Sam or the boys' affections. And speaking of affections, you look...different this morning.''

The truth was, Dani felt different. She had never been all that adventurous when it came to her personal life. Independent, yes. But as for taking risks in a romantic sense, she had always been sensible to a fault. Once again, with Beau, she hadn't exercised caution. Instead, she had recklessly given into temptation and satisfied her curiosity about what it would be like to make love to Beau—again. And she'd discovered being loved by Beau was every bit as good as it looked in the movies. No, Dani decided quickly, yesterday had been even better than that, because yesterday had actually *happened* to her. Just as, she was beginning to see, their lovemaking in Mexico had really happened. And it had obviously been as deliciously sensual and wonderful as her fragments of memory indicated.

She'd hoped, of course, that if they made love one more time they'd get each other out of their systems. Be able to move on with their lives. That hadn't happened. Instead, Beau seemed to want her more than ever. And she wanted him, too, even though she knew it wasn't wise and had no intention of ever giving into temptation that way again.

"What? No comment? No ready reply? You're just going to stand there looking secretive?" Jenna quipped after a moment, obviously frustrated that her fishing expedition had yielded absolutely nothing.

Jenna was not just the most creative of the four sisters. She was also the most curious. Which meant Dani was going to have to give her something if she wanted Jenna to drop it.

Dani held the front door while Jenna carried in a

white paper bag from Isabel Buchanon's bakery and two cups of decaf coffee, stacked one on top of the other. "Okay." Dani would take the lure. "How exactly do I look different?" Dani led the way to the living room, which—despite their nonstop efforts to arrange it satisfactorily the day before—was still a disorganized mess. She just did not have any talent when it came to home decor. And unfortunately neither did Beau.

"I don't know exactly." Jenna sat down on the sofa, which had been pushed to the far wall opposite the bay window overlooking the front lawn. Carefully she opened the lid on her coffee, while Dani sat beside her and did the same.

Jenna peered at her, taking in Dani's linen trousers and sleeveless shirt. "Flushed, I guess. Happy and excited and scared all at the same time. Sort of like when you've just come off a roller coaster at Six Flags." Jenna studied her intently as Dani pulled two buttery blackberry Danishes from the bag and set them on napkins, her concern as a big sister evident. "So what's going on?"

Nothing I can talk about, Dani thought as she took a bite of the delicious flaky pastry. But plenty she could *think* about. After they'd made love and she'd told Beau it wouldn't happen again, they'd spent a good deal of the rest of the day apart. She'd busied herself in her office. And Beau had gone off to parts unknown, returning only at dinnertime with some food from the Lone Star Dinner and Dance Hall for both of them. After they'd eaten, they'd retired to separate quarters of the house and gone to bed early, Dani upstairs, Beau on the sofa downstairs.

As a result, they'd also gotten up early. Dani had

heard him moving around, shaving and taking a shower before it was even light. When she'd emerged from the shower around six-thirty, he'd been talking on the phone downstairs. Shortly thereafter, he'd left, without a word about where he was going or why. Or even when he'd be back. Admittedly Dani, who'd spent half the night marvelling at the new life growing inside her, had been a little miffed. Even though she knew he didn't owe her any explanation. It wasn't as if they had to check in with each other just because they were married. She certainly wasn't informing him of her every decision, thought or whim. Yet it would have been nice to know where he was and what he was doing right this minute. It would have made her feel closer to him somehow. As if they were the kind of close-knit team they'd need to be for their baby.

"You can tell me," Jenna insisted compassionately.

"Obviously you think something potentially upsetting is going on," Dani said, studying her older sister carefully. "Or you wouldn't be here." Jenna was not one to offer sweet buttery Danishes and a shoulder to cry on unless she was pretty sure it was needed.

"Well…" Jenna started, clearly not wanting to offend.

Her impatience growing by leaps and bounds, Dani wiped her fingers on her paper napkin. "Stop trying to protect me, Jenna, and just spit it out." If there was anything Dani hated, it was a delay in bad news. If something awful had happened—and Jenna was acting as if it had—she wanted to know about it as soon as possible. This waiting for the ax to fall was for the birds.

Jenna took a sip of coffee and swallowed. "I just saw Beau Chamberlain going into the Lone Star."

"So?" Dani took a bite of her Danish. "He and Greta McCabe have been friends for a long time, you know that." Greta was Dani's friend, too. Dani knew there was nothing to feel jealous about there.

Jenna looked at Dani. "He wasn't with Greta. He was with Sharon Davis, his ex-wife."

Dani's heart did a somersault. Beau hadn't said anything to her about Sharon being in town, although after the way they had been skirting each other carefully since they'd made love, she could hardly blame him for not confiding in her. She had practically drawn the battle lines in her effort to maintain some independence from him, emotional and otherwise.

"Beau has a financial stake in Greta's dance hall," Dani reported numbly. That could explain why he was going into a place that wouldn't be open for hours, or even, she knew, have any staff there until much later in the afternoon.

Eyes narrowing suspiciously, Jenna persisted, "What does that have to do with Sharon Davis being here in Laramie, though?"

Dani didn't know. But ten to one it had something to do with money and the exposé Sharon was threatening to write about her life with Beau.

SHARON HAD NEVER BEEN a morning person, but Beau was, and it was a fact his ex-wife was well aware of. Hence, she'd known that the best time to catch him was early in the day. So she'd made sure she had a message waiting for him when he checked his voice mail at seven. And she'd made sure she was ready to meet with him at whatever location he chose after she flew in from Los Angeles. Knowing the last thing he wanted was his ex-wife and his new wife together under the same roof,

Beau had chosen the Lone Star. It was easy to find, even if you didn't know the area all that well, and Sharon didn't. Because he was Greta's silent partner, he had a key and could let them into the dinner and dance hall. And he knew it was one place in Laramie he could guarantee he and Sharon wouldn't be disturbed.

Now that they were here, however, facing off across the polished wooden dance floor in the center of the establishment, Beau was already regretting meeting with Sharon at all. Clearly she blamed him for everything that had gone wrong in her life. And that had been plenty.

"Our fans want to know why we split up," Sharon said, decisively tossing her sleek, dark, perfectly coiffed mane.

Beau walked over to one of the tables. He took down a chair, turned it around backward and straddled the seat. "Our fans don't need to know why we split up," Beau said, folding his arms over the top of the chair.

Sharon glared at him and continued to pace back and forth as dramatically as possible, glaring at him all the while. "*You* can say that. The mystery of our divorce hasn't hurt your career one bit."

The divorce hasn't hurt your career, either, Beau thought. *Your acting ability—or more precisely, lack of it—has.* But knowing better than to say that and risk ticking off his volatile ex-wife off any more, he kept silent.

"*My* career has suffered enormously," Sharon continued, pressing a hand to her ample chest.

Beau shrugged. Sharon wanted him to become emotional, too. That wasn't going to happen. "Painting me as an adulterer isn't going to help your career, Sharon," he told her in a low tone.

Sharon stalked closer, her three-inch heels making a staccato sound on the floor. "You're wrong there. People always feel sympathy for the wronged wife."

Beau's patience, what little of it was left, began to fade. "Except you weren't wronged and you know it." He pushed the words through clenched teeth.

Sharon's eyes glittered. "That's not so," she said fiercely. "You never really loved me, and you know it."

True, Beau thought on a tidal wave of guilt. Much to his chagrin, he hadn't loved Sharon. He just hadn't known it at the time. That didn't mean he had to keep paying for it, though. As far as he was concerned, he had more than paid for his sins. "I'm not going to let you do this to me," he said.

Sharon sashayed closer, her hips swaying provocatively in her short tight skirt. "Is that a threat?"

"It's a promise," Beau said quietly, looking her in the eye. "I will sue you if you persist in this course. And if you think your career is hurting now—wait until you see the damage that will be done if you are painted as a vengeful liar, as well as an adulterer."

Sharon's green eyes flashed with fiery temper and ugly intentions. She slapped her hands on the ladder back of the chair and leaned over, giving him a generous view of her breasts, spilling out of her low-cut top. "You forget who you're talking to. I work in this business, too. And I know exactly how much is at stake for you. You need a hit here, Beau, and a big one to keep your stratospheric salary and wealth of opportunities." She straightened slowly, then continued in a voice that was hard and clipped. "You're right, I may not win in the long run but I can certainly do enough damage to your reputation in the short term to keep women out of the theaters in droves. And perhaps create renewed interest in me and an opportunity or two for myself. By the time the truth about us comes out," Sharon smiled evilly. "You know how bad the press can be about printing retractions of any kind about anyone. Never mind about a story that's so old it's over. Well, by that time, the damage to your career will already be done, as well."

Unfortunately for Beau, Sharon's words had a ring of truth. She could not only drag him through the mud and make fools out of them both, she would inadvertently be dragging Dani—and their baby—into this mess. "So what do you want?" Beau asked gruffly.

"A part in the new Sydney Peterson movie."

Beau laughed and stood. "You're dreaming." The esteemed director had a rep for only working with the best. He was very particular about which actors he selected for his movies. A fact that did not deter Sharon in the least.

"You are one of Northstar Films' biggest actors," she said, pouting. "Your westerns, even when they get bad reviews—help keep them afloat. You have enough clout there to pull this off, Beau."

Maybe. Maybe not. But that really wasn't the issue, Beau thought, as behind him the front door opened and closed.

Sharon peered over Beau's shoulder and abruptly looked even more aggrieved. "What is she doing here?" Sharon turned toward Beau accusingly. "I thought you said we'd be completely alone this morning."

Regretting that he hadn't bothered to lock the front door of the dance hall after Sharon had come in, Beau turned to see who had entered. Somehow he wasn't surprised to see Dani framed in the dance-hall entrance. She looked even more beautiful than she had when he'd said good-night to her last night and—beneath her customary surface cool—even more distressed as she glided toward them. "I was looking for Greta."

"Greta is not here," Sharon said icily, shooting daggers at Dani with her eyes. "And you are not welcome here, either, after what you said about my last movie!"

It was all Beau could do not to grin. Dani's review of Sharon's most recent work had gotten her where it hurt and had been so on target it was almost funny. People were still quoting it.

Dani walked across the dance floor. As she neared Sharon, she shrugged. "If you don't want to have your work reviewed, don't act."

Sharon's jaw dropped. She shot a sharp look at Beau, then demanded hotly, "Are you going to let that little witch talk to me that way?"

Proud of the way Dani was standing up to his ex-wife, Beau shrugged. "I don't think anyone can stop Dani Lockhart from speaking her mind." He sure hadn't been able to. He turned back to Dani and held her eyes.

Her gaze didn't waver from his in the slightest. "How right you are about that," she remarked sassily.

Sharon released an exasperated breath. "Well, I am not going to stand here and take it," she declared emotionally. Tossing her head again, she gave Beau another dark meaningful look. "You remember what I said, Beau Chamberlain." She reached into her purse, pulled out a card with a phone number scrawled across the back. "When you have something to report, you can reach me here."

Beau lifted a brow. "A little beneath your usual accommodations, isn't it?'' Generally Sharon declined anything less than four stars, five hundred dollars a night.

"It's all this one-horse town has available right now, due to some wedding that went on last weekend! And don't think I'm happy about it, either!'' She left in a waft of expensive perfume.

"What are you doing here?'' Beau finally asked Dani.

Dani sauntered closer, looking pretty and trim in a sleeveless pink cotton tunic and matching trousers. "Call me nosy.'' Dani slid her hands into the pockets of her trousers. She stopped just short of him and tilted her head up to his, looking deep into his eyes. "I wanted to know what my husband was up to.''

Noting the unaccustomed possessiveness of her words, it was all Beau could do not to grin. Dani might not want to admit it, even to herself, but she was quickly getting as emotionally involved with him as he was with her. He tucked an errant strand of hair behind her ear. Damn but she was pretty, even this early in the morning, even when she was obviously determined to play it cool with him. "How'd you know I was here?'' he asked softly.

"My sister Jenna saw you enter the dance hall with Sharon, and she stopped by to tell me.''

Beau tensed at the accusation in her low tone. "And you and your sister immediately jumped to conclusions and thought the worst,'' he guessed.

Dani shrugged and continued regarding him warily. If this was a problem, she wasn't backing away. "I don't want to be made a fool of,'' she said bluntly.

Beau shot her an understanding glance. "No one does.''

Dani paused for a long thoughtful moment. She raked her teeth across her lower lip. "Sharon's still black-mailing you, isn't she?"

Beau nodded. Briefly he explained what his ex-wife wanted now.

Dani's amber eyes clouded with worry. "Are you going to do what she wants?"

"I don't know." Beau paused and looked down into Dani's upturned face. Taking in the compassion in her eyes, it was all he could do not to pull her into his arms and kiss her until she went limp with longing. Keeping his eyes locked on hers, he continued, "I'm against giving in to blackmail on principle. But I have to admit that right now, because of you and the baby, I'm tempted to do whatever's necessary to get her off my back, even if it means using every bit of clout I have to get her cast in another movie role." Right now he didn't want anything interfering with his relationship with Dani. He had an idea Sharon would like nothing better than to break them up, to assuage her own ego and wounded pride.

Dani shook her head and warned, "If you buy her off again, it'll be twice you've given in to her demands. She'll never stop."

Beau grinned. "I knew there was something I liked about you. Your voice of reason."

"I mean it, Beau," Dani said passionately. "Don't let that woman do this to you."

Beau took her hands in his. They were soft and slender and very feminine. "I'm not going to let her hurt you, Dani." He underlined every word.

Dani shrugged off his concern while still clinging to his hands. "She won't."

Beau frowned, his worry about the situation, his need

to protect Dani, increasing with every second that passed. "You say that now." He wrapped an arm around her waist and led her over to the chair he'd been sitting in, then guided her into it. "But, for our baby's sake and our own, we're going to have to announce our marriage soon." Beau lifted another chair down from the tabletop and positioned it so he and Dani could sit knee to knee. Once seated, he leaned forward and took her hands in his again. "And if we do that in the midst of all these bogus charges of Sharon's, it's going to put you right in the middle of a public slugfest. The press will scrutinize you and everyone close to you."

Dani was silent. He imagined she was thinking not just of the three of them, but her sisters, her nephew, Jeremy.

After a moment Dani released a beleaguered sigh. She withdrew her hands from his, got to her feet and began to pace. "How did you ever get involved with a woman like Sharon, anyway?"

Beau had asked himself that same question many times. As much as he was loath to admit it, a big part of it had been the sex. Sharon was very good in bed. But sex without love was—in the long run, when the lust and excitement wore off—worse in many ways than being alone. It wasn't a mistake Beau ever intended to make again. Good sex alone just wouldn't cut it. He needed more from the woman in his life. Much more.

"We were on location in the desert, filming *Lawless,*" Beau answered. "It was a tough shoot for a lot of reasons, and Sharon and I ended up turning to each other, initially just for camaraderie. But eventually things got a little more complicated—" *Sharon got a little better at playing me for a fool* "—and we continued our on-screen romance off-screen, too."

Dani held herself very still and studied him in silence. "Do you usually become involved with your leading ladies?" She searched his face.

"No." In fact, Beau thought grimly, he had a strict rule against it. One in the past he had religiously adhered to.

"Then…?" Dani continued watching him, struggling to understand.

Beau stood and looked Dani straight in the eye. "She needed me. Or seemed to, and for a while, anyway, it felt good to be needed that way. So we got married shortly after the movie wrapped." Beau knew, even as he said the words, how foolishly chivalrous it all sounded.

"When did you realize it was a mistake?" she asked softly, edging closer.

"When we returned to Los Angeles and attempted to settle into normal married life. She was jealous of the amount of work I was getting and resentful she wasn't getting more." Beau paused, remembering what a disillusioning time that had been. "I began to see a side of her I hadn't known existed." *And had liked even less.*

"But you hung in there, anyway." Dani regarded him with something akin to respect, for trying to do right by the woman he'd chosen as his wife.

Beau nodded. "I'd made a commitment. I felt honor bound to live up to it."

"And would have," Dani guessed softly, searching his face again, "if you hadn't caught her cheating on you."

"Probably." Beau sighed and moved away from Dani restlessly. "Although it was getting harder and harder, and since she didn't want kids and I did…" Beau shrugged his disappointment. "Well, suffice it to say, neither of us was all that happy." He moved back to Dani's side.

Silence fell between them once again, a more comfortable one now. Beau had never talked about his marriage to Sharon with anyone. It felt good unburdening himself to Dani. Better yet to know she understood the choices he had made, and the mistakes. Soon he hoped to understand her in the same way. But first he had to get her to open up to him. Not an easy proposition, considering how fiercely Dani guarded her heart. "That answer all your questions?" he asked.

Dani lifted her hands in an indifferent gesture. "I suppose."

Beau grinned. The one thing Dani was not was a good fibber. Beau smiled his satisfaction. "Admit it. You were concerned about me." His hands cupping her upper arms, he drew her nearer. "And you rushed over here to help."

Dani tilted her head back and favored him with a smile. "What if I was?"

Beau sifted his fingers through her hair, loving the feel of it. "Hey, if you want to act like a wife it's okay with me."

Dani's eyes sparkled and her deliciously full lower lip slid out in a kissable pout. "I am not acting like a wife!" she declared, arrowing a finger at his chest.

"Could have fooled me," Beau drawled, already lowering his mouth to hers. Ignoring her muted gasp of dismay, he kissed her the way he'd wanted to kiss her from the moment she'd walked in. With none of the caution their situation required and all of the heart. He kissed her to remind her what they could have, given half a chance, and what he wanted them to have. He kissed her out of frustration because they had let so many things drive them apart. And he kissed her in celebration of the baby they were having.

She fought him at first, using her hands to push against his chest. And still Beau persisted, parting her lips with the pressure of his, nudging his tongue inside, tasting the sweetness and the innocence that was her. He deepened the kiss, tormenting her with lazy sweeps of his tongue. His lips caressed hers, gently this time, and with incredible tenderness. Dani trembled and moaned. Her arms came up to wrap about his neck. The next thing he knew she was kissing him back with an urgency and an answering wonder that rocked him to his soul. Passion for passion, Beau met her needs, claiming her as his, until his blood began to heat and he knew it was either stop their embrace or end up taking her then and there. Slowly, reluctantly, he ended the kiss.

"Damn it all, Beau," she complained immediately, looking every bit as eager to continue as he. She swallowed hard. "You know we can't do this anymore, and you know why!"

All Beau knew was that every time he kissed Dani, he ended up feeling closer to her. He suspected it was the same for her, which was why she was now protesting so mightily. Having felt her response and experienced her need, which was so much more potent than her words, Beau felt a surge of male satisfaction much greater than his frustration at having to stop. "So you said," he murmured, not about to let her start another argument to try to keep them apart. He would wait, just as she wanted. But only because they were at Greta's dance hall. There would be a time and place to make love to Dani again much sooner than she knew. And this time when it came, there would be no turning back. He would see to it.

Chapter Eight

Back at the house, Dani once again got down to the endless overwhelming business of unpacking.

"All those clothes are never going to fit in that tiny little closet. What you need is an armoire," Beau said from Dani's open bedroom door.

As much as Dani hated to admit it, he was right. Aware she was still a bit peeved at him for stealing a kiss and even angrier at herself for letting him, she turned to Beau. Wearing a plain stone-colored shirt and jeans that seemed to underscore the healthy tanned hue of his skin, he looked handsome and sexy as all get-out. Worse, since they'd returned to her house, he only seemed to have time and attention for her. Which made concentrating on her organizational problems a very good idea, Dani decided pragmatically. What she needed to do here was pretend she hadn't a care in the world about anything except getting properly settled in her new home.

Dani forced a cheerful smile. "You're probably right. An armoire would be just the thing in this room. Unfortunately I didn't really consider the lack of closet space in the upstairs bedrooms when I bought the house."

Beau ambled farther in the room. "So let's go get one."

Dani blinked in astonishment. "Now?"

Beau shrugged. "Why not?"

Dani glanced at her watch and saw it was almost 9 a.m. "For starters, Billy should be showing up for work any minute."

Beau regarded her skeptically. "I wouldn't count on that if I were you."

Dani dropped the stack of shirts she'd been trying to fit into her closet on her bed, giving up for now. She whirled back to Beau and admonished, "Listen, cowboy, you may have thrown him out of here yesterday in a bad imitation of John Wayne, but he doesn't work for you. He works for me." And that was the way it was going to stay. As if on cue, the doorbell rang.

Beau scowled, knowing as well as Dani who it probably was.

"Stay out of this," she warned as she breezed past him. "I mean it."

She dashed downstairs, dodging moving boxes as she went to the front door. Billy was standing on the stoop. He looked as nervous and as stressed-out as it was possible to be. "I came to apologize," he said grimly, before she could get a word in edgewise. "I...I made a complete fool of myself yesterday."

"Yes," Dani said, looking Billy straight in the eye. "You did."

"But I swear it won't happen again," Billy persisted.

Beau appeared behind Dani. He glared at Billy, making it abundantly clear that if Billy wanted to get to Dani, he was going to have to go through him first. "How can we be sure of that?" Beau demanded, unconvinced.

"Because I give you my word," Billy said earnestly. "No more hitting on her." Billy turned to Dani. "No more fantasies of…well, you know."

Yes, Beau did, Dani thought uncomfortably, and as a consequence Beau once again looked ready to take Billy to the woodshed.

"Because I know it's not gonna happen," Billy continued, pleading his case. He swallowed and abruptly looked close to tears. "Just like I know I'll never be able to actually go to film school," he added hoarsely, looking deeply disappointed. "More than likely, sorting videos for you for a summer is as close as I'm ever likely to get, even if I did just get off the waiting list at USC."

Dani's eyes widened at that bit of news. The University of Southern California had a very prestigious film school. "You got in?" She had been mentoring Billy ever since he had confided his ambitions to her, when he was just starting high school, corresponding via e-mail and regular mail, seeing each other on her twice-yearly visits back to Laramie. Realizing just how bright and talented Billy was, she had encouraged him to apply to all the best film schools and had been as disappointed as he was when he was put on the waiting list by USC the previous April.

Billy reached into the back pocket of his jeans and withdrew a folded piece of paper. He handed it over. It appeared to have been read and reread many times.

Dani quickly scanned the contents. Beau did the same over her shoulder. "It says here you've got a week to send in your deposit to keep your place in the class," Dani said.

"And no financial aid," Billy reported glumly.

Dani ushered Billy inside and shut the door behind

him. "What do your parents say?" she asked gently as she led the way into the living room.

"That it's Texas A&M University or nothing, 'cause they aren't paying for anything else."

Billy sat down in a club chair while Dani and Beau took the sofa. "What about the University of Texas at Austin?" Beau said, getting involved in the problem despite himself. "They have a film school."

"My parents don't want me going there, either." Billy sighed. "They want me at A&M, studying cattle management, so I can work the ranch with my dad." He paused, then continued hopefully, "Maybe if you could talk to them, Dani, you could make them see this isn't just some fantasy, but a real opportunity for me. One I can't afford to pass up."

"I'll be happy to speak to them on your behalf," Dani said. She wasn't sure Billy's parents would listen to her. "But no matter what, you have to respect your parents' wishes."

"I'll go with you," Beau said.

Dani was happy about that. There was no doubt having someone along of Beau's stature in the film industry would help.

AN HOUR LATER she and Beau were sitting in the kitchen of the ranch house where Billy had grown up. As Billy had predicted, his parents were totally against him going to USC.

"But they have one of the best film schools in the nation," Dani said.

"Texas A&M has one of the best agricultural schools in the nation," Billy's dad countered.

Billy scowled and ran his hands through his slick-backed rusty-brown hair. "I don't want to be a rancher, Dad. I have no interest in cattle. Zero!"

"You're too young to know what you want," Billy's dad said, then took a long thirsty gulp of iced tea. He wiped the range dust from his brow.

"Maybe in four or five years, if you still want to do this," Billy's mom offered after a moment, smoothing the fabric on her long denim skirt.

"Four or five years is going to be too late!" Billy jumped up from the table and ran out of the room.

Silence fell among the remaining adults. "It really is a once-in-a-lifetime opportunity for him," Dani said gently. "And I have to tell you, aside from me and maybe Beau here, I've never met anyone who loves film as much as Billy does."

"Which is exactly the problem," Billy's dad said. He pushed his chair back with a screech and began to pace the cozy country kitchen. "It's all those movies that have put these crazy ideas in his head." Billy's dad scowled. "We don't want him going out there to California, spending all that money to go to a fancy private college and getting us into the kind of debt it'll take years to pay off, only to find out he can't get a job when he's through. We've seen it happen."

"And not just to kids who want to be in the movies," Billy's mom put in. "Only last year there were at least ten Laramie kids who graduated from college with degrees in art and music and philosophy and all sorts of other nonsense. Every single one of them applied for jobs all over the country, and not one of them found work in their field. You know what most of them are doing now? Waiting tables and working minimum-wage jobs."

Beau didn't try to dispute that. "There's never any

guarantee—even if you graduate with a degree in a sought-after field like engineering—that you'll get a job in your field," he told Billy's folks as he reached over and took Dani's hand.

"But this way," Billy's dad said firmly, "Billy will have a job in his field as soon as he graduates. Right here. On this ranch. Just like his momma and I always planned."

"I TOLD YOU IT WOULDN'T DO any good," Billy said as Dani and Beau met up with him outside the modest one-story ranch house.

Dani stepped beneath the shade of a towering live oak. "Don't give up just yet. There's still time for them to change their minds," she soothed.

"It'll never happen," Billy said miserably.

Probably not, Dani thought, forcing herself to be realistic. And for that, her heart went out to him. She and her sisters had all been encouraged to follow their dreams while their parents were alive and had, as a consequence, been even more determined to do so after their deaths.

"Let us both think on it and try to come up with a solution," Beau told Billy compassionately. He patted him on the back. "In the meantime, don't you go burning any bridges." Beau paused, then, sure he had Billy's attention, continued seriously, "I think you should go back in and apologize to your parents."

"Me!" Billy echoed, incensed.

"For running out of the house that way," Beau said. He gave Billy a stern look. "If you want them to help you, you've got to start demonstrating your maturity. Stop acting so hotheaded."

Dani nodded, knowing Beau had a point. "Then you

can go back over to my office and start unpacking and cataloging all the boxes of videos," she said.

"Dani and I won't be back till later," Beau said, linking arms with Dani.

Dani shot Beau an astonished look.

Beau smiled. "We have an armoire to buy."

"YOU WEREN'T VERY FIRM with Billy's folks," Dani said as she and Beau prowled the furniture store at the closest shopping mall, some forty-five minutes from Laramie.

"That's because I didn't want to get in the middle of what is essentially a family argument." Beau tested a sofa, then a chair.

Dani followed him from one furniture display to another. "This is Billy's future we're talking about."

"As well as his relationship with his parents." Beau finished his cursory tour of the entire store, then turned and went back to the far right corner, where they had come in. Standing in front of an armoire, Beau studied the display board with the manufacturer's specifications. "If Billy acts rashly now, he could do damage to his relationship with his folks that might never be repaired."

More interested in the subject they were discussing than the furniture, Dani slanted a curious look at Beau. "We're not talking just about him now, are we?"

Beau shrugged, hurt flickering briefly in his eyes. "I know what it's like not to have the support of your parents when it comes to following your dreams," he said quietly after a moment.

Dani touched his arm lightly as they moved on to the next armoire. "Your parents didn't approve of your wanting to be an actor?"

Beau grimaced. "That's putting it mildly."

"When did you know that acting was what you wanted to do with your life?" Dani asked gently.

Beau looked down at her and took her hand. "From the time I was a little kid, I wanted to act. My mother thought I was being cute to get attention and never took my declarations seriously."

"And your father?"

Beau's hand tightened on Dani's. His mouth set grimly, eyes averted, he continued, "Dad was career army and disgusted by just the thought of his son being a thespian. Every male in his family for six generations had graduated from the Citadel and been career military and he expected me—his only child—to do the same."

Dani could only imagine how much that must have hurt. "But you refused," she guessed.

Beau nodded. "I told him the family tradition ended with me." His shoulders tensing beneath the cotton of his shirt, Beau said, "Dad refused to accept that, of course. He figured he knew what was best for me, even if I didn't." Beau moved on to the next bedroom set. "He pulled a lot of strings and essentially put his own career on the line to get me a spot at the Citadel." Recalling, Beau shook his head. "I was furious when I found out what he'd done, told him no way in hell was I going to let my life be decided the way his had been, and that the closest I would ever get to a uniform was wearing one in a movie." Sadness filled Beau's eyes. "I didn't mean half of what I said, of course," he confided with a sigh. "Dad probably didn't, either. But the point is, we said some pretty ugly things to each other in the course of the arguments that followed. And once we said them, there wasn't any taking them back." Beau's face and tone hardened. "He didn't speak to me for a long time after that. Didn't acknowledge that he even had a son."

Knowing how it felt to lose your parents' love, for whatever reason—death, disagreement—Dani's heart went out to him. "That must have hurt."

Beau nodded. "Him, probably every bit as much as, if not more than, me, I'm sure." Beau paused, a distant look in his eyes. "Anyway, eventually, at my mother's urging, my father and I made up—at least on the surface—but things were never the same between us after that, and when he and my mom died in that train wreck in Germany a few years ago, well, let's just say I still have a lot of regrets about all the opportunities we missed to be close." Beau shook his head. "I wish we'd never let my choice of careers come between us like that."

"You don't want to see the same thing happen to Billy."

Beau looked at Dani, his blue eyes full of sympathy and understanding. "He's still young, Dani. He could change his mind a hundred times between now and then about what he wants to do with his life. I'm not all that sure it would hurt him to go to Texas A&M for a year, get some of the basic courses out of the way."

Dani sighed. "You don't know him like I do. If Billy goes to A&M, something in him is going to die."

"Or get stronger." Beau looked at Dani equably. "In the meantime he won't have totally alienated his parents or done damage to his relationship with them. Now, enough about Billy," Beau said. Keeping his hand linked with hers, he guided her over to the mattresses. "Come and help me pick out a mattress and box spring."

Deciding this was not a discussion she wanted to

have, even if they were the only two currently in that part of the showroom, Dani dug in her heels and wrested her hand from his. "Why? I already have a bed."

"I don't." Beau shot her a sexy sidelong grin as he tested first one mattress, then the next, with his palm. "And I'm not sleeping on the sofa again."

Dani huffed out a breath. "There is a remedy for that, you know."

"I tried that." Beau grinned and, finally finding a mattress and box spring he liked, stretched out on the king-size display bed. "Unfortunately," Beau lamented, too loudly for Dani's taste, "the lady of the house said no way was I sharing her bed." Beau tipped his hat over his eyes as if he was preparing to go to sleep. "In fact, the only time I'm allowed to be in her bed is when—"

Deciding he'd said quite enough, Dani sat down beside him and silenced him with a finger to his lips, "Hush," she admonished in a stern whisper. "Do you want someone to hear?"

Beau caught her by the wrist and pressed his lips to her skin. "You're my wife."

Tingling all over, and he'd barely touched her! "You know that."

Casting a look behind her to make sure they were still alone and finding to her relief they were, for the moment, anyway, Dani extricated herself from his grip. "I know that. But no one else here does."

Beau merely smiled and patted the mattress. "Come on. Try it out. Tell me what you think."

Dani had only to look at his face to know he wasn't giving up. Shaking her head, she lifted her feet off the floor and lay back, being careful to keep a good foot of space between them. The ceiling in the bed section was covered with blue velvet fabric, a curving yellow moon and a sprinkling of silver stars.

Beau looked up, too. "Romantic, hm?" He nudged her lightly.

Glad to be talking about something—anything—other than their sleeping arrangements, past or present, Dani nodded. "It reminds me—" She broke off as a fleeting picture of a pristine beach flashed in her mind. Without warning, she heard the sound of the ocean lapping gently against the shore. A man's voice, Beau's voice, whispering softly in her ear.

"What is it?" Beau asked, noticing the dwindling color in her face.

"I remember something," Dani said desperately, flashing once again to the private beach outside his villa in Mexico, the velvety blanket of stars overhead. She and Beau...tugging at each other's clothes...kissing wildly...

"Oh, my heavens!" Dani gasped, her hand flying to her chest.

"What?" He rolled onto his side, immediately concerned.

"Beau!" Dani trembled as even more potent images came flashing back.

"What!" he demanded just as urgently, leaning ever closer.

"The beach." In her excitement Dani grabbed the front of his shirt in both her hands and hauled him closer and didn't stop until they were nose to nose. "We didn't just make love in the hotel. We made love on the beach. Before we were married!"

Beau blinked at her once. And then again. A flash of recognition lit his face. She knew, even before he spoke, that he was starting to remember things, too. "You were wearing that—"

"Gauzy dress," Dani supplied.

"And we were arguing about something," Beau continued, looking stunned. "Just before I grabbed you and kissed you."

"And I kissed you back," Dani added. *More thoroughly and wantonly than I have ever kissed anyone in my life.* She sighed, recalling the passion, the wonder, of the moment. Even as she reeled from the knowledge that they had not just been together once, as they had first assumed, after their marriage, but *before.*

"And from the beach we moved to the villa—to the bed inside," Beau said, his memories of that afternoon suddenly coming as fast and furiously as hers. "Which means it wasn't just a one-night lapse in judgment," he concluded heavily, stunned.

For a long moment, they were both silent, thinking. Their eyes met, held.

"Just how serious were we about each other down in Mexico?" he wondered out loud.

Dani didn't know the answer to that, either. But she figured, as the furniture salesperson approached them to see if they needed any help, that it wouldn't be long before they remembered even more and found out.

"I CAN'T BELIEVE you managed to get everything delivered in an hour," Dani said as they reached the outskirts of Laramie once again.

"It's all in how you ask," Beau remarked as he drove his pickup down Main Street, waving as he spotted people he knew.

"Or who you are," Dani said, rolling her eyes at his cavalier attitude.

Beau pretended to be surprised. "You think that saleslady recognized me?" He gave Dani an innocent look.

"Oh, puh-leeze. She wasn't just salivating over the sale of the armoire, the fainting sofa, the dressers, china cabinet and dining-room table and chairs, pricey as they all were." To Dani's annoyance, the young woman had done everything but offer to take Beau on a date. And she'd been so ridiculously smitten with Beau she probably would have done so even if she'd known Dani and Beau were married. Which of course, she couldn't, since neither Dani nor Beau were wearing wedding rings. Dani sighed. She didn't like feeling jealous. It was a completely foreign emotion to her.

Beau stroked the chiseled contours of his chin with the flat of his hand. As they paused at the traffic light at the corner of Spring Street and Main, he slanted her a glance. He seemed to know she was annoyed with him. He didn't seem at all sure why, Dani noted. "You think I overdid it with the shopping back there?"

Which was another thing, Dani thought, feeling her annoyance increase. Couldn't the man do anything in half measures? But no. From his kisses to his acting to his lovemaking to his furniture shopping, Beau followed the all-or-nothing rule. Knowing that made her very nervous about their marriage. She was beginning to see he wasn't going to give up on that, either. Not now. And not eight or so months from now when their baby was born.

Aware he was still waiting on her verdict on the shopping and whether or not he had gone overboard, Dani said, "I think I got tired of arguing with you, of asking you *not* to do it." She shook her head, wishing he wouldn't look at her that way, as if it was all he could do not to haul her into his arms and kiss her.

"It's eventually going to have to go back, probably at considerable cost to you." Bottom line, she couldn't accept such a lavish gift from him. It might give him the wrong impression. Might make him think she had accepted him as a permanent fixture in her life, and as of yet, she had done no such thing. They were having a baby together. They'd made love a few times. But he hadn't said he loved her. He hadn't even come close. And she couldn't build a life with a man unless he loved her the way she was beginning—against her better judgment—to love him. She knew it, and she was pretty sure so did he.

But Beau merely smiled. The traffic light changed. He turned left and drove on.

As they neared her block, Dani said seriously, "I meant what I told you in the store, Beau. I am not going to accept all that from you."

Beau reached over and squeezed her knee. "Then accept it for the baby. Our baby," he said softly. "It doesn't have to be just you taking charge here. I want to do things for us, too, you know. All of us."

Yearning swept through her, so strong and sweet it brought moisture to her eyes. Dani swallowed around the growing lump in her throat and turned her glance to the house. It was the pregnancy. It was making her all emotional. Creating fantasies of the three of them— her, Beau and their baby—living happily ever after. Even when she knew the likelihood of such a fairy-tale ending was practically nil.

Dani blinked as they approached her house. "What are all these cars and that...other moving van doing here?" she demanded as Beau parked his truck at the curb several houses away. The only vehicle she recognized was Billy's beat-up blue Honda.

To Dani's mounting irritation and suspicion, Beau seemed not at all surprised by the vehicles surrounding her house. With an economy of motion, he got out of the pickup and sent her a deliberately mysterious look. "Let's go see what's going on, shall we?" He came around to help her out.

Dani focused more on what he hadn't said than what he had. "You know what's going on here, don't you?"

He didn't answer as he opened the front door of the house.

Dani blinked, and blinked again. Once more Beau was a steamroller, taking over her life.

A woman with a clipboard in hand rushed up to them. "We're almost done." The woman smiled at Dani cheerfully. "So! What do you think?"

Chapter Nine

Dani stared at the interior of her house. Gone were all the moving boxes she had left stacked every which way. The living room had been nicely arranged, with the sofa and two matching club chairs forming a cozy conversation area in front of the fireplace. One corner of the room held her stereo and compact-disk collection. Another nook held her antique writing desk and telephone. The three big bookshelves she hadn't been able to find room for had been moved to the wide front hallway, opposite the stairs, and were now filled with an orderly combination of books, plants and baskets.

The study across the hall was still a work in progress, but her desk, computer, fax and printer were all nicely arranged in a comfortable L, which would make working very pleasant. Her vertical files and sleek black office-supply cabinet had been set up neatly along one wall; her TV set and home-movie screen on another. Comfortable chairs, the kind used in movie-studio screening rooms, had been brought in and arranged nicely. Billy, who was busy arranging several thousand videotapes in the built-in bookshelves, merely grinned at her and kept working.

The formal dining room featured a beautiful Persian

rug and, minutes later, the dining set and china cabinet
Beau had just purchased. Thanks to the crew still working busily, the kitchen had also been transformed. The
shelves were lined and filled with her dishes. The ap-
pliances she used most were set up on the counters. The
pantry was stocked with all manner of gourmet foods
and neatly arranged. Fresh flowers and place mats
adorned the glass-topped table in the breakfast nook.
Directing all the activity was Kiki Harrison, one of the
most sought-after young set designers in Hollywood.

Spying Beau and Dani, a grinning Kiki came over to
join them. "I had hoped to be totally done before you
two got here. Obviously that's not the case."

"Close enough," Dani murmured appreciatively, still
looking around her in awe. "What you've done here is
nothing short of fantastic."

"I'm glad you like it." Kiki ran a hand through her
spiked blond hair. "Beau didn't give me much notice."

Eyes wide, Dani continued to look around. "He
didn't give me any at all."

"He wanted you to be surprised." Kiki squeezed
Dani's hand warmly, then winked at Beau. "I'm going
to have to get you to talk to my husband. These are the
kinds of things that warm a woman's heart."

Beau grinned back at Kiki. "I'll try to remember
that."

"Give us another forty-five minutes on the upstairs,"
Kiki said to Dani, "and then you can see that, too."

"So what do you think?" Beau asked after the
kitchen had cleared out, all the activity and workers
moving to the second floor, along with Kiki and the
furniture deliverymen.

"Is this a good surprise or a bad one?"

"Good," Dani admitted. She hated the process of

moving in and trying to sort out what went where. To have it all done for her—better than she could have done it herself—was a dream come true. She turned to him, grinning and propping her hands on her hips. "Okay now, fess up. When did you arrange this?"

"Yesterday when I stepped out to get lunch. Calling Kiki was the errand I ran off to do. I figured if we didn't have the professionals come in and help us out, we'd be forever trying to do it ourselves."

Dani blushed self-consciously. "True." Beau was right. This wasn't her forte. Nor was it his.

Beau laced his hands around her waist. Gently, he tugged her close, so that the length of her was pressed against his body. "And I wanted you, and your attention, all to myself." Sounding as pleased and happy as she felt, he nuzzled the sensitive skin on her neck.

And he'd done all this before they'd made love yesterday afternoon, Dani realized as she melted helplessly against him. Because he wanted them to be as comfortable and happy here as possible. "If I didn't know better," Dani said, swallowing nervously around the dryness of her throat, "I'd think this meant you were moving in here permanently." Not just until they decided what to do about the marriage neither could quite remember and the baby.

"That," Beau said quietly, looking deep into her eyes, "is exactly what it means."

Beau watched the gamut of emotions cross Dani's face. Shock, dismay, wariness, interest. She wanted to think this marriage of theirs—this family they were creating—was real enough to last a lifetime. Beau knew exactly how she felt. He wanted to believe that, too. The difference between them was, he was willing to work to make that happen. Dani had yet to make such a commitment. But she would.

"You work in Hollywood—when you're not off on location somewhere!" Dani sputtered finally, extricating herself from his arms and spinning away. Upstairs the sounds of activity continued unabated.

Confident that Kiki and her team of experts had things well in hand, Beau watched Dani pace the length of the sunny kitchen. Settling back against the counter, he braced his hands on either side of him. Dani was right. It was time they talked about this. "During pre- and postproduction, that's true," he admitted candidly, knowing even that didn't have to be a problem for them if Dani didn't want it to be. Plenty of spouses and kids who placed a premium on their family life accompanied actors to location for filming. Other actors filmed movies only in the summer, when their families could easily accompany them. Or lived in cities like Los Angeles, New York or Orlando, where film studios kept soundstages.

For anyone who wanted a family life, the possibilities were boundless. For those who didn't, well, he supposed, excuses would always be made. "As for the rest of the time, I tend to be in the Southwest, anyway— I've filmed nearly every movie I've made in either Texas or Mexico. We could do even more here if we had a soundstage, so I'm moving my production-company offices here and adding a soundstage, which I will also rent out to other film companies when not in use. I'll still have a branch office in Hollywood, but all the main work will be done right here."

Dani blinked, stunned. "In Laramie?"

Beau nodded, glad to see she seemed receptive to the

idea thus far. "I purchased several hundred acres of land just south of town last week."

"Before we—"

"—saw each other again. Knew about your pregnancy or made love again. Before any of that happened," Beau supplied, looking her straight in the eye. "I began making these arrangements."

Dani edged closer. "Why?" she whispered.

Beau reached out and took both her hands in his. "Because I don't do things halfway, Dani," he said softly, twining their fingers together intimately and searching her face. "I knew if I had married you I had a damn fine reason for doing so. And that I would see it through. I've already had one failed marriage," Beau said somberly. "I don't want another one."

Dani swallowed. Stepped back a pace. "I don't want that, either."

She withdrew her hands from his.

"But…?" Beau prodded, sensing there was more.

Dani raked her hands through her hair. "You're moving awfully fast."

Beau didn't discount that for an instant. He folded his arms, studied her bluntly. "I know what I want," he said softly, first meeting, then holding, her wide amber gaze. "The question is, do you?"

DID SHE? DANI HAD TO WONDER. Her heart was telling her to stop worrying about all the things she couldn't change and just go for it. Her head was telling her to stop now, before she got in any deeper, hurt any more. Because if and when her relationship with Beau did come to a grinding halt, it was going to hurt. More than anything ever had in her life.

"We're ready for you to see the upstairs now," Kiki said.

Beau gestured toward the back stairs, off the kitchen. "After you."

Dani followed Kiki to the sprawling second floor. All the moving boxes were gone. That, she'd anticipated. What she didn't expect to see was that her dresser and queen-size bed were no longer in the master bedroom. They had been moved to the smaller guest bedroom next to it. The master bedroom contained the king-size mattress and box spring Beau had purchased for himself at the furniture store. They had been set in a massive four-poster frame in rich cherry with a canopy over top. The bed canopy, bed curtains and coverlet had been done in a dark-blue damask that perfectly comple-mented the pale-blue wallpaper. Elegant lengths of rich blue fabric formed valances that had been draped along the windows.

There was a fainting couch, an old-fashioned vanity and padded stool, a large cherry bureau and matching armoire.

Plants, pillows and candles, artfully placed here and there, finished the room.

The master bath, located just across the hall, had been luxuriously outfitted, as well. Wicker shelves had been added. Linens, towels and bath products galore were luxurious additions to the gleaming white-and-blue ce-ramic-tile bathroom.

"If you don't like something, tell me, and we'll change it right away," Kiki said bluntly. "Beau said just to use my best judgment. The main thing is to get you situated so you can start working on your book right away, but I'm never quite comfortable doing that.

When it comes to personal surroundings, I think everything is highly individual.''

"It is, and you and your team have done a marvelous job," Dani said. Beau might not know it yet, but he was going to be sleeping in the guest room in her old bed. This was her house. She was not giving up her place in the master bedroom. He had come in and taken over enough of her life already. Much more, and she'd be buying into the same movie fantasy of the three of them living happily ever after just the way he was. And Dani knew she couldn't let herself do that. Life wasn't that easy. Only in the movies did things work out this neatly or easily.

Kiki smiled. "Then my work is done. So we'll all get out of your space right away."

"Thanks, Kiki," Beau said as he walked Kiki and other members of her team down to the front door.

"Don't thank me until you get my bill." Kiki's pleasant laugh drifted up the stairs. "All this last-minute stuff is going to cost you!" Dani imagined that was so. Beau not only would be paying for all the accessories and furniture Kiki had added, but travel, worker salaries and shipping expenses.

Short minutes later Dani heard car doors slamming out on the curb. Engines revving. The sounds of a moving van and several smaller vans and cars driving away.

Beau returned to find Dani sitting on the fainting couch. "I told Billy he could call it a day." Beau folded his arms and lounged in the doorway to the master bedroom.

Dani knew she should be angry about that—Billy was her employee, not Beau's—but she couldn't muster up the energy. So much had happened in so little time. Her heart pounding in her throat, she looked up at him. "So we're alone?"

Beau's eyes connected with hers and held for several breath-stealing seconds. "For the moment, yeah."

Beau crossed the room to her side. He hunkered down next to her, kneeling in front of her like a knight paying homage to his queen. "Something on your mind?" he asked gently, taking her hand, lifting it to his lips.

Dani tingled at the feel of his lips caressing her skin. Heat started low in her body and rose to her chest, neck and face. "Should there be?"

His eyes locked on hers. He traced the back of her hand with his lips. "I thought this would be a good surprise."

Trying not to think how very much she liked the tantalizing scent of his aftershave, Dani shrugged. "It is and it isn't." Beau had a reputation for getting totally engrossed in whatever project he was working on. It was part of what made his movies so appealing to the public. He left no part of the fantasy untapped.

With a bantering smile meant to disguise the way she felt, she said, "It's like I had a fairy godmother come in, wave her magic wand and take care of everything." She felt as if she was an actor on a movie set and it was all pretend.

"That was the plan."

Dani ignored the possessive way his hands had tightened on hers. If she didn't know better, she'd think he was not just married to her, but desperately in love with her. Fortunately she had never been one to get totally wrapped up in fantasies of any kind. "Only there are no fairy godmothers," she reminded him unsteadily. And there was nothing dreamlike about her pregnancy.

The baby she was carrying was very real and becoming more real by the moment.

"That's true," Beau said, his midnight-blue eyes darkening. "You've got a husband, instead."

A husband who might or might not stay once the movie magic ended and he moved on to his next project.

Dani looked at him, wishing he didn't have the ability to tap into her fantasies quite so accurately, wishing she didn't know what an insatiable lover he was. He was making it impossible for her not to fall in love with him. She swallowed around the sudden tightness of her throat. "You're telling me to get used to this kind of star treatment."

Beau lowered himself onto the fainting couch beside her and shifted her onto his lap. He wrapped his arms around her lovingly. "I'm telling you that, as long as we are married, I will stop at nothing to make you happy," he whispered in her ear, his warm breath sending a thrill down her spine.

Dani inclined her head as he pushed back her hair and rained kisses down her neck. "What happens when the clock chimes midnight and I turn back into Cinderella before the ball?"

Beau kissed her cheek. "That's not going to happen," he promised amiably.

Dani flattened both hands on his chest and wedged distance between them. He was acting as if this was all very simple and easy, when Dani knew it wasn't, because life, especially her life, never was. "You forget," she reminded solemnly, "I don't believe in happily-ever-afters, Beau. I haven't for a very long time."

"Because of the way your parents died?"

Once again, he was cutting too close to the bone, bringing up things Dani didn't want to discuss, not with him, not with anyone. The doorbell rang. "Saved by the bell," she said lightly.

Beau frowned. As far as he was concerned, they had just started to get somewhere. "Don't answer it," he said gruffly, more determined than ever to unlock the mystery that was his wife.

"I have to," Dani said, looking over her shoulder and glancing out the window. A familiar sunshine-yellow pickup truck was parked in front of the curb. "It's my sister, Kelsey." The baby of the family, who was as changeable and capricious as the day was long, Kelsey was in some kind of jam more often than not. If not for her three older sisters, all of whom were constantly bailing her out one way or another, Dani didn't know what Kelsey would do. She certainly couldn't rely on any of the men in her life—Kelsey couldn't decide on any one man any more than she could decide on any one profession. In the years since she had left home, Kelsey had held more jobs and dated more men than the rest of her sisters put together.

"Hope I'm not interrupting anything." Kelsey winked slyly as she breezed in. Dressed in the usual jeans, long-sleeved shirt and bandanna tied jauntily around her neck, a Stetson tilted on her head, she made a fetching picture of youthful exuberance.

Dani blushed at the teasing innuendo in Kelsey's tone. "Of course not," Dani said stiffly, giving her sister a stern look.

Ignoring Dani's unspoken order to cool it, Kelsey merely grinned and looked at Beau. He wrapped his arm around Dani's waist and tugged her newlywed-close. "It's nothing that can't be continued later—in even greater detail," he reassured Kelsey.

And unfortunately Dani knew that was true. Beau

would start up with the questions again first chance he got.

Kelsey grinned. ''Good.'' Not bothering to take off her hat, she led the way into the living room and dropped onto the sofa. ''I can't believe how quickly you moved in.''

''I had help,'' Dani said dryly.

''I'll say.'' Kelsey leaned forward abruptly and clasped her hands between her knees. ''Listen, I came over to tell you something.''

''Okay.'' Dani sat down opposite her.

''I finally did it,'' Kelsey said.

Forever cautious where her baby sister was concerned, Dani narrowed her eyes. ''Did what?''

''Bought back the ranch.''

''What ranch?'' Beau said as all the color left Dani's face.

''The ranch where we grew up,'' Kelsey said. ''Brady Anderson and I closed on it earlier today.''

Beau sat down beside Dani and took her hand in his. ''What does he have to do with it?'' Beau asked curiously, taking the words right out of Dani's mouth.

''He's my partner,'' Kelsey explained as if it was obvious. ''I didn't have enough money to buy it on my own, and since I couldn't convince any of my sisters to go in on the deal with me, I decided to go fifty-fifty with Brady.''

''You hardly know that cowboy!'' Dani exploded. This time Kelsey had gone too far in her recklessness.

Kelsey's lower lip pushed out in a determined pout. ''I know him just fine. We've worked together for a month!''

Her patience fading fast, Dani rolled her eyes. ''Exactly my point,'' Dani said tightly. ''You can't just go and buy property with some cowboy you met just a month ago!''

"I not only can," Kelsey shot right back, her attitude as smug as Dani's was derisive, "I did. And furthermore, I will be moving in there next week, Brady by the end of the summer."

Dani drew in a long slow breath and struggled to hang on to her escalating temper.

"Meanwhile, we're off to buy horses, ranch equipment and cattle," Kelsey continued as if it was the most natural thing in the world.

Dani's eyes narrowed suspiciously. "Where are you getting all this money?"

Kelsey sat back in a relaxed manner and explained confidently, "Technology stocks. That broker I dated a few years ago? He taught me a thing or two about investing while we were still an item. Ever since, I've been investing every cent I could in the market. 'Course I had to cash in almost all of it to make the down payment on the ranch to the bank, but I'm sure I can build it back up again. If I did it once, I can do it again."

Dani shook her head. She was pretty sure this was not what her parents would have wanted for Kelsey had they still been alive. "Have you told Jenna and Meg you're going to be living and working with some cowboy you barely know?" Dani studied Kelsey carefully.

Resentment clouded Kelsey's green eyes. "Yes, as a matter of fact, I have."

"And…?"

Kelsey blew out an impatient breath. "Meg is worried sick, as usual. Jenna is encouraging me to go for it. Neither of them like the fact that I've entered into a partnership with Brady any more than you do."

Dani tensed. "I didn't say that."

Kelsey shot to her feet. "Oh, for heaven's sake, Dani,

you don't have to. It's written all over your face. Yo
think we all need to stay as far away from the ranch as
possible. That somehow we'll be safe if we just pretend
none of it ever happened."

Dani stood, too. "We can hardly do that."

Kelsey whirled on her. "But you'd like to, wouldn't
you?"

Beau got to his feet and looked from one to the other.
"What are you two talking about?"

Kelsey scowled at Dani as she spoke to Beau. "Dani
hasn't been back to the ranch since the day our parents
died. She wouldn't even go back to the house to help
us move out."

"With good reason," Dani said, pushing the words
through gritted teeth. Already she could feel moisture
gathering in her eyes.

Kelsey's expression turned pleading. "You have to
put it behind you, Dani, once and for all," she counseled gently, as if she was the older sister, not the other
way around. "Just like I'm trying to do."

Dani folded her arms. "This is *not* the way," she
retorted stonily.

"Well, your way certainly isn't, either!" Kelsey rummaged in her pocket for a key, then thrust it into Dani's
hand. "Do yourself a favor. Take today. Go back. Look
around. I guarantee no one else will be there." Kelsey
gave her a long searching look. Settling her hat more
squarely on her head, she strode to the door. "I'll call
you when I get back!" The door slammed behind her.

Dani stood rooted to the spot, the key to the ranch
house still in her hand. "I'll go with you," Beau said.

"I'm not going," she responded flatly.

He moved closer so he could see her face and
touched her arm lightly, just above the elbow. "You
have to go."

Dani plucked his fingers from her arm like some odious piece of trash. "Says who?"

"Dani—"

"Just because Kelsey's gone off the deep end doesn't mean I have to do the same."

Beau rubbed the back of his neck. He looked at Dani for a thoughtful moment before he spoke. "What she's doing sounds gutsy to me."

"That's because you don't know the whole story," she said. Tears once again threatened.

"Then tell me," Beau pleaded softly, edging closer.

"No." Dani put up her hands to ward him off. She didn't want him touching her. She didn't want anyone touching her. All she wanted, all she had ever wanted, was to be left alone, where no one and nothing could hurt her.

"Dani—"

Ignoring Beau's outstretched arm, Dani dropped the key Kelsey had given her on the coffee table and rushed past him. "I have to get out of here."

Beau picked up the key she had dropped. "Where are you going?" he asked.

"I don't know," Dani said emotionally, grabbing her purse and rushing out the door. She just knew, once again, it felt like the whole world was closing in on her.

DANI ENDED UP at the highway that ran past the ranch. And once she was there, she knew Kelsey was right about this much—she had put off coming back for far too long. Maybe, she thought, her hands clenching the steering wheel until her knuckles turned white, it would even prove cathartic. But it didn't feel cathartic as she turned her car into the long gravel lane and drove through the open wrought-iron archway. The two locked hearts—which had been their brand—and the letters proclaiming it the Lockhart Ranch had long since been removed. But Dani could see them in her mind's eye as clearly as if they were still there.

Just as she remembered rushing home from school with her mother on that last fateful day.

Dani realized there were tears streaming down her cheeks. A fierce Texas storm brewing on the horizon. And another vehicle—a vintage red truck—right behind her.

Furious to find Beau had followed her, Dani proceeded to the ranch house. Formerly a pale sage-green, with dark-green shutters, the rectangular two-story home was now a gray-blue with black shutters; but the paint was peeling in places, and the place had an overall air of neglect. Which wasn't surprising. Dani had heard from her other sisters that the ranch had been standing empty for six months now, because the previous owners, who had relocated to a property closer to Dallas, had set the sale price way too high.

And now it belonged to Kelsey and some cowboy she barely knew!

Miserable beyond words, Dani turned off the ignition and slammed out of her car into the fiercely blowing wind. Beau parked right behind her and climbed down from the cab of his truck. Dani strode toward him, aware that the air felt damp and markedly cooler on her skin. Another sign of impending rain. Knowing full well how fierce and unrelenting the rain could be on the flat open terrain of the ranch, Dani stabbed a finger at his chest. "I want you to leave. Now." It would be bad enough to be stuck out here during a storm. Never mind with the ever-inquisitive, ever-bossy and interfering Beau at her side.

Stubbornly he held his ground. "Tough," he said,

his tall strong body braced for a battle he didn't intend to lose.

Problem was, Dani thought, *neither did she.*

His eyes radiated unchecked interest but no anger as the escalating wind buffeted his body, plastering his shirt against the muscular contours of his chest. "I'm not going anywhere."

Frustration flowed, hot and potent, through her veins. In the distance, lightning crackled against the black clouds. "Darn it all, Beau Chamberlain! I don't want you here!" Dani stepped closer.

He shrugged, clearly not the least bit perturbed by her unwelcoming attitude. His eyes roved her upturned face. "Well, I don't want you alone when you are clearly this upset!"

Dani glared at him. "It's none of your business."

Beau's lips thinned authoritatively. Clearly he was not used to having his wishes disregarded, and he was fast losing patience with her. Bracing his hands on his waist, he leaned down so they were face-to-face. "The heck it's not," he said just as firmly. "In case you've forgotten, you are my wife."

And she was carrying his child. Much as she was loath to admit it, he did have a right to be concerned about their child. Dani drew a deep calming breath. "I'll be all right."

"Yes," Beau said succinctly, looking every bit as fiercely determined as she was to come out of this situation a winner. "You will."

"But I need to do this alone." Dani's voice dropped a persuasive notch.

Beau shoved his hat a little farther back on his head and regarded her skeptically. "After how many years?"

Too many, Dani thought. And at the same time not nearly enough. She only knew she wanted the hurting to go away, the ongoing feeling of loss to dissipate, and after nearly seven years, it hadn't begun to happen.

Beau's voice gentled. He touched her shoulders and looked at her in a way that let her know he was remembering her parents, too. He'd met them briefly once or twice during one of his holiday visits to his aunt. The same way he'd met Dani. "What happened, anyway?"

The storm clouds gathering on the horizon grew more ominous. Looking at them made Dani feel even more nervous and upset. "I don't want to discuss it," she said, then whirled away from him and headed for the overgrown trail behind the house that led to the rise where the old barn had stood. She didn't want to think about the kindness Beau had shown her the few times they'd met when they were kids. Or now.

"Fine. I'll ask Kelsey," Beau said, the challenge in his voice unmistakable.

"Don't," Dani said shortly as she pushed her way through the trees, bushes and weeds.

Beau followed, one of his strides matching her every two. "Why not?"

"Because it will bring up all sorts of things she doesn't need to dwell on, either."

Thunder rumbled overhead. "She seems to be handling this just fine," he observed.

Her whole body throbbing with tension, Dani pushed on. "Kelsey's surface calm is deceptive. She isn't handling this any better than the rest of us, as has been evidenced by her constant switching of jobs and boyfriends and every other significant detail of her life!"

With Beau right beside her, keeping pace, Dani reached the top of the rise just as the rain started. There, where the old barn had stood, was a building that couldn't have been more than two years old. It was bigger than the original, painted the same ugly gray-blue as the house, but in her mind's eye, Dani could see the old barn, which had been gray, splintered and falling apart to the point where play had been forbidden.

"Tell me what happened," Beau insisted as the rain came down harder.

Dani turned to him and sighed. If she didn't tell him, someone else would. She didn't know why it mattered so much. She just knew she didn't want him hearing this from anyone else but her. Feeling as though her heart was breaking all over again, she took a deep bolstering breath, gathered all her courage and said, "My parents died—both of them—right here, in front of my eyes."

BEAU HADN'T KNOWN if Dani would confide in him, even if he followed her all the way out here. He did know that she was used to handling things more or less alone, that she kept her feelings buried deep inside. That she'd trusted him enough to tell him anything meant a lot. Because she had to trust him in order to love him. But there was still a lot more to be said. And no reason on earth they should stand out here in the storm to do so.

Past arguing about anything, Beau lifted the latch and pushed open the barn door. Seeing what he intended, Dani blanched. He took her by the elbow and guided her inside. Outside, the wind picked up. As Beau closed the door, shutting out the storm, the wind and the rain, tears flooded Dani's eyes. Not sure what else to do—her pain was so great—he closed the distance between them swiftly, took her in his arms and held her against him.

Determined to get her talking—Kelsey was right, Dani needed to confront this and talk about it—he stroked his hands through the silken strands of her hair.

"So what happened?" he prodded gently as her sobs began to subside.

Dani pulled away from him. Struggling to compose herself, she wiped her face with her hands and began to talk in a hoarse choked voice. "The barn that was here then was nearly twenty years old and had suffered structural damage in a previous thunderstorm. My parents were waiting to have it torn down and we'd been forbidden to play here. But it was such a great place, one of the few places on the ranch where any of us could go to be alone."

Dani gulped. A distant look came into her eyes. As she continued, her voice began to shake. "That day…that last day Kelsey and I had come home from school with Mom—she was a teacher at the high school—Jenna had stayed in town for an after-school prom-committee meeting." Fresh tears glistened in Dani's eyes. "We knew there was a tornado watch on, but there were always tornado watches during the spring storms and we didn't really take it seriously, until it suddenly began to get very black out and very quiet, very still. We didn't know it then, but a tornado had formed just outside Laramie, and touched down on several ranches in the area, overturning tractors, uprooting trees and knocking over power lines, and causing all manner of havoc. It was heading our way."

Dani's breath hitched. "Mom and Dad told me to get to the storm cellar in the basement, but Kelsey was nowhere around. They assumed she was in the old barn or down at the stables, which are a little farther out, with her horse. Mom said she'd check the barn. Dad went off to check the stables. They wanted me to stay in the house in case Kelsey showed up here." Turning away from him, Dani began to pace, her sandals tap-tapping on the cement floor.

"I guess Mom had just reached the old barn when the tornado appeared." Dani closed her eyes briefly, shook her head, her pain at remembering evident. "Whether the tornado actually hit the barn or the high winds alone did it, we'll never know. But it collapsed on top of her."

Beau could only imagine how horrible that must have been.

Covering her ears, Dani pushed on. "I heard the crash all the way over at the ranch house. So did my dad. As soon as the tornado roared by, we both made a mad dash for the barn." Dani swallowed. She turned to Beau, the detached distant look back in her eyes. "It was like a big pile of kindling, but miraculously my mother was still alive," she whispered. "My dad told me to go back and call 911 while he went in to see what he could do for my mom. So I did—only to find out the phone lines were down." Dani gritted her teeth. Tears rolled down her face. "I ran back. What was left of the barn collapsed just as I arrived. And that was…it." Dani lifted her hands helplessly, then let them fall as she concluded, "I knew they were gone."

Knowing she needed him now more than ever, Beau strode to her and took her in his arms.

"Were any others killed?"

"No, just my folks, although there were a few other ranchers and their families injured, too. Overall, the town and the county got off lucky. Many more could have been killed had the tornado touched down in a heavily populated area."

"That's why you never wanted to come back here." He stroked her back.

Dani buried her face in his chest. "Can you blame me?"

No, he couldn't. But he also knew that you never

solved a problem by running from it. Pain had to be faced. The sooner, the better. "Yet you came back to Laramie."

"To be close to my sisters again, to have a real home," Dani confided emotionally. "Not to relive the past!" She pushed away from him and scrubbed at the fresh flow of tears. "Damn Kelsey and her lamebrained ideas, anyway!"

"You ought to be thanking her," Beau replied.

Dani stared at him. She should have known Beau would take the opposite view. Didn't he always? "For what?" Dani snapped. If there was one thing she didn't want today, or any other for that matter, it was Beau's criticism.

Beau paused. His glance was loving and tender. His words were anything but. "It's pretty clear you haven't moved beyond your parents' death. And until you do, no really happy future is going to be possible. Bottom line, Dani. You either come to terms with what happened here and move past it. Or you get mowed down by it. Those are your choices."

Hot angry tears glimmered in Dani's eyes. "I should have known better than to confide in you. I should have known you wouldn't understand!"

"I do understand you, Dani." Beau's voice lowered a husky notch as he grabbed her and held her in front of him when she would have run. "Just the way you have always understood me!"

Dani struggled unsuccessfully to be free of him. "What are you...?" she sputtered. "I never..." And then it hit her at the same time it hit him. With the force of a locomotive speeding across the Texas plains.

They'd been in Mexico, at his villa, trying to end their feud for both their sakes, with Dani insisting she'd been right to systematically dismantle the fantasy element of all his movies and Beau insisting she'd been wrong. Dead wrong to deprive people of their hopes and dreams. He had insisted that the all-consuming love depicted in his movies did exist. And so did the eventual triumph of good over evil, right over wrong. Lasting happiness was within reach of everyone, Beau had said. What was wrong, he had continued, was telling people over and over in her reviews that "real life" just wasn't like that. That real life guaranteed only heartbreak and, at best, fleeting happiness.

The hell of it had been, Dani had feared Beau was right, even if she was scared to admit it. Maybe other people did have better, happier and more satisfying lives. Maybe it was just her who'd never been meant to be happy or to have all that life could offer.

Hurt, for no one had ever talked to her like that, she'd lashed back at him. Demanded to know why he was taking her reviews so personally. Demanded to know why he was so wrapped up in what she said about his work when he clearly didn't give a hoot what other critics said about his films.

Beau had readily admitted that Dani got to him like no other. Maybe because Dani was harder on him than any other actor in Hollywood. So relentlessly critical, in fact, that if he didn't know better, Beau had alleged hotly as they carried their argument from the patio of his villa down onto his private beach, he'd think she was in love with him.

"You said I loved you," Dani remembered, color blooming in her cheeks as the memory of that fateful night hit her full blast. "On the beach outside your villa in Mexico, you said I loved you!" she repeated, stunned and amazed.

Beau nodded as if this was something he'd come to terms with long ago. "And you admitted it was so," he replied.

Chapter Ten

"And then you kissed me and told me you loved me, too," Dani said, marveling at the return of the memories. It was happening just the way Lacey and Jackson McCabe had said it would. Out of the blue, they were remembering things in bits and fragments. One fact leading to the recollection of another.

And what she was remembering now, Dani realized in wonderment, was one of the most romantic moments of her entire life. The kind that was so movie perfect and wonderful she had never expected to have it. The kind that happened to other people. Never to her. But this had happened to her, Dani realized in trembling amazement. She didn't even have to close her eyes to recall the warmth of the sand beneath her bare feet or the wind blowing over their bodies. She didn't have to struggle to remember Beau's arms around her holding her close, or his lips on hers, kissing her with more tenderness and passion than she had ever dreamed existed. She didn't have to wonder how and when and why he had made her his woman, because suddenly she knew. And so, Dani realized as she looked deep into his eyes, did he.

"And we made love right there on the beach," Beau

said, the passion in his low voice fueling her own. As he looked at her, his hands moved down her back and tightened on her spine.

Her heart pounding with the enormity of what they were discovering to be true, Dani pulled away from him. She ran her hands through her hair.

"Not just on the beach," she said in a low trembling voice as memories of that weekend in Mexico continued to come back at a dizzying pace. "On the patio." She had an image of Beau stretched out on top of her. "Inside the villa." Another image of them impatiently making love against the wall. "In the bed." Their bodies intertwined. "The shower." Beau soaping her, then holding her close, so close... Never had she been loved so thoroughly or so well. Never had she felt as loved as she had that night. Never had she known such passion, tenderness or understanding. Never had she felt such happiness or hope for the future. As if it was all there, waiting for her. She needed only to stay with Beau, and everything she'd been afraid to yearn for would come true.

Beau's eyes darkened as his memory returned with the force of the storm pounding outside. "We couldn't keep our hands off each other for most of that night and all the next day," he said softly, drawing her into his arms once again.

Dani splayed her hands across his chest. She looked up into his face. "And then we went into town for dinner." She'd been wearing that white off-the-shoulder dress. Beau had stopped to buy her a bouquet of fragrant flowers from a street vendor. They'd been walking hand in hand down narrow cobblestone streets.

Beau nodded. A smile curved his lips as he recollected, "It started to rain." A gentle warm rain that soon picked up in force, threatening to drench them both.

"So we ducked into that church," Dani continued, remembering the beauty of the candlelit chapel.

"And the priest thought we were there wanting to get married," Beau recollected, all the love Dani ever could have wanted in his eyes.

Dani nodded. She remembered turning to Beau in surprise and embarrassment at the misunderstanding, only to realize the two of them were thinking the same thing after all—that it wasn't such a farfetched idea. "And suddenly it seemed like the most natural thing in the world," Dani concluded softly.

Beau smoothed a hand up and down Dani's back. "So we did."

Dani closed her eyes briefly, remembering how it had felt to stand before the altar, pledging to love Beau as long as they both lived. She remembered how it had felt to know he loved her enough to promise the same. "We didn't have any rings," Beau said huskily, "but it didn't matter. We said we'd get them later."

Dani nodded. "And then we went to that restaurant, and the restaurant owners were so happy for us they made us those special drinks to celebrate."

Beau nodded. "You remember everything."

"So do you."

Silence fell between them once again. Dani felt as though she was standing on a precipice. On one side, all the joy and happiness she had ever hoped to have. On the other, a fall to misery. Only now it wasn't just herself she had to be concerned about. She had her baby—their baby—to think about, too. She didn't want that baby to suffer the kind of loss she had. One moment having a father to love and nurture her and make her feel safe and secure the way only a daddy could, the next losing him forever.

"I do love you, Dani," Beau murmured as he gazed into her eyes. He threaded his fingers through her hair, trailed a hand down her face.

"And I love you, Beau," Dani whispered back emotionally. So much that she wanted to believe in the fantasy as strongly as he did.

"But...?" Beau prodded at the lingering doubt in her voice.

Dani swallowed. She knew she had to be completely honest with him if this relationship of theirs was to work. "I still don't believe in happily-ever-afters. And certainly not the lifelong kind." The kind always denied her.

"That's only because you won't let yourself believe," Beau said sternly, looking all the more determined to convince her otherwise.

"Beau..." Dani drew in a ragged breath.

Beau tilted her face up to his. "When we were in Mexico, you opened up to me for the very first time. You let yourself trust. Not just in me but what—if we're honest—we've both been feeling for each other for a very long time. What happened with the amnesia changed all that. Made us go back to flirting and feuding again. But it doesn't have to stay that way. We can love each other again. You can stop being afraid of life and start taking risks again." He looked at her as if he was betting everything on the two of them. "All you have to do is let go," he whispered urgently.

Dani groaned. Tempted, yet so afraid of being hurt again, of having her whole life turned upside down, the equilibrium she'd fought so hard to get back destroyed.

"Let the fear go, Dani." Beau lowered his lips to hers. "Replace it with love for me and our baby."

She read the intent in his eyes: to make love to her here, now, while the storm raged outside. Bending closer, he pulled her against his hard length and used his other hand to brush the hair from her nape. His warm breath touched the curve of her cheek, the bow of her lips, then moved to her chin, the soft vulnerable underside of her jaw. Trembling with pent-up desire, Dani wreathed her arms about his neck and turned her lips to his.

His lips came down on hers, firm and sure. A disquieting shudder ran through her. Her whole body trembled, and then she was throwing caution to the wind, following her instinct and rising on tiptoe to deepen the kiss. Beau reacted in kind, his next kiss forcing her lips apart. His hands moved sensuously in her hair, then glided lower in long smooth strokes over her shoulders, back, breasts and hips.

Unbuttoning as he kissed, his mouth still moving ardently over hers, he opened her blouse and unclasped her bra. Dani offered no assistance or resistance as he pushed the rain-drenched fabric aside and cupped her breasts. It was everything she could do to keep her soaring feelings in check. But when he uttered a soft male groan of contentment as he brushed her hardening nipples with his fingertips, then bent to kiss the taut aching crowns, desire swept through her in powerful waves. Dani knew what he was doing. Trying to replace the bad memories with good. It shouldn't have worked, but it did. And she wanted more, so much more than just a few kisses and the feel of his hands and his lips on her breasts. She wanted to know all of him, here and now. She wanted to feel connected with him again, the way they'd connected with each other in Mexico, not just in body, not just in want and need, but in heart and soul.

"Make love to me," Dani whispered urgently, aware once again the world had narrowed to just the two of them. Taking his hand, she led him to a sheltered alcove in the barn. "Make love to me here, Beau. Now."

Beau hadn't meant things to go this far. He'd wanted to kiss her, touch her, make her believe in the two of them. He'd wanted to make her see how right they could be together, the fact that they were married and she was pregnant with his child aside. He wanted to see how much they were meant—no, destined—to be together. Not just for now but for the rest of their lives. And the best way he knew to do that was by letting their feelings run rampant, in kisses and in touch.

Whether she wanted to admit it or not, Dani had been his ever since they had made love that first time, and she always would be. He could feel it in the possessive way she held him and the ardent way she returned his kiss. Awed by the beauty of her, the perfection of her supple curves, he undressed her slowly, touching and caressing as he went. Dropping to his knees, he lingered in the V of her legs, kissing and caressing until she trembled and moaned, until she could no longer contain the wild pleasure he was evoking.

Dani dropped to her knees right along with him. And then her lips were on his, kissing him with a hunger and desperation he not only understood but felt. Trembling, Dani unbuckled his belt, and slid down his zipper. More ready for her than he had ever been, he wanted to hurry. She wouldn't let him. As the rain drummed on the roof, she eased open the buttons on his shirt.

Drew that off and ran her hands across the hard muscles of his chest. Like hers, his skin felt so hot it almost sizzled. And still she continued, slowly, lovingly helping him off with his boots and jeans, kissing everywhere she looked, touching everywhere she kissed, until at last she'd aligned their bodies, bare flesh to bare flesh, and looked up at him with eyes that were glazed with passion, dark with need.

"Now?" Beau asked, his voice ragged.

"Yes," Dani whispered.

His arms around her, his body trembling with the effort it took to contain his own pressing need, Beau rolled so she was beneath him. Shifting their clothes beneath her hips, he raised her knees and then entered her, watching her face as he did so. She gasped and moaned as he kissed her. He obliged her with slow deliberate thrusts, and she met each one with an abandonment of her own. He slipped a hand between their bodies. And her hips rose instinctively to meet him as he touched and rubbed and stroked. Desperate for more, unable to get enough of her, he kissed her with an intensity that took her breath away. And then there was no more thinking, only feeling, nothing but the slow inexorable climb to the edge, a blazing explosion of heat, and the slow contented slide back to reality.

AFTERWARD, TREMBLING, cuddled in his arms, Dani rested her head on his chest. Beau could tell by her silence that she was as shaken by everything they'd remembered and done as he was. "It's going to be all right," he said.

"I know that." Dani released a ragged breath.

"But...?" Beau asked, seeing there was more she needed to confess.

Dani swallowed. She clung to him tightly and her voice dropped as she confessed emotionally, "I just never thought I'd be married and having a baby without my parents here to share it. Because they'd be so happy about the baby, Beau. They'd be so happy about us." Bitterness clouded her eyes. Her future and her past joined as Dani shook her head miserably. "Oh, God, Beau, I don't want to know firsthand how unfair and terrifying life can get. But I do know and I...I can't shake the fear I've felt deep inside ever since my parents died."

Much as Beau wanted to, he couldn't restore Dani's innocence any more than he could restore his own. They were adults. They had learned the hard way that life wasn't always fair and that some unhappiness and pain came into everyone's lives. But he could give her hope and faith in their future. Wanting to comfort and protect her in every way and any way he could, he anchored her against him tightly. "We're going to be okay, Dani," he said fiercely. "You, your sisters, our baby, everyone. I'll make sure of it."

Eventually Dani's heart slowed. Her body relaxed. "Feeling better?" Beau asked as he stroked her hair.

"Yes." Dani sighed her relief. "Although—" her breath warm and soft against his chest, her body cuddled snugly against his, Dani's voice and mood lightened considerably "—I don't think this is what Kelsey had in mind when she asked me to visit the ranch again."

Beau rolled so she was beneath him again. Enjoying the new hint of mischief in her eyes, he gently kissed her lips, then framed her face with his hands. He knew she was still afraid of her happiness, afraid it would be snatched away. But that wasn't going to happen to her, not again, and with his help, one day soon she would know that. "And I think—" Beau kissed her gently

"—that when it comes to you being loved the way you should be loved, the way you need to be loved, all your sisters, heck, even your parents would approve."

And just to make sure she knew that, he made love to her again, then and there.

"GOSH, YOU GUYS LOOK happy this morning," Billy told Dani and Beau the next morning when he reported for work. "Did something happen?"

You might say that, Dani thought. But since she and Beau had yet to discuss when and how they were going to tell people about their relationship, she merely smiled. "It just feels good to be settled in. And speaking of settling in, I've got a column due later today. And I've yet to watch the movie."

"Then you better get started," Beau said.

"What are you going to do this morning?" Dani asked. They'd spent so much time making love they hadn't discussed that, either.

"I think I'll give Billy a hand sorting and cataloging some of those videos. It's time we got to know each other better."

Billy beamed. "Way cool," he said.

"Any change in your parents' attitude about USC?" Beau asked as Dani headed off to the library to watch the movie she was supposed to review.

"No," Billy said. "But I haven't given up yet. I called the financial-aid office. They're going to see what they can do for me. They said worst case, I could ask for delayed admission and wait to start there next fall. Which would give me a year to work and save up enough to go."

Dani grinned as she shut the door behind her. Billy and Beau were actually bonding. Whoever thought that would happen? Then again, she wondered blissfully, whoever thought that she and Beau would fall head over heels in love? But they had. And now they were married, they had a baby on the way, and life was settling into a nice little routine. It was almost too good to be true, which was, of course, what bothered Dani the most. Their happiness seemed movie perfect. And movie perfect was the kind of happiness that never lasted.

But maybe this time it would, she told herself resolutely as she got out the preview film the studio had sent her and settled down to view it. Certainly she and Beau both wanted it to work. And where there was a will, there was a way. There had to be, Dani thought as she turned off the lights and switched on her projector.

DANI SPENT THE REST of the morning screening the new romantic comedy and then writing her review. When she emerged from the study, Billy and Beau were deep in conversation. Unaware that Dani was standing in the portal, listening, Billy continued eagerly discussing several recent movies. By the time he'd finished, Dani and, apparently, Beau were both extremely impressed. It was rare for anyone outside the industry to be aware of the difference lighting and camera angles made in a film. Rarer still for someone of Billy's age, who had just graduated from high school, to be so knowledgeable.

"Nice to see you two bonding," Dani teased.

Beau grinned and pushed to his feet. Closing the distance between them, he wrapped an arm about her waist. "Get your review written?"

"Yep," Dani reported happily. "All faxed in."

"How many stars did you give it?" Billy wanted to know.

"Two and a half."

Billy did a double take. "Only two and a half?"

Dani understood his surprise. The prerelease buzz on the movie had been fantastic. But that was, Dani felt, due to the charisma of the stars, not the story line, which had been heavy on fantasy and short on reality. Feeling Beau tense, Dani eased herself from his loose embrace. She moved toward the windows that overlooked the front lawn, then smiled and explained regretfully, "Not that it'll matter. It will do super box office in any case."

But once again Beau seemed to be thinking, to Dani's increasing regret, *You've missed the point.* Knowing her work—and Beau's reaction to it—might continue to come between them, Dani tensed, too. Billy picked up the tension between them. He glanced from Beau to Dani and back again. Beau, however, wasn't about to get into whatever he was thinking or feeling about Dani's views in front of Billy.

"Before I forget," he said, changing the subject pleasantly and crossing to Dani's side. His eyes held hers "Meg called. She wondered if you could baby-sit Jeremy for a little while this afternoon. She's got to go to the hospital to meet with the entire nursing staff."

Dani knew Meg was swamped. She was taking over for Lilah McCabe and was the new nurse supervisor at Laramie Community Hospital. The least Dani could do for her older sister, who'd put her life on hold for all three of her younger sisters when their parents had died, was help out with Meg's son. "Here or there?" Dani asked cheerfully, happy to change the subject and even happier to be able to spend some time with her nephew, whom she hadn't seen nearly often enough when she lived in California.

"Her place." Beau wrapped an arm around Dani's

shoulders and coaxed her into the warm curve of his body. ''She said it would probably be easier, since Jeremy has all his toys there.'' He lifted one of her hands to his lips and caressed it softly. ''Plus, she sort of promised him he could hang out in his wading pool.''

''Want to go with me?'' Dani asked Beau as she reluctantly extricated herself from his arms and reached for the phone. She couldn't think of a better way to spend the afternoon than hanging out with Beau and her beloved nephew. But to her disappointment, it didn't seem to be in the cards.

''I'll try and join you later,'' Beau promised, an enigmatic expression on his face. ''Right now I've got some matters of my own to take care of.''

DANI THOUGHT BABY-SITTING her nephew would be easier than talking about her work with Beau. She was wrong. Jeremy's questions started practically the moment Meg left for the hospital, and they weren't ones Dani could answer easily.

''Do you know who my daddy is?'' Jeremy asked as Dani turned on the hose and began to fill the extra-large wading pool Meg had set up in the backyard.

Dani shot Jeremy an apologetic look. ''I can't answer that for you, honey.'' *No one, save Meg, can.*

''Does Mommy know?'' Jeremy stood on first one foot, then the other while Dani spread sunscreen on his shoulders.

It would be hard not to, Dani thought as she put the cap back on the bottle. ''Jeremy, I think this is something you should talk about with your mom.''

''I did.'' Jeremy scooped up his boats and carried them over to the wading pool. ''She says it's too complicated, that we can't talk about it until I'm older, that

I'm too young to understand. But she's wrong.'' Jeremy dropped his boats, one at a time, into the water. ''I'm a big kid now—I'm almost six.''

Dani smiled as she looked at her nephew's fair freckled face. Maybe she was prejudiced, but as far as she was concerned there wasn't a cuter little boy in all of Laramie. His dark auburn hair was cut in a Prince Valiant style that framed his adorable handsome face. An intriguing mixture of intelligence and curiosity sparkled in his chocolate-brown eyes. ''You *are* growing up fast.''

Jeremy sighed. His lower lip shot out petulantly. ''So how come my momma won't tell me about my daddy?'' he demanded unhappily. ''How come it has to be a secret?''

Because she's protecting someone and she has been for the past six and a half years.

''Everybody else at school has a daddy,'' Jeremy continued unhappily. ''Even if their momma and daddy are divorced, they got one,'' Jeremy said. ''Please, Aunt Dani, can't you make her tell me?'' Tears of frustration glimmered in his eyes as he stepped into the wading pool with Dani's help.

Dani made sure he had a sure footing before she let go of his hand. ''I'll talk to your momma. See what I can do. But it's going to take time,'' she warned gently. ''Meanwhile you are going to have to be very patient and not pester your momma about this until I can make some headway with her, okay?''

''I guess.'' Only partly mollified, Jeremy made a face.

Beau suddenly appeared. He was carrying a paper bag from the Snack Shop on Main Street and a cardboard tray of drinks. He winked at Dani sexily before turning to smile at Jeremy. "I come bearing gifts."

"Presents?" Jeremy asked.

Beau dropped into the lawn chair next to Dani and settled his tall frame comfortably. "Freshly baked pretzels and ice-cold lemonade."

"Mmm," Dani said, not just meaning the delicious yeasty aroma wafting up from the bag.

"The soft pretzels, with salt on 'em?" Jeremy asked, scrambling out of the wading pool.

The kind Dani had always liked. And Beau knew it.

Beau ruffled Jeremy's hair. "I take it you like them?"

"Oh, yeah!" Jeremy said enthusiastically, his earlier questions about his father forgotten, to Dani's relief.

"Well, sit down on your towel and I'll fix you right up," Beau said, then stopped. "That is, if Dani says it's okay."

Dani grinned and leaned over to plant a kiss on Beau's cheek. "It's more than okay. It's great, thanks."

Beau got Jeremy settled with pretzels and drink and then did the same for the two of them. As they munched on their warm delicious pretzels, Beau inclined his head at the large turn-of-the-century Cape Cod house next door. "Given the size of the place for sale, roughly as big as yours, I'm surprised you didn't buy it, so you and Meg could live side by side."

"I might have, had it not needed so much work." Dani sighed. "But as you can see—" she pointed to the lavender paint, green shutters and deep-purple trim "—it needs a lot of work."

"Have you seen the inside?" he asked.

Dani nodded. "Talk about garish! The wallpaper is hideous, the kitchen completely antiquated to the point of ridiculousness. Although it's structurally very sound, and spacious, to boot. Bottom line, I just didn't have the time or patience for all the interior and exterior painting that place is going to need. But even in the condition it's in, it will sell eventually to some brave soul willing to weather the extensive updating, especially since the owners just dropped the price again.''

Beau nodded thoughtfully. "In comparison, Meg's little two-bedroom, one-bath Cape Cod—once the guest cottage to the larger home—is a dream.''

Dani nodded. "Hers has been completely redone inside and out. Of course, it had different owners.''

Beau studied the lemon-yellow cottage with the striking green trim. "Ones with taste?''

"Exactly.'' Dani tilted her head to the side and peered at him, as Jeremy, finished with his snack, climbed back into the wading pool. "Get whatever it was you had to do done?'' Dani asked Beau. In deference to the heat of the summer day, he had dispensed with the usual oxford-cloth shirt and put on a snug-fitting white cotton T-shirt that defined his wide shoulders, brawny upper arms and flat sexy abs to perfection. Faded jeans covered his taut lower torso and long muscular legs in a way Dani—as well as every other woman in America if they could see him—couldn't help but find enticing. His tanned skin glowed against the white of his smile, and even though it was only midafternoon, the faint hint of beard already edged the handsome contours of his jaw. His sexy blue eyes glimmered with affectionate lights, and he looked relaxed and at ease, despite the lack of sleep they'd had the past couple of days. Just being near him like this made Dani tingle deliciously from head to toe.

Beau smiled mysteriously. "Yep. I'm all done with

what I had to do," he drawled. He tossed off his hat and raked his fingers through his black hair, but to Dani's frustration didn't explain further what he had been doing or why.

Beau glanced at his two companions. Jeremy was once again seated in the middle of his wading pool, in the shade, his sailboats all around him. Dani, who was sitting in the shade, too, had on shorts and a tank top. Beau's eyes darkened ardently as he noted the relaxed way she was sitting in her lawn chair, her feet stuck in the pool, water halfway up her calves. "You two seem to be having fun." Beau took Dani's hand in his and twined their fingers intimately. "Mind if I join in?"

"Okay with me," Dani said, loving Beau's gentle touch. Reluctantly she tore her gaze from Beau's and turned to her nephew. "Jeremy, what do you think?"

Jeremy grinned at Beau, with a nearly-six-year-old's exuberance. "Want to play with my boats?" he asked.

"I sure do. I haven't seen any this neat in I don't know how long," Beau said, levering himself out of his chair and dropping to the grass. He tugged off his boots and socks and set about getting as comfortable as they were. "First thing I think we should do is make a marina," Beau decided. As usual, he wasted no time in taking charge.

"What do cowboys know about marinas?" Dani teased.

Beau winked at Dani sexily, then turned back to Jeremy. "Let me tell you, pardner. Cowboys *know* about a lot of things."

They sure do, Dani thought. *Especially when it comes to lovemaking and bedrooms...and how to make a woman feel more wanted and more alive than she ever has before.*

In the next hour Dani was sent into the house half-a-dozen times for aids to their experiments. They used an eggbeater and a spatula to create choppy water and waves, an aluminum cookie sheet for a boat ramp, shoe-strings for ropes, rocks from Jeremy's collection for anchors and upside-down plastic storage containers for docks. Beau was patient, kind and caring. He could have been every little boy's dream-come-true daddy. Jeremy, who had never known a father of his own, was particularly enamored.

Meg noticed, too, when she got home and breezed out to the backyard to join them. She was still in her nurse's uniform. Her rich auburn hair tucked into a tidy French twist on the back of her head, she looked tired and stressed. "Well, this is the first time I've had a movie star up to his elbows in our wading pool," Meg said cheerfully.

Jeremy frowned. "He's not a movie star, Mom, he's a cowboy. Aren't you, Beau?"

"Either that or I play one on-screen." Beau smiled up at Meg. "Hi." He stood, wiped his hands on a towel and extended a hand.

"Nice of you to let me borrow Dani for a while," Meg said, taking in the great way Beau was getting along with her son.

"Family's important," Beau replied somberly.

"And speaking of family," Dani interjected, looking at Meg. Her sister wasn't going to want to hear this, but Dani had no choice but to tell her. "May I have a word with you alone?" Dani asked casually.

"Sure." Meg's aqua-blue eyes telegraphed curiosity as they retired to the kitchen. Briefly Dani filled Meg in on her earlier conversation with Jeremy, finishing plaintively, "You've got to tell him something."

"I know," Meg said, wringing her hands. She paced back and forth, her slender frame drawn tight as a bow. "The question is what."

"The truth," Dani urged quietly. *To all of us.*

Meg frowned. "It's not as simple as that," she argued, as emotional on the subject as ever.

Dani quietly studied her super-responsible older sister. If she didn't know better, she'd think Meg had gotten herself involved with a married man or something equally scandalous. What other explanation could there be for Meg's continued secrecy? Especially after all these years.

"It's only going to get more complicated if you don't," Dani warned.

Beau walked in, Jeremy bundled up in a colorful beach towel, trotting along beside him. Ignoring the obvious tension between the two sisters, Beau announced amiably, "Jeremy wants all four of us to have dinner together. What do you two ladies think?"

Happy for the reprieve, since it was clear nothing was going to get settled or be revealed this afternoon, Dani smiled. If they couldn't assuage Jeremy's questions, at the very least they could distract him, wonderfully and warmly. "I'll go you one better. Let's round up the other two Lockhart sisters and make it a real family party."

THEY ENDED UP cooking at Meg's. Beau grilled the chicken. Meg prepared the scalloped potatoes. Dani made a garden salad. Kelsey pitched in where she could. And Jenna brought a lemon meringue pie from Isabel Buchanon's bakery and made the iced tea. To Dani's pleasure, Beau got along with all three of her sisters; it was as if he'd known them for years. And seeing how happy he made Dani, her sisters had no problem welcoming him into their family with Texas-style enthusiasm and gusto.

"Admit it," Dani teased him gently as the two of them walked the six blocks home in the dusky evening light. She couldn't recall ever being as happy as she was at that moment. "You loved being surrounded by all those women!"

Beau slanted her an acknowledging grin. "With every one of your sisters as warm and loving and lively as you? You bet I did."

There was no doubt about it, Dani thought. Beau was going to be an asset to her family. He was going to be an excellent daddy to their child, as well as a good role model for her nephew, and her sisters all liked and respected him.

Dani smiled at Beau again, thinking how nice it was just to be with him like this, strolling through Laramie as if they hadn't a care in the world, talking and enjoying each other's company. She never would have imagined it. As recently as a few days ago it had been a stretch to think they might even be just friends again. And yet now they were so much more than that. So much more than simply husband and wife. They were lovers and soul mates, too. She tucked her hand in his and teased gently, "What happened to the Lady with the Poison Pen?"

Beau turned to her, and the vulnerability in his eyes got to her the way no smooth seduction technique or carefully crafted words ever could have. He wrapped an arm around her waist and lifted her chin. "She disappeared the day I married you," he said huskily.

The next thing Dani knew, their lips had locked in a searing kiss. His tongue swept her mouth and desire poured through her in mesmerizing waves. Her muscles, deliciously relaxed only moments before, now stretched and strained. She arched against him wantonly, no longer caring who saw them together like this, no longer caring that they were standing on the street where she lived, in plain view of anyone who might happen by. She cared only that this never end.

She could feel his arousal pressing against her and knew he was just as deeply caught up in the changes happening between them as she was.

And there were changes, Dani admitted to herself as they slowly, reluctantly, let their kiss come to an end. Because it was true. She did feel different now. And it was all because of Beau. For the first time since her parents' death she was beginning to think maybe life wasn't all leading up to tragedy. For the first time in years she was beginning to think that maybe there was still a chance for her to have the kind of life she had always wanted as a kid. With a satisfying career, a husband and children to love.

Still holding her in his arms, Beau traced the dewy moisture on her lips with the pad of his thumb, whispered, "You are one sexy lady. You know that, don't you?"

The look in his eyes made her breath stop. She had never seen—or felt—such desire. "You certainly make me feel that way," she admitted huskily.

"Good." Beau's arms tightened around her possessively. His expression was grave. "And I intend to keep on making you feel that way."

Dani gave a soft shuddering laugh. "Then we better get home," she said, happy they were so much in synch in their wants and needs. "Before we really give the neighbors something to talk about."

"And speaking of home," Beau said as they turned and continued walking—faster now. "Isn't that Billy's car up ahead?"

Dani nodded at the beat-up Honda with the FILM-BUF plate. "It looks like he's still at the house," she murmured, frowning because she hadn't meant for Billy to work so late.

But Beau apparently felt no such compunction. "Good. I need to talk to him." Still holding her hand tightly in his, Beau headed for the front steps.

"About what?" Dani slanted Beau a curious glance as they crossed the front porch.

"His future." Beau smiled and held the door.

As Dani had feared, Billy was still working feverishly, entering cataloged films into the computer database he had set up on Dani's computer. "I can't believe you're still at it," Dani scolded as she glanced at her watch.

"I'm going to take a dinner break soon," Billy said.

"You mean you haven't eaten yet?" Dani said, incredulous.

"No, but..." Billy blinked as he looked past Dani at the dusky light outside. "Is it that late?"

"It's almost nine o'clock. You've worked almost twelve straight hours today, Billy."

He looked bewildered. "Wow. It felt more like, I don't know, seven or eight."

Beau looked at Dani. "Why don't you rustle up something for Billy to eat while he and I talk man to man?"

Billy's eyebrows lifted at the idea of anyone giving a woman as independent as Dani orders, no matter how much she liked Beau or how politely they were worded. Indeed, had such a suggestion come from anyone else, it would have been promptly volleyed back or ignored. But Dani had only to look at the determined set of Beau's jaw to know that the conversation between him and Billy was going to take place whether she wanted it to or not. Hence, it might as well be here and now, she reasoned practically, still bristling a little at Beau's take-charge kick-butt cowboy attitude. This way, she'd have a better chance of finding out what it was all about.

Nevertheless, very much aware it wasn't in her nature to take orders from any man, she smiled and excused herself. Then went back to the kitchen to prepare a sandwich and salad for Billy. When she returned, tray in hand, Billy and Beau were seated in the living room, conferring earnestly.

"Basically I can offer you two options," Beau was saying as Dani entered and set the tray in front of Billy. "The first is to take a one-year internship with my production company in either the Los Angeles office or the new satellite office here in Laramie, defer admission to USC for one year and save your earnings. This would give you a chance to see if you like the business side of moviemaking before you start an expensive education. The second option is to go ahead and enroll in USC in the fall and take a part-time internship with my company's L.A. office during the school year to pay your living expenses. In either case, my production company is awarding you a scholarship for tuition. But there's a catch. Actually, three catches." Beau waited a beat. "One, you have to work for my company after you graduate for every year of tuition paid. Hence, if we pay for four years of undergraduate education, you owe us four years at the regular entry-level director's salary.

"And two," Beau stated firmly as Dani sat down on

the arm of the sofa next to him, "no more passes at Dani. She's my woman now and that's not going to change."

"Beau!" Dani protested, face flaming. Honestly, sometimes he carried his John Wayne attitude too far.

"And three," Beau continued, pausing only long enough to clasp Dani's hand and shoot her a hotly possessive grin before he turned back to Billy, "you have to get your parents to agree to whatever option you choose."

Billy, who'd looked quite excited up to this point, predicted dourly, "Well, that'll never happen."

"Actually," Beau said as he rested their clasped hands on Dani's thigh, "you might be surprised. I spent a couple of hours with them this afternoon."

So that was where he'd been when she first went over to baby-sit Jeremy, Dani thought.

"I told them how impressed I was with your drive and your knowledge," Beau continued. "I went over all the financial details of my proposition with them."

"And?" Billy waited with bated breath.

"They were okay with it." Beau smiled, explaining, "They were just worried you'd get an expensive education and graduate and not be able to find a job. Since that's been taken care of, they're seeing things in a new light."

Billy got choked up. Dani was feeling a little overcome herself, finding out Beau was every bit the softhearted mentor to young people she was. "I don't know what to say," Billy stammered finally.

"You don't have to say anything right now," Beau said. "Just go home and talk to your folks. You can let me know what the three of you decide in a day or two. From there, we can notify USC."

"Well, you made his day," Dani said after Billy had left and Beau had led her back into the living room.

"Think so, hm?" Without letting go of her hand, Beau sat in one of her large comfortable club chairs.

"I'm impressed." Responding to the gentle tug on her hand, Dani sat on Beau's lap.

Beau grinned at her praise. "Finally!"

"Although—" Dani's sultry voice took on a teasing note as she settled more squarely on his lap "—I'm not sure whether I should be pleased or annoyed at your high-handedness in ordering me around and calling me your woman and basically just throwing your weight around that way." Not that his take-charge demeanor hadn't been sort of sexy, because it had been. She liked that she never knew quite what her new husband was going to do next. Just as she loved the solid warmth of him, his inherent dependability, his strong sense of responsibility. Beau was the kind of man you could depend on through thick and thin, the kind of man who would never use or betray you.

Beau's eyes glimmered. "I would hope," he said, slipping one arm around her and threading his fingers through her hair, "that you'd be pleased by my chivalry in protecting you against unwanted advances and young overeager suitors. In any case," he confessed with a cocky grin as he slipped his hands beneath the hem of her T-shirt and unfastened the front clasp of her bra, "now that you are my woman and my wife, that's just the way it is."

Their lips met. Feelings soared. His mouth was hot and demanding above hers, and Dani put everything she had into the kiss. She wanted him with every part of her heart and soul, and she wanted him to know it.

Commanding everything she had to give, he tangled

his hands in her hair, holding her head just so. As they continued to kiss, mating lips and teeth and tongues, sensations sizzled through her, and the scent of his cologne, so brisk and masculine, filled her senses. Twining her arms about his neck, Dani surged with heat and arched against him. She wanted to feel all of him against all of her. And she wanted it now.

Moaning in frustration, she whispered, "Darn it all, cowboy, we've got on too many clothes."

Beau chuckled. "My feelings exactly." He kissed her with a thoroughness that took her breath away, then lifted his head and looked deep into her eyes. Never had Dani seen such desire, and she moaned as he tugged off her shirt and bra, baring her breasts to his view. "Better," he murmured as he bent to kiss her again, beginning yet another slow voluptuous exploration of her mouth as his hands explored her soft curves, his thumbs and fingers playing over her breasts, the shadowy valley between and her nipples until they were tight aching buds. The heat of his caresses shattered her.

"We're not going to make it up to the bedroom, are we?" she whispered shakily as Beau set about unfastening the waist of her shorts.

"Nope. We're not." Beau lifted her off his lap long enough to draw off her shorts and then her bikini panties. "That going to bother you?" he asked as Dani knelt in front of him and whipped off his T-shirt, boots, jeans and shorts. She took the velvety length of him in hand.

"Not at all."

Bending her head, she loved him with the same thoroughness as he had loved her, learning anew the sleek contours of his hips and buttocks and thighs. She loved him until he was hot and dewy and shuddering with need.

"My turn," Beau said on a ragged breath. He tugged her to her feet, then drew her onto the chair, so she was sitting and he was kneeling in front of her.

As his warm hands slipped between her thighs, it was all she could do not to cry out. "I already want you," she whispered as his lips trailed across her tummy.

"I know." Beau dipped his tongue into the well of her navel, causing Dani to part her thighs and lift her hips and tremble all the more. He fit his lips around the tip of her breast and suckled lightly, until she strained impatiently against him. "Just not enough." He moved to her other breast. "But you will," he promised huskily. "That I promise you."

His lips dropped to the most delicate part of her. Hands on her thighs, he pushed her legs even farther apart. And then he kissed and caressed her with a wild sensual pleasure that seemed to have no end. Over and over he loved her, until she was shuddering and trembling, every secret silken inch of her. "Now," she murmured, pushing him to the floor. Needing to give, even as she took, she straddled his hips, then knelt, her knees astride his thighs. Slowly she lowered herself, took the hot velvety length of him inside.

Beau groaned and caught her hips in his hands, drawing her into an even deeper union. Then his fingers were moving between their bodies, caressing and loving, enhancing her pleasure. The need within her exploded and her self-control evaporated. Dani cried out. Next thing she knew she was on her back again. Beau was on top of her, rubbing his chest across her bared breasts, tantalizing her budding nipples with his silky mat of chest hair and the hard muscle beneath. Dani rocked against him, shuddering uncontrollably, even as Beau took her lips in a slow mating dance and trembled with the need to hold back his own release.

"Deeper," Dani whispered, lifting her knees and holding him tight. She knew he wanted their lovemaking to last and she felt the same. She wanted his slow sensual possession of her to never stop. And yet...she was half out of her mind with wanting him, quaking with sensations she could hardly bear. She was so aroused, in fact, she could barely breathe.

"Like this?" Beau loved her an inch at a time, going deeper, deeper still.

"Yes." Dani kissed him again as he pressed into her as far as he could go, then withdrew and filled her again. "Just like this." The love she felt for Beau pouring through her, she surrendered herself to him, luxuriating in the emotion, the longing and tenderness, and yes, love in his eyes. And then they were kissing again, desperately, sweetly, passionately. Commanding everything they had to give. Surging. Writhing. Cresting together, wave after wave. Lost in the passion and the need. And each other. Then the world fell away and they were lost in the cascading pleasure.

Afterward Beau held her close and stroked her hair. Dani had never felt as close to anyone. Never loved anyone, as much as she loved Beau at that moment. She wondered if he felt the same. Resting her chin on her hand, her forearm on his chest, she looked up at him. He was deliciously disheveled, sexier than ever. But there was a tenderness in his eyes, a gentleness she hadn't seen before. Her heart swelling with love, she decided to put her observations to the test, asking, "You don't have any regrets about marrying me, do you?"

Beau grinned as if that question was a no-brainer. "Best thing I've ever done," he asserted confidently, lifting his head and kissing her once more. "What about you? Regrets?" he prodded as desire shimmered through her anew.

"Not a one," Dani said just as confidently, looking deep into his eyes and finding they had never been so blue. She kissed him again as she sought to make all his wishes come true. Just as he had hers. "And I mean that, Beau, with all my heart."

Chapter Eleven

Beau had just returned from his morning run when
Sharon Davis drove up and parked in front of the house.
He could tell by her made-up appearance that she was
ready for a showdown. Knowing what a stir it would
create if the neighbors saw him and his ex-wife having
an emotional confrontation on Dani's front lawn, Beau
ushered Sharon inside.

"How did you find me?" he asked wearily, hoping
Dani did not come back in time from her jaunt to the
office-supply store with Billy and witness any of this.
They'd had such a great night. A great week. He didn't
want anything to ruin it now, and it was pretty clear,
from the ugly resentful look on Sharon's face, that this
was her agenda.

"Just because you didn't tell me where you were
staying in Laramie doesn't mean I can't track you
down," Sharon said sweetly. "Everyone in town is talking about how tight you two are—someone even saw
you kissing on the street last night." She chided him
with a scornful shake of her head, "Not very discreet,
darling ex."

Beau supposed it hadn't been. Not that he cared. He
was damned eager to tell the world he was married to

Dani. He just didn't want her in the middle of this on-going mess with Sharon. And until that was resolved…

"I didn't know you were tuned in to local gossip," Beau said tightly. He grabbed the towel he had left on the stairs and headed for the kitchen.

Sharon sauntered after him, her vampy high heels clicking on the polished wood floor. "It's not just local anymore, sugar. The tabloids are going with a page-one story next week. 'Beau Chamberlain makes peace with his most passionate critic.'" Sharon looked at him with new venom as Beau uncapped the bottle of water he had chilling in the fridge. "The copies will be out just in time for the premiere of your new movie, of course," Sharon finished with relish.

Beau swore and mopped his face with the end of his towel. Who wasn't out to destroy *Bravo Canyon,* the best movie he'd made in years? he wondered futilely.

Sharon sat down on a stool, hiking the skirt of her revealing sundress well above her knees. "Everyone in Hollywood is buzzing, you know, wondering what in blue blazes you're doing in this one-horse town." Sharon leaned forward, giving him a generous view of her cleavage. "Never mind considering opening a sat-ellite office of your production company here. Or is that just a ploy—" she paused and searched his face "—to get the Lady with the Poison Pen on your side?"

Aware he had never been more turned off by his vin-dictive ex-wife, Beau drank greedily from the bottle, then asked impatiently, "What do you want?" *Whatever the hell it was, he wanted Sharon to get it over with and get out of here.*

"I am here merely to remind you that the clock is ticking. And we still haven't found a solution to our little dilemma."

Beau wondered if Sharon's deal for her tell-all book had fallen through, or was about to, due to the defamation and libel threats issued from his own lawyers to hers. He regarded her grimly. "I'm not giving you any more money, so you can forget that."

"There are other options." Sharon gave him a sultry look as she played with the pendant nestling between her breasts.

"Such as?"

Sharon slid off the stool and grabbed his sweaty T-shirt with both hands. "How about a reconciliation between the two of us, or at least the hint of one, just in time for the premiere of *Bravo Canyon?*"

Beau pried her fingers from his shirt and turned away from her. Undeterred, Sharon continued, "Imagine what a buzz it would cause if I were to show up at the premiere, on your arm, the two of us looking happy as could be."

Beau stared at her. Were there any limits to how far she'd go? It did not appear so. "You've got to be joking." *The only person he was taking to his premiere was Dani*

"It wouldn't have to be a permanent thing," Sharon suggested sexily, batting her eyelashes at him. "Just long enough to raise speculation about us again."

"And help you peddle your tell-all book of lies? No thanks. You try to sell it and I mean it, I'll sue. That simple. You'll have an army of lawyers on you before you can spit."

Briefly, fear flickered in her eyes. A second later determination returned, icier than ever. "I need work," Sharon said flatly. *And she was willing to do anything to get it.*

"You have an agent. And a publicist." Beau took

Sharon's arm and guided her toward the closest exit, the back door. "Use them," Beau counseled sternly.

"I have," Sharon replied emotionally as she wriggled free of his grip. "But since we split, I can't even get arrested."

Beau did a double take. "And you're blaming that on me?"

Sharon scowled. "You're a powerful man in the business, Beau." She reached into the leather carryall draped over her shoulder and pulled out a dog-eared copy of a script. "I want the part of Maizie. One phone call from you is all it will take."

Beau snorted in derision. His ex must have lost her mind.

"I'm running out of patience, Beau," Sharon threatened. She closed the distance between them, not stopping until they were nose to nose. "You can make this happen for me."

Beau knew he could if he wanted.

"If you do it, the tell-all will be forgotten. Like that." Sharon snapped her fingers.

Beau clenched his jaw and hung on to his skyrocketing temper with effort. "You're wasting your time." He had given her a generous settlement at the time of the divorce for two reasons. He had wanted out as quickly and quietly as possible. And he'd felt guilty for ever marrying her when it was clear in retrospect that their relationship had been based on infatuation, not love.

"Am I?" Sharon lifted one exquisitely plucked brow. "I don't think so."

Beau swore softly as a muscle ticked convulsively in his jaw. Sharon had made a fool of him once. He wasn't about to let that happen again. "Do yourself a favor and get the hell out of Dodge."

"Don't you mean Laramie?" Dani interrupted dryly from the entrance to the kitchen, Billy right beside her.

THE MOMENT SHARON was out the door, Dani turned to Beau. "She's blackmailing you, isn't she?"

"I can handle her." Beau was only sorry anything had spoiled what should have been a delightful morning with his new wife.

Billy piped up with, "You shouldn't have to handle her alone." He looked ready to join the posse on Beau's behalf. "Not when you've got Dani and me on your side."

Beau smiled at Billy. Dani had been right—he had initially misjudged him. He was a pretty good kid. "What do you mean?" Beau asked.

Billy scowled. "Sharon Davis talked to you that way just because she thinks no one else will be able to see or hear her do it," he said.

"But Billy and I have an idea how to change all that," Dani added, grinning mischievously.

Beau gazed at Dani. She had never looked more beautiful or feisty than she did at that moment. It occurred to him that she was protecting him every bit as fiercely as he had protected her. He liked it. "What are you suggesting?"

"That we do what people do in the movies," Billy said.

Dani nodded. "And bring the truth to light."

Minutes later Beau set the phone back in the receiver. "It's all set. I'm meeting her late this evening."

"That should give us plenty of time, don't you think?" Billy looked at Dani hopefully. Dani nodded.

"Meanwhile," Beau said to Billy, "have you made any decisions about your future?"

Billy nodded. "I talked to my folks. We decided that it makes the most sense for me to spend a year living at home and working out of your offices here. That way I can save as much money as possible and learn as much as possible about the film business before I start college. And they can watch over me and see that I don't turn nutty on them—you know, pierce my tongue or something like that—just 'cause I'm now working in the film business. They hate my goatee enough as it is."

Beau knew there was an easy solution to that—shave. But Billy would have to come to that realization on his own. "Please don't pierce anything," Beau said earnestly. He angled a thumb at his chest. "I'd be blamed."

"I know." Billy chuckled, then promised, "I won't. So, anyway, back to business. With my mom and dad's blessing, I accept your offer of a one-year internship first, and the four-year scholarship after that."

Pleased, Beau shook hands with him. "I'll have the production-company attorneys express-mail the papers to you and notify USC right away."

"Thanks." Billy looked at his watch. "Well, if we're gonna do that tonight, I better get moving on the setup."

"Call if you run into any trouble," Beau said.

"Yes, sir." Billy gave a sharp two-fingered salute, then grinned and slipped out the door.

Beau turned to Dani. He wanted nothing more than to take her to bed and keep her there, make hot passionate love to her all day. But her totally businesslike demeanor said she had other plans. "What's on the agenda today?'' he asked as he headed upstairs to shower.

Dani followed him into the bedroom, where he'd hung his clothes. ''I have to watch and review your new film.''

Beau tensed. There had been so much going on he had almost—but not quite—forgotten about that.

''I think I should watch *Bravo Canyon* alone,'' Dani said. It would be easier to concentrate, get her review written and sent in.

Beau shrugged off his sweaty T-shirt and running shorts and dropped them in the laundry hamper. ''I've got to meet with my agent and publicist, anyway, at the temporary office space I rented on Main Street.'' Beau reached for his razor and shaving cream.

''I'll see you later, then?'' Dani said, already backing away.

Beau nodded. ''I'll go as soon as I get cleaned up, then be back in a few hours.''

EDIE AND ELLSWORTH GLITZ were waiting for him. The trio settled down in the sparsely furnished office while he passed out the cups of lemonade he'd picked up from Isabel Buchanon's bakery.

Edie handed him a printed schedule of events. ''You leave the day after tomorrow for the two-day publicity blitz. It's going to be in Dallas, since that's also where the premiere is going to be held.''

Beau knew all that. They had gone over it several times in the past few weeks, either by phone or fax. He scanned the pages impatiently, then listened absently as Edie filled him in on the post-premiere-party details, as well. Noticing his lack of attentiveness, Edie frowned.

"You might demonstrate a tad more excitement," she said.

Ellsworth looked concerned, too. "If you can't sell your own movie, no one can." He paused, abruptly becoming more personal. "I know how much this movie means to you. The considerable risk you took in accepting a part that—on the surface, anyway—is not the least bit sympathetic."

Edie put in with a publicist's single-minded concern, "Not to mention you almost blew everything with that very dramatic set-to with Shane McCabe a few weeks ago."

Beau shrugged, having no regrets about the ploy that had served to help Greta and Shane realize how they really felt about each other. "It all worked out in the end, and I got a little free publicity for the movie, to boot."

"True. But now the tabloids have gotten wind of Sharon's tell-all project, as well as your relationship with Dani Lockhart. They're going to publish stories alleging that this is only the second in a round of publicity stunts. They're going to wrongly hint that you're only shacking up with her to elicit a good review from her, thereby insuring a big opening weekend for the new movie."

Beau grimaced. He should have seen this coming. Would have if he hadn't been so enamored of Dani and wrapped up in the love they'd discovered. He looked at Edie and Ellsworth. "We aren't shacking up." Furthermore, anyone who knew him would know he would never use a woman that way.

"Temporarily residing beneath the same roof, then," Ellsworth said impatiently. "It will all look the same in the *National Inquisitor*."

"Which reminds me." Edie referred to her notes. "*Personalities!* magazine called this morning wanting to know if the scoop on the street is true. Are you living with the Lady with the Poison Pen?" She shook her head. "I put them off, said I'd have to check with you, but they won't wait long before sending someone out to see for themselves if we don't get back to them. So," Edie concluded abruptly, looking more like family than business associate, "you want to tell us what is going on with you and Dani Lockhart?"

Beau took a long swallow of lemonade while he considered how best to protect Dani from any scandal or heartache. She was just beginning to believe in happily-ever-afters. He didn't want anything spoiling that now.

"It's personal."

"That may be," Edie said, her pen and paper at the ready for drafting a press release. "But we have to tell them *something* if you don't want whatever is going on between you two to become hopelessly intertwined with the scandal brewing with Sharon and or to overshadow the debut of your new movie."

"On the other hand, if you were to announce you'd made peace with Dani Lockhart after your long-standing feud with her, and were having some sort of romance with her, that would knock Sharon's bogus charges of past infidelities off the radar screen, at least in terms of publicity value," Ellsworth predicted.

"A new romance beats an old one any time. The more sensational or surprising, the better. And a romance with Dani Lockhart is certainly that," Edie remarked sagely. "So. What do you want me to say?"

"Nothing yet," Beau replied. He had to talk to Dani first. But if he had his way, they'd be announcing their marriage pronto.

WHEN BEAU WALKED IN, Billy was still toiling away, cataloging the massive collection of videos. Dani was nowhere in sight. "Where is she?"

"Still watching the movie. She hasn't come out of there since you left." Billy nodded at the closed library doors.

Beau was nervous about Dani's response to the movie. He'd put his heart and soul into it. If she didn't like the film, it would be a very personal, very hard hit. One best handled alone between Dani and himself. "Listen, you've been working hard," Beau told Billy. "Why don't you take the afternoon off? We'll meet you at the place where the sting will take place."

"Are you sure? 'Cause I've got over five hundred of these left to go. And Dani wanted them done as soon as possible so she can get started on her book."

Beau put his hand on Billy's shoulder, gave him a man-to-man look. "Dani and I need some time alone."

Flushing, Billy grinned. "Why didn't you say so?" That quickly, he was already shutting down the computer, getting up and out of his chair.

"Do us a favor?" Beau tossed him a notepad, pen and roll of tape. "Put up a Do Not Disturb sign next to the doorbell on your way out."

Billy gave him a thumbs-up. "No problem."

As soon as Billy left, Beau rapped on the library door. No answer. Sure the movie had to have been over for at least thirty minutes, if not more, he walked in. Dani was curled up on the sofa in front of the projection screen, crying softly. Embarrassed, she wiped the tears from her eyes. Beau's heart took a nose-dive. "That bad, huh?"

Dani reached for the tissue box. Pulled one out. Blew her nose, then launched herself into his arms for a congratulatory hug. "Don't be silly," she murmured affectionately. *"Bravo Canyon* is going to be a huge hit for you."

Beau wondered if Dani still felt there was too much fantasy in the movies he made, then decided against asking her opinion. There was no sense in letting their work cause problems between them. What did it matter how she viewed the film professionally? It was her devotion as his wife, her love and understanding that he wanted and needed. He held her close and kissed her passionately.

"So how did your meeting with Edie and Ellsworth go?" Dani asked long minutes later, when they finally drew apart and had gone into the kitchen to get something to drink.

Beau watched her pour them both some milk. Frowning, he took the glass she handed him. "That's what we need to talk about." As much as he was loath to tell her, he knew he had to. "The tabloids are on to us. We're going to have to publicly announce our marriage or face all sorts of wild speculation."

Dani took a stool next to his. "What do you want to do?"

Beau drummed his fingers on the butcher-block surface of the work island. "Part of me wants to keep our marriage quiet forever. Just enjoy being married without dealing with all the media hoopla the announcement of our marriage will create. But I also know it would be easier on you and your sisters if we just took the bull by the horns and told it all now. That we were married in Mexico in a small private ceremony several weeks ago and are now expecting a baby."

Dani drew a tremulous breath and set her glass down on the work island. "If we announce it, Beau, there's no going back.'' She looked at him, worried her happiness was going to be taken from her as swiftly and unexpectedly as before.

Beau covered her hand with his, letting her know with the steady warmth of his touch he had no such qualms. "I know."

As she looked into his eyes, Dani began to relax and was able to concentrate on things that were a little less grave. "We don't even have wedding rings, Beau!"

Beau glanced at his watch. "We can fix that this afternoon."

"We're supposed to meet Billy."

"Not until seven. We've got plenty of time to do this before that if we want. Say yes, Dani." Beau leaned forward and gently kissed her lips. "Say yes, Dani," he whispered persuasively, "and make this marriage of ours a real and lasting one in every respect."

Dani hesitated once again, uncertainty welling up inside her.

Determinedly she pushed it away. Love like this came along once in a lifetime. She'd be a fool to let it go. Even if it was all happening a little too quickly for comfort. "Yes," Dani whispered, kissing him back, putting everything she felt, everything she hoped for, in the sweet caress. "Yes...yes...yes..."

As BEAU HAD PREDICTED, buying rings went off without a hitch. And he and Dani arrived at his newly leased office on Main Street a good hour before Sharon arrived. Billy had set up earlier, just as Beau had directed, and had phoned to let them know he, too, was on his way.

Meanwhile, Dani thought, she and Beau had a few moments alone to continue the discussion they'd started on the way home from their secret meeting with a prominent Dallas jeweler at a midpoint between Dallas and Laramie. "You're sure you want to announce our marriage at the premiere of your new movie?" she said nervously. She knew she was in love with Beau, and he with her. That as lovers and friends they were great. But as for marriage...somehow that still seemed like an enormous step, one with long-term implications, and deep down Dani wasn't sure she was ready for all that pressure. Since her parents' deaths, she'd had trouble trusting in the future. Marriage to Beau required a lot of trust in not just today and tomorrow and next year, but the far-distant future. Dani had trouble believing that future could be happy and trouble-free when she knew darn well that all her happiness could easily end the very next day. She'd had the rug pulled out from under her once. She didn't want it pulled out from under her again.

As long as their impetuous union had been a well-kept family secret, of course, their marriage hadn't been that difficult to deal with. Maybe, Dani thought, because she'd sort of had one foot out the door, so to speak, knowing they could easily change their minds and end it all at any time with no one having been the wiser about how foolishly romantic and naive they had been. But if they announced it...went public...well, there would be no turning back, no renegotiating the terms of their relationship, for either of them. The pressure would be on to make this work for the long haul. And it was a pressure that Beau, unlike her, did not seem to be feeling at all.

"We'll put out a press release in the morning," he continued enthusiastically. "You'll attend the premiere and the post-premiere party as my wife. As soon as the publicity jaunt is over, we'll head off on a honey-moon."

And what about my book, Dani wondered. *The dead-line I'm going to have trouble making even without a honeymoon?* Beau hadn't asked her if it was a good time for her to take off. But she supposed she could always work on her honeymoon, if need be. Maybe they could even watch some of the movies she needed to review together. And then she could take a few notes and write about them later. Reassuring herself it would all work out if she just gave it a chance, Dani smiled and decided to go for the gusto this time. "You don't waste any time taking charge, do you?" she teased, stepping into his arms.

"Not when it comes to something I want as much as you." Beau kissed the top of her head. "And now that's been decided, I think it's safe to do this." He removed the velvet box from the inside pocket of his tan blazer, took the diamond engagement and wedding ring they had purchased and slid them onto her finger. "Just what all the best-dressed women are wearing this season," he teased.

Dani slid the wedding ring they had purchased for him onto his finger and went right back into his arms. "I know how you feel about fashion for men," she said, loving the strong solid feel of him next to her.

"A giant waste of time," Beau agreed.

"But I'd like to see you in this—" she indicated his ring and waggled her eyebrows at him suggestively "—and nothing else." Maybe if they went back to bed and stayed there for a while, all these doubts she was having would fade. Heaven knew she never felt as safe or loved as when she was in Beau's arms.

"That can be arranged," Beau said, kissing her

deeply, until a wave of tenderness washed over them both. "Just as soon as we get this nasty business with Sharon over with."

Dani sighed and laid her head on his chest. She wrapped her arms around his waist, cuddling close and listening to the steady beat of his heart. "I'm all for that," she murmured affectionately, her anger about that unabated. "That woman has tortured you long enough."

Beau smoothed a hand over her hair. He laughed softly at the unusually protective note in Dani's voice. "Can't disagree with you there."

Downstairs a door opened, shut. Beau slid off his wedding ring and handed Dani the box for safekeeping just as Billy bounded in the door. "I think she's coming," he announced breathlessly.

Beau's dark brows lifted in surprise. "If Sharon is early, she must be anxious to get this over with, too," Beau said.

"Good luck." Dani kissed Beau's cheek.

Billy and Dani disappeared into the next room and shut the door behind them.

Dani settled down before the TV monitor to watch, while Billy put the digital camera and sound system through a quick check. They heard the click of high heels on the stairs. A moment later Sharon Davis breezed into the office next door, where Beau was sitting with his feet propped on an old wooden desk.

"I'm glad you came to your senses." Looking every inch the femme fatale in a low-cut red dress, she reached for the file of papers in his hand.

Just as swiftly Beau snatched them out of his ex-wife's reach. "Not so fast," he warned sternly. "Before we get to our transaction, I want to get a few things clear."

Sharon made a face.

"I can get you the part you want, but first you have to pull the plug on this exposé you've been peddling," Beau said firmly.

Sharon folded her arms. "Consider it done."

"And you've got to tell the truth about why our marriage ended."

Sharon shrugged. "It ended because you wanted to end it."

Beau said nothing, just looked at her steadily.

After a moment Sharon exclaimed, "Surely you don't expect me to tell people that you wanted a divorce because you found me in bed with the pool boy!"

"Why not?" Beau said. He steepled his fingers together and propped them on his lap. "It's the truth." Beau continued to regard Sharon steadily. He finished grimly, "And he wasn't the only one, either."

"Yes—" Sharon uttered a bored sigh and shook her mane of sleek dark hair over her shoulder "—but you never caught me in bed with any of them."

Beau dropped his feet to the floor and vaulted out of his chair. "So you're admitting it?" He faced his ex across the surface of his desk, his fury rising as he remembered what a fool she'd made of him. "You slept with a lot of other men while we were married."

Sharon regarded Beau impatiently, displaying a coldness and a meanness that was completely at odds with her public persona. "I told you," she said. "None of those men meant anything to me." She sat on the edge of his desk, hiking her dress halfway up her thighs.

Ignoring the show she was putting on for his behalf, Beau regarded her coolly. "Then why did you do it?"

he demanded impatiently, his loathing and disillusion-
ment evident.

"Because I like sex," Sharon said bluntly. "And I
like men. A variety of men. I didn't see why that had
to stop just because we were married." She leaned
across the desk and ran a finger down his chest. Cast
him a sultry look. "You could have done the same
thing, you know. Experimented with others. I wouldn't
have minded." Infuriated by Beau's lack of reaction to
her, she pushed him away. "But no, you had to be such
a prude and act as if our marriage had been permanently
damaged by my little fling." Sharon slid off the desk
and stalked away from him.

"Maybe because it had," Beau said quietly.

Sharon glared at him. "But your chivalry worked
against you in the end, didn't it?" she taunted nastily.
"Because you didn't want the whole world to know
how provincial and narrow-minded you'd been."

"Or what a tramp you'd been," he said.

Sharon propped her hands on her hips. "This is a
new century, Beau."

Unmoved by her taunting, Beau stared her down.
"Some things shouldn't change. Honor. Fidelity. Commitment in a marriage are among them."

"If you say so." Sharon rolled her eyes. "I don't
give a horse's rear."

"That was clear to me then," Beau agreed smoothly.
"And it'll be clear to the rest of the world soon, too, if
you don't back off."

Sharon narrowed her eyes at Beau "What are you
talking about?"

"Smile," Billy said, walking into Beau's office exactly on cue. He pointed to the air vent above Sharon's

head, where the recording devices had been set up just behind the grate. "You're on camera!"

Sharon sputtered and swore and tossed her head. She glared at Billy, then at Beau. "You're lying," she told Billy. Storming past him, she headed out into the hall, down the corridor and into the room where Dani was still sitting. She saw the video equipment that was still running and the TV monitor that quite clearly delineated the room where she and Beau had been talking.

Beau had followed her. Sharon's fury was replaced by panic. "What do you want?" she demanded hoarsely.

"I would think that's obvious," Beau replied grimly. "You, out of my life forever. The blackmail and extortion and lies to stop."

Sharon began to pace. "You can't expect me to tell everyone the truth about our divorce."

"No, I guess I can't," Beau drawled. "That would be too out of character, even for an accomplished actress like yourself. But I can promise you this. If you continue with the autobiography filled with your lies or ever again come after me for money or imply to anyone—however indirectly or subtly—that my infidelity caused the breakup of our marriage, this tape will be released to every major news organization and TV show in the world. And then see where your career is!"

Sharon's lower lip trembled. Tears appeared in her eyes. If Dani hadn't known better, she would have thought they were for real. Sharon might not be all that talented of an actress, but she was a wonderful fraud.

"What about the new movie and the part of Maizie?" Sharon asked in a low trembling voice that begged everyone to take pity on her.

To her chagrin, no one did.

"What do you think?" Beau said, making it clear with one sardonic glance that he wouldn't wish Sharon on his worst enemy, never mind people he considered his friends.

Realizing none of this was going the way she'd planned, Sharon glared at Dani. Then she turned back to Beau to work yet another angle. "I can't believe you could be so...so cruel and underhanded," she said.

"Neither can I, but then, I learned from a master," Beau answered sarcastically.

Infuriated that none of her manipulations were working, Sharon continued to glare at both Dani and Beau. "Did she put you up to this?" she asked after a moment.

"No," Beau said. "But she gave me the courage to do whatever it took, no matter how loathsome, to get you out of my life once and forever. And for that alone," Beau said, drawing Dani against him and kissing her soundly, "she's worth her weight in gold."

"THANK HEAVEN THAT'S OVER," Dani said as they entered the house a scant half an hour later.

Beau felt as if a giant load had been lifted off his shoulders. He reached over and squeezed Dani's hand, aware he'd never been happier or more in love than he was at that moment. "Now all we have to do is announce our marriage to the world," he said.

Compared to what he and Dani had already been through since they'd discovered they were in love with each other, having a press conference to announce their marriage and that they had a baby on the way was going to be a piece of cake.

"And get something to eat," Dani said, her stomach

rumbling, reminding them both they hadn't yet had dinner. "I don't know about you, but I'm starving."

As they passed the library on the way to the kitchen, they saw that the light on Dani's answering machine was blinking. She went to check her messages. There were two, both from her publisher, wanting to know why she hadn't faxed in her review of *Bravo Canyon*. Dani made a face and pressed a hand to her forehead. "Oh, darn, I forgot all about my deadline." Dani switched on her printer and pushed a button on her desktop computer. "You might as well read what I wrote." She handed him her review.

Remembering the last review she'd written about his work, Beau hesitated. Her eyes glowing affectionately, Dani pressed it into his hands. "Just read it," she said softly. "Please."

Beau swallowed and turned his gaze to the page in his hand.

The early buzz about *Bravo Canyon* was overwhelmingly bad, but I'm here to tell you it was wrong. Dead wrong. The love story at the heart of this film involves a loner and a battered wife. The victim of a cheating wife himself, Grady Bodine (played by Beau Chamberlain) is reluctant to get involved in a romantic relationship of any kind, never mind an adulterous one with the wife of the richest man this side of the Rio Grande. But when he realizes that the fate of this smart spirited woman is in his hands, when he realizes no woman should ever have to be treated with such unremitting cruelty, he decides to rescue her. And while rescuing her, goes against everything he believes in and falls in love with her. And she with him.

Starved for love, in need of a tender touch and understanding, the two lovers fall into each other's arms. And thereby put the lives of themselves and everyone close to them at risk.

In the hands of a lesser actor, this would have been a standard western, at best. In the hands of Beau Chamberlain, *Bravo Canyon* becomes a masterpiece, one with the epic sweep of a John Ford film and the carefully nuanced performances of Chamberlain and all those interacting with him. You'll want to see this movie more than once...

Suddenly feeling like the world's biggest fool, Beau said gruffly, "You don't have to go easy on me now that we're married, Dani. That wasn't part of the deal."

Dani blinked at him in confusion. "What do you mean?"

Beau studied her, not sure when he had ever felt so disappointed in someone. Dani had always had a reputation for fairness. To watch her squander it now was like watching her self-destruct. "You've never really liked my acting," he reminded her impatiently. "I don't care. That's not what we're about."

Dani's eyes widened. "You think I gave you a free ride on this one because we're married?" she asked in a low incredulous tone.

Maybe, Beau thought, she hadn't realized until now what she'd done. "Yeah, to make up for all the things you said about me before. And I'm telling you—" he gave her a level look "—you don't have to do that."

Dani drew herself up indignantly. "I didn't cut you any slack."

Beau sighed. Now he had offended her pride. "Maybe not intentionally," he said gently, "but it's obvious your love for me has colored your feelings here.''

"I beg your pardon. It has not! You did a damn fine job in that movie, Beau. People are going to be talking about your multilayered performance for years!"

Beau knew he'd given the performance of his life in *Bravo Canyon*. Right now that was the least of their concerns. "Even so, your review is likely to be suspect because of our relationship," he explained patiently, taking her hands in his. "I think you should consider pulling it before you end up making fools of us both. In fact, I think you should stop reviewing my movies altogether now that we're married. It'll save a lot of trouble if you do."

Dani withdrew her hands from his and crossed her arms. "Reviewing movies is my job."

Hating the businesslike look in her eyes, Beau sighed in exasperation and shoved his hands through his hair. "I know that, and you can review every other movie, just not mine anymore."

Dani stepped behind her desk and sank into her chair. "What are you saying here, Beau?" she demanded, her demeanor cool and unruffled. "That I am so unprofessional I can't be objective where your movies are concerned?"

A muscle ticking in his jaw, Beau braced his palms on her desk and leaned forward, lowering his face so that they were at eye level. "I'm saying it will save us from arguing and hurt feelings and everything else rotten that goes along with the two of us being on different sides of the same business."

Dani picked up the copy of her review and walked over to the fax machine. "I have never skipped a movie for personal reasons and I am not about to start now."

Beau watched her feed the review into the fax and punch in the appropriate number. "Not even for us?"

Dani stopped and looked him straight in the eye. "If I stop reviewing your movies, then I am as much as admitting I can't be impartial where you are concerned, and I *can* be. I am a professional, damn it."

Beau caught her hand before she could push the start button. "So am I. But that doesn't mean I would deliberately do something likely to cause trouble in our marriage," he said, his fingers tightening on hers.

"Fine." Dani jerked her hand from his restraining grip. "Then *you* give up making movies."

Realizing he couldn't stop her from faxing indefinitely, Beau grimaced and stepped back. "Now you're being ridiculous," he said. Worse, she was acting like a stranger to him. Nothing like the woman who had shared his bed and warmed his heart the past few days. But maybe, Beau thought, he had only been seeing the parts of Dani he wanted to see, needed to see, to make this hasty badly thought-out marriage of theirs work. Maybe he'd been deluding himself about Dani's potential for a lasting commitment.

Dani edged away from the fax machine. "So are you," she muttered, heading for the door.

Not about to let her run off before they worked this out, he caught her arm and backed her up against the bookcases. "All I ask you to do is recuse yourself from reviewing any movie I'm in. That's not so hard." And if she took the time to think about it, she would know that.

"And I told you I can't do that," Dani shot back stubbornly, splaying her hands on his chest and pushing past him. "Not without impugning my reputation." Narrowing her eyes, she reminded him in a flat implacable voice, "I treat everyone the same in this business. I always have. I always will. I've worked hard to be fair."

Beau knew that. He had always admired her integrity, even when he didn't agree with her reviews. But none of that was the point. "No one would think less of you for passing on your husband's movies," he said, refusing to let her direct their argument to less-intimate ground.

"Maybe they would." Dani lifted her shoulders in an indifferent shrug. "Maybe they wouldn't." She looked at him steadily. "But I would think less of me. Darn it all, Beau—" she aimed a lecturing finger his way "—I don't want to be one of those reviewers who does favors for family and friends. And, bottom line, this is what your request amounts to."

There was no missing the boiling fury in her eyes. "Meaning you aren't willing to give an inch on this issue, even for your husband," he ground out, aware he was growing more disappointed—and disillusioned—by the second.

"Not even half an inch," Dani countered flatly.

"Fine," Beau turned away from her, his own temper flaring.

"Now you're angry." Dani followed him to the library doors.

"Yes." Figuring the last place they needed to be was her office, Beau headed for the living room.

"Why?" Dani stamped down the hall after him.

In the living room Beau crossed his arms and assumed a no-nonsense stance. "Because I think there's at least part of you that wants this marriage to fail."

A rush of indignant color swept into Dani's cheeks.

"That's not true!" She looked every bit as hurt and frustrated as he felt.

"Then why won't you do the one thing that's guaranteed to give us a smoother ride?" Beau asked with mounting impatience.

Dani didn't answer.

"I'll tell you why," Beau said softly when she started to turn away. Closing the distance between them swiftly, he caught her by the shoulders and forced her to face him. "I think you've just been waiting for an excuse, any excuse to walk out on our marriage because you're scared to love. You're scared to rely on anything or anyone other than yourself because of what happened to your folks."

At that, her face grew pale, her shoulders stiffer. "If you really think that, you don't know me at all," she said, appearing no less hurt and disillusioned, no more ready to meet him halfway. "Furthermore," she continued, standing as still and unresponsive as a statue in his arms, "I am not the one who is making impossible demands here. You are."

Was he?

Beau didn't think so.

Dani was the one who was being unreasonable. Dani was the one who was afraid to love. Afraid if she did, the whole world would come tumbling down around her once again. Beau regarded her with growing helplessness, his gut telling him that if it wasn't this issue driving them apart, some other one soon would be. "I've done everything I can to show you that you are safe with me and always will be," he said quietly. But to his chagrin, Dani didn't seem to want to hear that, any more than she wanted to confront—and conquer—her fears. She had gone into this relationship with him with both feet out the door, and even after all the love they had shared, she was still ready to bolt at the slightest provocation.

Tears flooding her eyes, she brushed past him. "This isn't a movie, Beau, or some fantasy of life as it should be. As much as you might want to, you can't control the ending or make it happily-ever-after. This is real life, and in real life things don't always work out the way we want. How well I know that," she finished bitterly.

"Meaning what?" Beau shot back, finding her remote attitude and cold sad voice much more terrifying than her anger. "That because we disagree on something our marriage is over, just like that? Meaning I'm supposed to stand by and watch you sabotage our marriage and make fools of us both by insisting your career comes first and always will?"

Unable to dispute the truth of that, Dani grabbed her purse and her keys and headed for the door. "I should have known my career is the only thing I can count on in this life! I should have known this happiness, like every other, wouldn't last!" she said emotionally. "Darn it all, Beau, why did you do this to me? Make every aspect of our life together movie-set perfect right down to the interior of my house? Why did you make me believe we had a love that was wonderful enough to be in one of your movies if it wasn't going to last?"

"I'm not the one throwing it all away!"

"Aren't you?" Dani asked, her disappointment in him like a dagger to his heart. "You know if I do a favor for you, it won't be long before other actors come to me, too, asking for the same kind of 'special consideration' because that's the way it works in this business. You treat just one person different—a little better, a little worse—and before you know it people think maybe you can be swayed to give a better review just because you happen to like someone or see them socially, and everything you do or say becomes, if not suspect, at least a lot less respected. I've worked too hard to let that happen. I don't want to have my integrity, my ability to be objective, questioned, because once that happens, my career as a respected critic is finished. And I'm not going to let that happen, not even for you.'' Giving him no chance to respond, she stormed away.

Beau caught up with her in the front hall. Their eyes met. The air between them fairly crackled with electricity. They were at a turning point here, whether Dani wanted to admit it or not. Up until now, she had only let herself really rely on two things—her sisters and her career. For their marriage to work she had to rely on him, too. She had to be ready to risk conflict and turmoil and stay around and work things out. She couldn't just run every time they hit a rough patch. But that was, it seemed, exactly what she was determined to do. He had only to look into her eyes to know that was so.

''Let's just face it before we do any more damage,'' Dani said, hurt radiating from her eyes. ''This—us—isn't right.'' Her tone was low, bitter. ''We never should have even started.''

Aware it was all he could do not to take her in his arms and kiss her senseless, he said softly, ''You already walked out on me once, Dani. In Mexico. You walk out that door this time and I am *not* coming after you.'' He wouldn't put either of them through that again.

Dani glared at him, her expression stony with resolve, the hands-off warning still in her eyes. ''I don't want you to come after me," she insisted quietly, stubbornly, her heart encased in stone once again. "All I want is for you to leave so I can put my life back together— without any of the movie-set fantasy you're so fond of." Shaking her head, she turned away. "I'm going to spend the night at my sister Jenna's apartment. I'll give you until morning to clear out your things."

Chapter Twelve

"Bet you didn't know Dani still had any of these things, did you?" Kelsey Lockhart asked as she, Jenna and Meg placed a gauzy white dress, a dried bouquet and a white lace mantilla on the desk in his production office the following morning.

Beau stared at the belongings, which still bore the fragrance of Dani's perfume and the feminine essence of her skin and hair. He wasn't surprised she'd kept these things. She was a very sentimental woman at heart, capable of an amazing amount of love. It was just too bad she wouldn't let herself give it. "Maybe they're a reminder of what not to do again," he said gruffly, pushing the things away.

"Like get involved with someone like you?" Meg asked quietly.

Beau sat back in his chair, silent, waiting. These Lockhart women stuck together, that much he knew. Not one of them would be leaving until they had their say.

"You two love each other," Jenna began.

I sure thought we did. That was why he'd thrown down the gauntlet, telling her if she walked out the door, it was over. He wasn't coming after her again.

Because he wanted to shake her up, make her realize what was important. Their marriage. Not their careers. Not their fears. But all the love—the family—they could have together. Now, given the way she had walked out on him again... Beau sighed wearily, unable to recall when he had felt so lonely and unhappy.

He dropped his pen on his desk.

"You really love each other," Kelsey added.

"And what makes you think that?" Beau asked coolly.

"The way you look at each other when you're together," Jenna said.

The night they'd had dinner with all the Lockharts had been fun, Beau admitted.

"Not to mention the way she talked about you incessantly, even before the two of you ran off to Mexico," Kelsey said.

Beau hadn't been able to stop thinking or talking about her, either.

"And let's not forget the way she looks right now," Meg added, worry etched on her face.

"Why? What's wrong with her?" Beau demanded, leaning forward in his chair.

All three Lockhart sisters scowled at him. "You broke her heart," Jenna said.

Beau didn't know whether to laugh or argue. He arrowed a thumb at his chest and said, "She broke her own heart when she turned her back on me and our marriage."

"You never should have let her walk out on you." Meg shook her head reprovingly.

"And what was I supposed to do? Keep her prisoner?" Beau shot right back, refusing to feel guilty about anything that led to their breakup. How was he supposed to know that Dani wouldn't come to her senses last night and return? How was he supposed to know that their marriage really meant so little to her when it meant everything to him? "I can't be with a woman who doesn't put us first," he said. He picked up a pen and turned it end over end.

"We totally agree with you on that, Beau," Jenna said gently.

Kelsey nodded. "We think Dani should stop reviewing your movies, too."

"But we also think if she chooses to continue reviewing your work that you should accept that," Meg added.

"*Especially* now that there's a baby on the way," Jenna said.

Beau paused at the mention of the child he and Dani had created in an act of love. Warm feelings flooding his heart, he regarded them uncertainly. "She told you about that, too?"

They nodded in unison. "She was going to have to sooner or later," Kelsey said.

"She'll need our help more than ever if you're not going to be in the picture," Jenna warned.

Beau scowled. The thought of Dani having their baby without him was unbearable. He stood up restlessly, braced his hands on his waist. He was letting Dani go because he loved her, hoping she'd come back on her own, not because she felt obligated to, because of their baby or their hasty marriage, but because she loved him. Enough to want to spend the rest of her life with him and make theirs a real marriage in every respect. He wanted her to come back because she loved him enough to risk her heart.

"I'm not abandoning the baby," Beau said flatly.

"Any more than I'm abandoning Dani." The pregnancy was going to be an emotional time for her. Whether they were married or not, he was going to be there to see her through it.

Skeptical looks were exchanged all around. "You may not think that's what's happening now..." Kelsey began.

"...but ten to one Dani sees it that way," Meg finished.

"No matter how much you both love the baby, it won't be the same, either, if the two of you aren't married," Jenna warned.

Meg's eyes telegraphed a boatload of concern. "Don't make the same mistake I did. Don't put your pride ahead of what's in your heart," she advised, clearly speaking from bitter experience.

Beau thought about the problems Meg's son, Jeremy, was going through now because of Meg's decision to go it alone, without a husband or father to help her. "Is that what you think I'm doing?" he asked eventually. "Deserting Dani? Deserting our baby? Deserting the two people who—" at least until his argument with Dani last night, he thought "—were going to be my family?"

Meg lifted a brow. "Aren't you?"

"WHAT DO YOU MEAN you can't review *Bravo Canyon?*" Dani's publisher, Hank Mortimer, asked later the same morning. "You got the film, didn't you?"

"Yes, I got it." The phone cradled against her ear, Dani paced and paced. She didn't know what it was about her house now, but it seemed so big and empty since Beau had packed his bags and left. Worse, she had never felt lonelier. And she had cried all night at Jenna's apartment.

"Did you watch it?" Hank demanded.

"Yes, I watched it." Doing her best to take care of her baby, even under such enormous stress, Dani sipped a glass of milk.

"And…?" Hank waited for the verdict with bated breath.

Dani sighed and sat down at her desk. "It's the best film Beau Chamberlain has ever made."

"So what's the problem?" Hank sounded thoroughly exasperated.

Dani rubbed the tense muscles at the back of her neck. "I'm just not sure I can be objective."

"When have you not been objective?" Hank demanded.

When I fell in love with Beau. Common sense had gone right out the window. She had acted on feelings, and feelings alone. And as a result had made a complete fool of herself, thinking that their marriage could ever work.

"Keep this up," Hank said, clearly trying to tease her into cooperating with him, "and people are going to think he charmed you into not reviewing his movie."

Dani stiffened. "I would never let that happen." Nor did she want to make fools of both her and Beau, as Beau had suggested she'd be doing by printing such a glowing review of his work. Granted, she didn't think she had written anything that wasn't true. *Bravo Canyon* was the best western she had ever seen. But it had also starred Beau and been made by his production company. And she loved Beau more than she had ever loved anyone in her entire life. So maybe Beau was right.

Maybe, given what was in her heart, she wasn't able to be objective where he was concerned.

Hank exhaled loudly on the other end of the connection. "Up till now, you've never refused to review a movie, either."

That's because I've never been in love. And she did love Beau with all her heart and soul, no matter what he thought. Otherwise, she wouldn't have been up most of the night waiting for him to charge over to Jenna's like some big-screen-western hero, claim her as his woman and sweep her up into his arms. And take her home.

Hearing the sound of a car door slam out front, Dani moved to the window just in time to see Ellsworth and Edie Getz coming up the stairs to her front porch. "Hank, I have to go."

"Fine. Just make sure that review is in by six o'clock. Or else." Giving her no chance to reply, her publisher cut the connection.

Still stinging from her boss's rebuke, with no clue as to what she was or wasn't going to do about that, Dani stepped out onto her porch. No doubt Beau's agent and publicist had an opinion about what she should do, one she was quite sure they were just dying to share with her. "Don't tell me," Dani said drolly, taking in the superbly dressed power couple from Los Angeles. "Beau sent you."

Edie and her husband exchanged a look. "Actually," Edie said, "Beau would probably fire us both if he knew we were here."

Dani noted that didn't seem to be stopping them. "Then…?" she prodded.

Edie sighed as Dani escorted them into the living

room. "We're here to talk some sense into you, since talking sense into Beau failed."

Ellsworth settled on the sofa beside his wife. "We know what happened in Mexico."

Dani's shoulders stiffened with dismay. "Then you know Beau and I made a giant mistake." One that had been unequivocally confirmed when Beau, perhaps the most determined man she had ever known, had passed on the opportunity to take charge of the situation in his usual big-screen-hero way and "allowed" her to walk out on their life together last night.

Edie frowned. "The only mistake I see either of you making is right now."

Ellsworth continued, "Stubbornness can be a great asset to a person in the entertainment field. It keeps you drumming away when others around you give up. But it's a very bad trait for a marriage."

Edie nodded in agreement. "Married couples need to be able to give and take, and sacrifice their own agenda for the benefit of the union."

Dani knew that was true. And if she thought there was a real chance she and Beau could fix things, she'd be back by his side in an instant. But they couldn't. Beau had been very clear about that. He had asked her not to review his work for the sake of their marriage. Hurt by the attack on her integrity, she had refused his request. He had told her not to walk out on him again. And she had.

Aware Edie and Ellsworth were waiting for some explanation, Dani said finally, "Beau and I didn't have a real marriage."

"You would never know that by the way he's behaving," Edie murmured, smoothing her skirt.

"I haven't seen him this upset since he came back from Mexico several weeks ago," Ellsworth agreed.

Dani's chin jutted out. "I didn't force us to break up. He's the one who made the demands and issued the ultimatums."

Again the Getzes were in agreement with each other and disagreement with Dani. "He thinks just the opposite happened, that you're the one who walked out on him," Edie said.

Dani knew that Beau had never cared what anyone said about his work as long as he felt he'd made an entertaining movie that left people feeling that right always prevailed over wrong. But he had cared about what *she'd* said about his work, just as she had always been more intensely interested in his work than anyone else's. Like it or not, because of their feelings for each other, this was a personal issue and probably always would be.

Edie stood and crossed to Dani's side. Patting her gently on the shoulder, she said, "The point is, it doesn't matter who did what to whom when. What matters is that the two of you are miserable without each other. You have a chance to be happy, Dani. And so does Beau. But for either of you to get the chance to have it all, one of you is going to have to make the first move."

Edie and Ellsworth were sounding more like Beau's family than agent and publicist. But then, wasn't that what the duo was famous for—supporting and nurturing their clients? "Shouldn't you be having this conversation with him?" Dani asked, refusing to budge.

"We already have." Edie sighed and shook her head. "He's as stubborn as a mule."

Ellsworth's brow furrowed. "He says he's not going

to force you to come back to him again. 'Been there, done that,' is how he put it.''

Dani took a deep breath. Was it too late? What would Beau do if this time *she* went back and said she wanted to try again, instead of just sitting here and waiting for him to chase after her? Meanwhile there were other problems to be dealt with. Deciding to seek Edie and Ellsworth's advice on the rest of the dilemma, Dani confided, ''I'm under considerable pressure professionally to publish my review of *Bravo Canyon*. Beau, on the other hand, thinks it is way too glowing and has asked me to pull it.''

''What do you want to do?'' Edie asked gently.

Dani shrugged, her heart in turmoil. ''I want the same thing I wanted yesterday—to publish it.'' She knew it was personal—and personal feelings of any kind had no place in her work. She knew it didn't make sense for her to be feeling this way. But the fact remained she wanted everyone to know how proud she was of Beau and what he had done in *Bravo Canyon*. Dani looked at Edie and Ellsworth. ''What do you think I should do?''

''I think you have to go with your gut feelings on that,'' Ellsworth said.

Dani hedged. ''But when word gets out we're married...'' Which would be soon, since they knew the tabloids and other celebrity magazines were on to them.

Edie held up a hand. ''I wouldn't worry about that, Dani. You've established quite a reputation for yourself. People will understand that you love Beau, but that you are also a talented critic capable of moving beyond your personal feelings to the work at hand.''

They made it sound so easy, so logical. If only it was! Dani bit down on her lower lip as anxiety and regret welled up in great powerful waves. "You think Beau and I have made a mistake, breaking up over this, don't you?" she asked, studying their faces.

Edie and Ellsworth exchanged a look laced with meaning. Then Edie turned back to Dani and spoke for them both. "We think a love as powerful as yours comes along very seldom in this life. If the two of you are wise, you'll both put your pride aside and do everything you can to preserve it."

DANI PACED THE INTERIOR of her house after Edie and Ellsworth left. As much as she hated to admit it, she knew they were right. But was it too late? The premiere of *Bravo Canyon* was in a matter of hours. Beau was already ensconced in his Dallas hotel room. There was no guarantee he would even be willing to try to work things out, come to any sort of compromise. And yet, if she didn't try, wasn't she consigning them both to a life of heartache and misery? Never mind the baby they were expecting?

Dani went to the phone and dialed Wade McCabe, an investor, and his wife, Josie, the wildcatter who had struck oil for him. "Guys," Dani said as soon as she got them on the line, "I need a favor."

An hour and a half later Wade was landing his chopper on the rooftop of the Dallas hotel where Beau was staying.

But to Dani's surprise, instead of Edie and Ellsworth Getz—who'd been supposed to meet her on the rooftop and escort her down to see Beau—Beau himself was standing there waiting. Framed in the Texas sun, aviator sunglasses covering his eyes, wearing a white shirt, jeans and hat, he had never looked sexier. Or more unapproachable.

"Good luck, honey," Josie said.

"Thanks," Dani murmured as she gathered up her luggage and stepped out of the chopper. Judging by the wary expression on Beau's face, it looked as if she was going to need it. Her heart pounding in her throat, she looped her garment bag over her shoulder and dashed across the rooftop to Beau's side.

The chopper lifted off with a great gust of wind. Dani waved once, then turned to Beau. There was so much to say. She didn't know where to begin. So he did it for her.

"I'm sorry," he said huskily, taking her in his arms and hugging her. "I never should have let you go off alone last night…"

Dani looked into his eyes as they slowly drew apart. "You're not the only one responsible for making our relationship last, Beau. No matter how frightened I was, I never should have walked out on you…"

But before she could say anything more, Beau whipped off his sunglasses and touched a finger to her lips. "Hear me out, Dani. For both our sakes, I need to say this." His voice dropped a notch. "I know I accused you of being afraid to love me last night, but the truth is, you weren't the only one who was having second thoughts about putting it all on the line. All my life I've believed everything was within reach. All I had to do was want it and work for it. Then you came along. Suddenly, nothing was easy or predictable. Right off the bat you had me pegged. I could tell you were attracted to me, but you wouldn't do anything but flirt or feud with me. Then you married me. You made love with me. But you wouldn't stay with me. Not all that willingly, anyway. After a while I began to wonder if what you'd said to me when we first met, about life not being this easy, wasn't right, after all. I knew what had happened to your parents, how you and your sisters had all suffered as a result…the injustice of it all. And I began to wonder if maybe you and the baby weren't the one thing in my life that would be taken away from me for no reason any of us can comprehend. Not because of death, but because of an inability to trust in the strength of our marriage, on both our parts. I knew you'd been through so much that you no longer had faith that life would bring you any lasting happiness. And the same went for our marriage. And I didn't have confidence that you would be tenacious enough, or love me enough, to stay around and work through our problems. Instead, I expected you to bolt at the first signs of any real difficulty. So when trouble came, as it inevitably and routinely does in all marriages, I practically pushed you out the door. Instead of doing what I should have done, which was to move heaven and earth, make whatever sacrifice or compromise necessary, so you would stay."

"Oh, Beau…" Dani's heart broke for him. She knew how it felt to be filled with hurt and uncertainty, to want to be happy, but fear you never will be.

"And my mistakes didn't stop there," he continued gruffly, moving away from her and beginning to pace. He shook his head in mute regret. "I had no right to accuse you of trying to make fools of us both or ask you to pull your review of *Bravo Canyon*. In fact, the more I think about it—" Beau's lips twisted ruefully "—the more I feel I should stay out of your work entirely. Because that really isn't the function of a husband or a wife."

Dani's heart pounded. Unable to help herself, she moved a step closer, so they were standing just inches apart. "Even if I can no longer treat you the same as everyone else in the business?" she asked slowly.

Beau grinned—he obviously liked the sound of that—and then his eyes darkened. "I'll be honest with you, Dani. It meant a lot to me that you were proud of my performance." Abruptly he grew very still. "I don't need your approval. But I want it."

"I want yours, too." Tears of happiness and relief stung Dani's eyes. She wrapped her arms around his neck and kissed him sweetly. "More than anyone else's in this world."

"You've got it," Beau said thickly as he hugged her back. They kissed again, more passionately this time. "Because you're the best critic in this country and everyone knows it. Your reviews are so insightful and fair they put everyone else's to shame."

"I wouldn't go that far," Dani said, blushing, as she leaned back against the warm cradle of his arms to gaze into his face.

"I would," Beau said firmly as he stroked warm loving hands down her spine. "But it's not your reviews that I'm interested in, Dani." He paused to kiss her temple. He lifted a hand and drew it tenderly down the side of her face. "It's you. And the baby." Gently he touched her tummy. "And the life we can have together if we put everything else aside and just concentrate on making our marriage a real and lasting one."

Euphoric relief surged through Dani as she lifted his hand to her lips and kissed it. "I agree that's what we should do," she said seriously, knowing if they were going to be together again, they couldn't be afraid to lay it all on the line and talk out their problems, even when it was uncomfortable to do so. "But I also think I need to set the record straight in a lot of ways, and that's why I'm publishing this one last review of your work before I call it quits.''

Beau gave her a steady assessing look as some of the light left his eyes. ''What about the conflict of interest?''

''I took care of that.'' With a reassuring glance, Dani extricated herself from his arms. ''But just to make sure it all meets with your approval before it actually hits the newspapers, why don't you check out the amended version?'' She reached into her pocket and pulled out a neatly folded copy, then watched in silence as Beau began to read what she had written.

It isn't often real life is imbued with movie magic, but that, dear readers, is exactly what's been happening to me.

I fell in love. I married. And I'm going to have a baby with the man I love more than life itself.

What's surprising about that? you're probably asking yourselves. It happens every day.

And you're right. It does. Absolutely.

Usually not with a man who has been doing nothing but flirting and feuding with you for the past two years, but that is exactly what happened.

I finally made peace with Beau Chamberlain, America's big-screen hero and movie star extraordinaire. And once the two of us finally buried the hatchet, it didn't take us long to realize there was still considerable energy between us. Of a completely different, very romantic, kind.

For that reason, I almost passed on reviewing *Bravo Canyon*.

And then I decided I didn't want to leave it like that.

So, before I exempt myself from ever reviewing one of Beau Chamberlain's movies again (in the interest of marital harmony), here is what I think, what I *really* think, of *Bravo Canyon*...

Beau scanned the unremittingly favorable review, which he had already read back in Laramie, then looked at her in wonderment. "You didn't have to do this," he said huskily. "Bring our personal situation into your column. I know how much you've always prided yourself on keeping your work completely separate from your private life, that you've built your reputation on not doing favors for family and friends."

"I know I didn't have to do it," Dani agreed, her heart soaring at the new peace and understanding between them. "But I wanted everyone to know how I feel about you. I wanted them to know that my feelings, my commitment to you, are so deep and abiding they aren't ever going to disappear."

Touched by the public display of her affection, knowing how much it had cost her, Beau smiled. "I reckon you've done that, seeing as how your column runs in dozens of newspapers across the country." He folded the review, put it in his pocket and took her back into his arms. He ran his fingers through her hair and looked deep into her eyes. "Soon everyone will know how much I love you, too."

Dani grinned. "And how exactly are you planning to do that?" she asked.

"By holding your hand and kissing you every chance I get, starting with tonight's premiere of *Bravo Canyon*," Beau promised, sweeping a hand down her spine.

"Speaking of which," Dani said between more

kisses, her enthusiasm for Beau's latest project undaunted, "*Bravo Canyon* is going to be the big hit of the summer. In fact, I'll be surprised if anything surpasses it this year."

Beau kissed his way down her neck and brushed aside talk of his latest movie. "I don't care about that."

"Sure you do. We both do. But," she cautioned soberly, luxuriating in the cozy feel of his arms around her, "the difference is, we both know now that our work isn't the only thing. The most important thing is us. Our marriage. Our baby. Our family." Tears of joy misted her eyes as she stood on tiptoe and kissed him once more. "I don't ever want to be without you again."

"I don't ever want to be without you, either," Beau replied, pulling her even closer, letting her know with the tenderness of his touch that they had their whole lives ahead of them, and this time, nothing would force them apart. Not their pride. Not their work. From now on, they would weather things together, as husband and wife, mom and dad.

Dani looked into his eyes and saw all the love she could possibly have wished for. "So it's settled?" she asked huskily. "We'll put on our wedding rings and tell the world what an incredibly wild and wonderful thing we've gone and done?"

"You bet we'll tell 'em," Beau declared. As prepared as ever, he grinned and pulled the velvet ring box out of his pocket. "I've got them right here." He flipped the box open.

As Dani slid the wedding band on Beau's finger, she realized that only a few days had passed, but in those days, her life had changed remarkably. At long last, all her dreams were coming true. She was no longer afraid of the future. There were no guarantees, of course, but with Beau's love and their rock-solid commitment to each other, she knew that she, Beau and the baby could weather anything.

Her future with Beau beckoning like a bright rainbow, Dani was unable to contain her euphoria as Beau slid her engagement and wedding rings on once again. "Oh, Beau, I owe you so much," Dani murmured happily as she went back into the warm inviting circle of his arms.

"And how's that?" Beau drawled as he indulged in a long steamy kiss that left them both feeling glowing and alive.

Eager to share her revelation, she whispered softly, "Because you've made me realize I can have my happily-ever-after—with you."

"And I'm having mine," Beau whispered back, all the love he felt for her reflected in his eyes, "with you."

SEVERAL HOURS LATER Meg, Jenna, and Kelsey gathered around the TV in Meg's living room. Impatiently they waited for the late edition of the evening news and a glimpse of Dani and Beau at the star-studded Dallas premiere of *Bravo Canyon.*

"Think they made up?" Kelsey asked, as they passed around the popcorn bowl.

"As crazy in love with each other as the two of them are?" Meg quirked a brow and shook her head at the silliness of the question. "Of course."

"Think they're going to stay married?" Kelsey persisted. "Or even tell anyone they are married?"

"We're about to find out." Jenna pointed excitedly at the TV screen.

The news anchor said, "Sorry to disappoint all you

ladies, but one of the biggest movie stars in this country announced his marriage tonight. And he did it right here in Texas. That's right. Beau Chamberlain, star of the new movie *Bravo Canyon,* is married. And to none other than film critic Dani Lockhart.''

The three other Lockhart sisters grinned.

''Look! They're even wearing wedding rings now!'' Kelsey said exuberantly.

''This is so great,'' Jenna said, beaming at the happy looks on Beau and Dani's faces.

''Not to mention romantic,'' Kelsey said on a wistful sigh as the telephone rang. Meg got up to answer the phone.

She said hello, then listened. ''Hi, Lilah. John.'' She covered the mouthpiece. ''It's the McCabes. They're on speakerphone,'' she said.

''Uh-oh,'' Kelsey murmured. If anyone in Laramie felt a parental responsibility to the girls, it was John and Lilah McCabe.

''Yes. We saw it. We knew about it.'' Meg blushed fiercely as she listened to John and Lilah. ''I don't know. We'll have to get back to you on that,'' she said finally, then hung up, still blushing.

''What did they say?'' Jenna asked, still studying the TV and the way Dani looked in the evening dress she had given her. A better commercial for one of her designs couldn't have been made. The photos of Dani and Beau would be printed in tomorrow's papers. Everyone would want to know where Dani had gotten her dress.

''They wanted to tell us they're expecting all four of us to get married and settle down just like their sons did,'' Meg reported, as the TV reporter also made mention of the baby Beau and Dani were expecting.

"So?" Kelsey challenged, for a moment looking as wild and untamable as the horses she liked to ride.

"So," Meg said, looking steadily at her sisters, "they want to know which one of us is next."

Chapter One

"I need a favor. And I need it from you," the low distinctive male voice drawled.

As the velvety sound surrounded her, tingles of awareness slid down Jenna Lockhart's spine. She knew that rich murmur. And unless she was hallucinating... The blood rushed hotly through her veins. She turned slowly toward the door, telling herself she had to be imagining it. That the romantic notion was prompted by the equally shocking elopement of her sister, Dani, and Beau Chamberlain several weeks before. Just because Dani had found the man of her dreams and married him, just because wedding fever was sweeping through the town of Laramie, Texas, did not mean that the man of Jenna's dreams would waltz back into her life on a moment's notice. Did it?

Drawing a deep breath, Jenna lifted her gaze, curious to see who had entered her exclusive boutique just seconds before closing time. And promptly felt her knees turn to jelly. Well over six years had passed since she'd seen the man who had broken her heart, but Jake Remington hadn't changed a bit. Except, perhaps, to become even handsomer and more self-assured. He was a good six inches taller than her five-nine frame, with a penchant for casual clothes and an even more casual manner, which belied his enormous wealth.

"What are you doing here?" Jenna demanded.

Looking completely at ease with himself in the ultra-feminine surroundings, he circled the one-of-a-kind wedding and evening dresses on display. Once at her side, he tipped his black Stetson, revealing layers of thick deliciously rumpled jet-black hair. As he scanned her from head to toe, pleasure seemed to tug at the corners of his mouth. "I wanted to congratulate you on your success." Jake brought his gaze back to hers. "Your clothing designs have been in the news all month. Your sister Dani created quite a stir when she wore one of your dresses at the premiere of Beau Chamberlain's new movie. Reportedly every starlet in Hollywood wants one of your dresses."

That was true. Jenna was booked solid with appointments. She was taking the time between now and then to prepare for the onslaught. And perhaps look at hiring someone besides Raelynn to help her in the shop. But not wanting to disclose all that to Jake, Jenna merely shrugged and returned his steady glance, albeit with a lot less admiration. "You've done very well for yourself. J & R Industries is a multimillion-dollar conglomerate."

Jake propped his hands on his hips, which pushed back the edges of his black sport coat. His sexy grin widened. "You've kept up."

Jenna turned away, trying not to notice how taut and trim his midriff was beneath his olive-green shirt and snug black jeans. "Hard not to if you read the business pages of the major Texas newspapers, and I do."

Following her around the shop, Jake said, "I would

have called for an appointment, but I didn't think you'd see me.''

Trying hard not to recall how good it had felt to be held against that warm strong chest, Jenna refused to look at him as she shut down her computer for the night. ''You were right.'' She remembered without wanting to how much he had hurt her, abandoning her the way he had. ''I wouldn't have.''

Jake looked at her steadily, his face serious now. ''What happened between us was a long time ago.''

Funny, Jenna thought. It seemed like yesterday to her. Though in reality it was six years, eight months, ten days and...nineteen hours before. But who's counting?

Jenna smiled thinly. ''What's your point?''

Jake's expression was suddenly as vulnerable as it was grave. ''I want us to be friends again.''

Jenna didn't want to think of Jake as vulnerable, because if she did it almost meant he had a heart, and that was *definitely* not true. She locked the cash register. ''Not possible.''

He leaned across the sales counter. ''How do you know unless you try?''

Every muscle in her body went stiff with tension. ''I'm not interested in trying, Jake,'' she told him flatly, ignoring the unsettling way her senses stirred at his close proximity.

Jake regarded her with so much smug male assurance it took her breath away. ''Same old stubbornness and fiery temperament.''

''Same old arrogance and conceit,'' she shot back, refusing to be distracted by the enticing woodsy scent of his skin.

Instead of being insulted, Jake merely grinned, and looked all the more entranced. ''Jenna, I have a proposition for you.''

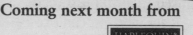

If you enjoyed what you just read,
then we've got an offer you can't resist!

Take 2 bestselling love stories FREE!
Plus get a FREE surprise gift!

**Don't miss
an exciting opportunity
to save on the purchase of
Harlequin and Silhouette books!**

Buy any two Harlequin or
Silhouette books and save
$10.00 off future Harlequin
and Silhouette purchases

OR

buy any three
Harlequin or Silhouette books
and save **$20.00 off** future
Harlequin and Silhouette purchases.

**Watch for details
coming in October 2000!**

PHQ400